HAIR OF THE DOG

ASHLYN KANE
& MORGAN JAMES

Dreamspinner Press

Published by
Dreamspinner Press
382 NE 191st Street #88329
Miami, FL 33179-3899, USA
http://www.dreamspinnerpress.com/

Hair of the Dog

Cover Art by Catt Ford

ISBN: 978-1-61372-346-3

Printed in the United States of America
First Edition
January 2012

eBook edition available
eBook ISBN: 978-1-61372-347-0

For the man behind the woman
behind half the magic.
(That's you, Brandon.)
Love you.
A

For KM,
champion and confidant.
M

Prologue

The Hunter

RUN.

The scent was fresh. He caught it smeared against the corner of a building, alcohol and wanting. It smelled of man, and it smelled of prey. He pressed his nose to the concrete and followed the scent.

Run.

He would find the man that smelled so good, and he would rip into his flesh. He would bite and bite and bite. He would spill the blood—red under the waning moon's light. Then the man would belong to him. He would keep the man for his own. And he would find others. Others that smelled as good, as sweet, as... intoxicating.

Run!

His long nails scraped across the concrete every time one of his paws hit the ground, but he could hardly hear it now under the sound of his own panting. He was excited—soon he'd have the man. Each exhilarated breath came out loud. Soon, soon, soon....

Around another corner—so many buildings, but... *there*! The man was only ten strides away! *Stop!*

Stop, stop, stop.

The man was prey and should be attacked like prey. He was the hunter. He would hunt.

Quiet, quiet, quiet, he crept. So close, so close. The man saw nothing. The man was nothing, but soon the man would be better. So much better.

Thump-thump went his heart. *Ta-da-dum* sang the man.

To the ground, low, low, he readied himself to pounce.

The man stopped.

Low on the ground, he tightened his muscles, opened his mouth, bared his teeth. Snarling, ready to take down his prey, he leapt.

Chapter One

The Wolf at the Door

THERE was a tiny spider spinning a web in the southeast corner of Ezra's bedroom, just above his bed. A breeze was coming in through the open window, and every few minutes it blew hard enough to set the spider swinging.

Then a harder gust blew it all the way into the east wall, and Ezra blinked hard and realized he was awake. Had been for a while now.

Exhaling noisily, Ezra rolled over and sat up, then immediately regretted the first part of that decision when his shoulder screamed in agony. "Jesus, what the fuck—?"

When he looked, his shoulder was an ugly mess of dried blood and yellow-purple bruises. *What the hell did I get up to last night?* he wondered.

But he couldn't seem to remember.

Automatically, he staggered to the bathroom. This time it wasn't just his shoulder protesting. His legs were sore, too, and his stomach muscles. In fact, there didn't seem to be any part of his body that was pain-free. Had someone roofied him, then attacked him on his way home from the pub last night? Had he gotten into a bar fight? Been mugged? "That's the last time I walk home from the bar," he grumbled aloud. Definitely taxis from now on. Even his voice sounded strained.

In the bathroom, his reflection offered nothing but more questions. To put it bluntly, he looked like crap. Blood had matted the hair on the left side of his head, turning it rusty brown from its usual dirty blond. His blue eyes were red-rimmed and bloodshot enough to rival any drug addict's. The bruising wasn't limited to his shoulder but had spread across his chest and legs.

And—Ezra inhaled deeply, then coughed—he desperately needed a shower.

Well, with any luck some hot water would clear his head and help him remember the events of the previous night. Ezra stumbled into the shower and turned the hot water up high, planting both hands on the tiled wall and letting the heat and steam soothe him.

Red water pooled on white ceramic before swirling down the drain, and gradually Ezra began to wash himself, starting gingerly with his hair. The blood must have been from his shoulder, because his head didn't hurt—not so much as a bump, which he supposed made him very lucky, though it just raised more questions about why he couldn't remember.

Getting soap in the gashes on his shoulder was an experience he had *no* desire to repeat, but he couldn't risk getting an infection. He didn't have health insurance, and he wasn't going to waste his inheritance because he couldn't handle a little sting.

Finally he was clean and as ache-free as he was going to get without painkillers, so he reluctantly shut off the water and patted himself dry before digging through his father's medicine cabinet for a first aid kit. A few squirts of Bactine and some fresh gauze later, he was about as close to healthy as he was going to get.

And still just as clueless about what had happened last night as he had been when he woke up.

Ezra ran the towel over his hair again quickly before limping back into his bedroom and gazing down at the pile of clothes he'd thrown around the room the night before. They were a total loss—all of them torn to shreds or bloodstained—but they didn't smell of alcohol. He knew he'd had a few drinks at his father's wake, but he hadn't had enough to warrant a blackout. Besides, alcohol didn't explain the clothes.

With a sigh, he bundled his ruined clothes up and shoved them into a garbage bag. They obviously weren't going to offer him any answers.

Dressing seemed to take eons. Every muscle resisted movement. The process of pulling a sweatshirt on over his head left him exhausted.

Maybe coffee would help, Ezra thought hopefully, and then he meandered into the kitchen to put on a pot. If not, he could always call his cousin; he was sure Dominic had been at the bar with him. In fact, they had decided to walk home together. He'd left Dominic in front of his apartment building ten minutes or so from the bar, and then… then he must have walked home himself.

The streetlamp two blocks from his apartment had flickered, he remembered now. And—had he heard a noise?

No, he couldn't have heard what he thought he'd heard. His mind was just playing tricks on him now, after the fact. Obviously he'd made it home safely. Sort of.

A brief search turned up a bottle of aspirin hiding beside the microwave, and Ezra popped three of them while the coffee percolated, strong-smelling and too loud.

He needed to be mobile today—he had too much to do to just sit around. There were papers to be signed, accounts to be closed out. He'd have to see his father's lawyer to make sure the ownership transfer of the apartment was in order.

He desperately wanted to crawl back into bed.

He was halfway through his third cup of coffee before he realized his dad had switched to decaf. No wonder he didn't feel any better.

Thunk thunk thunk.

Christ, was that—was that someone at the door? What the hell were they using to knock with, a battering ram? And anyway, who would be visiting *him*?

Probably one of his new neighbors wanting to convey condolences. Or maybe the superintendent? Ezra limped over to the door and pulled it open. "Can I—?" he started to ask, but then his voice deserted him.

There were two Mafiosos standing in the hall.

Or, well, Ezra assumed they were Mafiosos, because it was either that, or he had called for a couple of really high-class hookers before he'd blacked out. Who else would go around making house calls in expensive-looking black suits and wear sunglasses indoors? Oh God, had his father died owing the mafia money? Had they come to collect on his loan?

"Good morning." The man in front nodded to him. He didn't sound like he particularly meant it. "May we come in?"

No! Ezra's common sense screamed at him. *Do not let the organized crime boss and his bodyguard into your apartment!* But he found himself stepping back, out of the way.

The two of them walked into the apartment like they owned it, and Ezra shut the door after them, pulse pounding. "I—who are you?"

"My name is Callum Dawson," the same man said. From his tone, he expected Ezra to know who that was. "This is my associate, Blaise LaPorte."

The huge man still standing slightly behind him—Blaise—gave Ezra a cold nod, his ponytailed dreadlocks bobbing.

"Hi," Ezra said finally, when it seemed like they were waiting for him to speak. "What do you want?"

Uh oh. That was apparently the wrong answer. Blaise folded his—Jesus, *massive*—arms. If Ezra hadn't been in fear for his life, he would definitely have considered trying to hit that.

Dawson raised an eyebrow over the top of his sunglasses, then reached up with one hand to take them off. His eyes were a deep chocolate brown, just a shade lighter than his hair.

Ezra lamented his bad luck. He absolutely would have hit that too.

Dawson lowered his voice. "You don't have to say anything aloud. Just point to where he is. We won't let him hurt you. Help us to help him and you won't be in any trouble."

Trouble? Won't let who *hurt me?* "Did I do something illegal that I don't know about?" That explained it—maybe they were detectives? FBI or something? That guy Mulder always wore a suit, didn't he?

The guy must have finally sensed Ezra's confusion—and hopefully his innocence—because he took a step forward into Ezra's personal space, searching his face.

And then sniffed.

Seriously, what the hell?

"Alpha...." The bodyguard seemed wary.

"Do you smell that?" Dawson asked the room at large, though Ezra assumed he was talking to Blaise.

"Um, sir," Ezra began warily, trying to meet the bodyguard's eyes over Dawson's shoulder to discern if this was normal behavior.

Dawson reached out his hand and touched Ezra's shoulder right above the bandage, his gaze suddenly very sharp. Ezra's eyes were drawn to his as though they were magnetized, and he swallowed. A surge of adrenaline coursed through him; Ezra could barely feel the pain. There was a waft of clean, pine-scented air, warm somehow, and comforting. Then Dawson said, "Take off your shirt."

He *should* have thrown a fit—or at least thrown the two of them out on their asses. This was definitely not typical FBI behavior. Besides, those guys had badges. He should definitely *not* have reached for the hem of his sweatshirt with his good arm and started wriggling carefully out of it, but that was what he found himself doing, contorting his body until the skin-warm garment was balled up inside-out in his hands.

It was suddenly too hot in the apartment anyway.

Callum Dawson was staring at his bandaged shoulder. Ezra watched as if mesmerized as he reached out again and ran his finger along the edge of the tape until he found the end and began peeling it away.

Ezra shivered. "What—?" he started again, but when the gauze peeled away, he saw that the gash had scabbed over completely and the skin at the edges was already shiny, healthy pink scar tissue.

Dawson said, "You should sit down."

That sounded like a fantastic idea. Ezra did as he was told.

Across the room, the bodyguard snorted. "Well, at least he knows his place."

Dawson shot him a dark look, but then he turned back to Ezra and sat on the couch across from him, and most of the hostility in his posture evaporated. "I need to ask you some questions," Dawson told him. He put his sunglasses down on the coffee table. "And I need you to answer me honestly."

"Okay," Ezra said hollowly, looking down at his shoulder.

"First—" He stopped, and when Ezra managed to tear his eyes away from his crazy mutant skin, Callum Dawson had become an entirely different person, kind and quiet. "What's your name?"

"Ezra."

"Okay, Ezra. You can call me Callum."

Ezra nodded.

"I need you to tell me what you did last night."

He blinked. "I… I don't remember."

"Think," Callum persisted. "What's the last thing you remember?"

Shaking his head, Ezra forced himself to concentrate. The bar. He'd been walking home. "I was walking home from my father's wake. With my cousin."

Callum and Blaise exchanged a dark look. "Which bar?"

"Uh. O'Callahan's? On Higgins?" Ezra took a few deep breaths and closed his eyes. "Dominic was plastered. He decided to walk home to sober up so his girlfriend wouldn't be mad at him, and I thought he needed a chaperone. So we walked to his place on Chestnut. After that I figured I might as well walk the rest of the way home. It was only another four blocks."

"Did you notice anything strange?"

"You mean like when I woke up with a gash in my shoulder and bruises all over and no recollection of what happened?" Ezra raised a shaking hand to his face and realized he was shivering. Maybe he should put his shirt back on.

"Blaise, find Ezra a blanket," Callum said calmly without turning around. "And something to eat with sugar in it, if you can."

Ezra looked down at his hands. "I thought I heard a noise," he admitted. "But then I convinced myself I was crazy. I mean—I guess it could've been a stray dog or something just—growling. Must've been the full moon," he joked weakly.

Blaise wrapped the blanket around his shoulders, which helped with the shaking a little bit. Then he shoved a cookie in Ezra's face.

"Eat it," Callum advised. "You'll feel better."

Ezra had the somewhat stale cookie halfway swallowed before a thought occurred to him. He licked the crumbs from his lips before speaking again. "You're very bossy."

From behind him, there came a cough that sounded suspiciously like a laugh. For the most part, Callum ignored Ezra's comment, though he did look up long enough to roll his eyes at Blaise.

"Why are you asking me all these questions?" Ezra said suddenly, feeling a bit more energized. He'd apparently really needed that cookie. "Am I in some kind of trouble?"

The air filled with a tension. Ezra could practically taste Callum's reluctance as he sighed. "In a manner of speaking, yes. Last night you were bitten by a lycanthrope—a werewolf."

Great, now Ezra was looking for hidden cameras. "I'm sorry, I thought I just heard you say I was bitten by a werewolf."

"That's what I said. This one escaped from a correctional facility two days ago. We've been tracking him since. That's how we ended up here."

"You can't be serious." Could he? "I was bitten by an escaped convict werewolf? That's the line you're going with? Really?"

"No. He was a psychiatric patient. Sort of. And we prefer lycanthrope, or lycan."

Oh, so it was a *crazy* escaped were—sorry, *lycanthrope*. That... really didn't make Ezra feel better. "Listen, buddy," he began, "you need to lay off the HBO."

Callum sighed. "If I prove it to you, do you promise not to panic?"

Ezra didn't think it was too likely that this guy—who was, he now realized, obviously crazy himself—was going to convince him of the existence of werewolves. He shrugged. "Sure, boss. Whatever you say."

And then Callum pulled his lips back in an unattractive expression, and Ezra watched as his teeth grew and sharpened into something that was definitely not human. Just as quickly, they reverted to their earlier form, and Callum said, "Remember, you promised."

Ezra swallowed, shaken to the core. "So what you're saying is, I'm a were—uh, lycanthrope."

"Well, not yet." For the first time, Callum looked unsure. "I've never seen anyone change—there's usually a lot of paperwork involved before a human can be turned. Background checks, psych evaluations, that kind of thing. But from what I've read, it takes anywhere from a few days to a full month for the lycanthrope DNA to splice into the human sequences."

"Splice?" Ezra echoed. He was definitely regretting that he'd taken only three aspirin.

Ignoring him, Callum turned to Blaise. "See if you can find a bag or something. Pack for at least a week."

"Sure thing, boss," Blaise rumbled, disappearing again into the depths of the apartment.

That snapped Ezra out of his daze. "Excuse me? Were you going to ask before you just carted me out of here? Or don't I get a say?"

"It's not safe for you here," Callum said dismissively, checking his watch and then standing and reaching into his pocket and drawing out a cell phone.

"I can take care of myself!" Ezra stood up, letting the blanket fall to the couch.

Callum looked pointedly at the healing wound on his shoulder and said, "Obviously," before putting his phone to his ear. "Bring the car. Five minutes." Then he snapped it shut. "You should put your shirt back on. It's cold out."

Ezra gritted his teeth. "I'm not going outside."

"Yes, you are. You need my protection, and I need answers about what happened to the wolf that bit you." Callum shoved his phone back into his pocket just as Blaise reappeared from the bedroom. "It's in everyone's best interest. Just until your DNA is done rearranging itself."

"I don't even know you!"

"Well, that's about to change."

"You got any medication I should know about?" Blaise asked, slinging an ancient Coors Light duffel bag over one shoulder.

"Not yet I don't," Ezra snarled.

Then he looked down and noticed he'd put his shirt back on.

And he was sporting wood.

Fuck my life.

Callum gave him a knowing look. "The car's waiting. Let's go."

EZRA was feeling less shaken and much more in control by the time they pulled up to a tall, nondescript office building in the center of the city. The driver of the SUV, a slender woman with curly dark hair and her eyes hidden behind dark aviator glasses, put the vehicle in park. "Pick you up at six?" she asked, all business.

In the front seat, Callum shook his head, reaching for the door handle. "Take Blaise home. I'll use one of the fleet vehicles." Then he looked over his shoulder at Ezra. "You're with me."

Ezra supposed he really didn't have much of a choice. He unbuckled his seat belt and slid out of the SUV behind Callum, then quickened his steps to match the other man's stride. "What is this place?"

They went past the reception area and stopped at a security checkpoint, and Callum flashed an identification badge at the two uniformed men at the desk. "He's with me," he said shortly, taking the time to scrawl Ezra's name and the date and time on a generic sign-in sheet.

"Yes, sir," the guards chorused.

What the hell was up with these people?

The shorter of the two men handed over a bright pink visitor's pass, and Callum passed it to Ezra with barely a look. "Here, put this on."

Ezra was beginning to see that *very bossy* did not even begin to cover it.

Once you got past the security guards, the office building seemed to be just like any other. The floors were a polished engineered stone, and large terra cotta pots held a variety of plants, both real and fake. In the center of the lobby was a bank of elevators.

And that was where things started to get interesting. Callum pressed the call button and motioned for Ezra to follow him inside the first elevator, but when he selected the sub-basement level, a mechanical voice spoke seemingly out of nowhere: "Voiceprint confirmation required."

"Dr. Callum Dawson, head of research and development."

"Voiceprint confirmed."

As if this day could get any more *Twilight Zone*. "Are you going to tell me where we are now?"

"You're at the CDC's Center for Lupine Research." The elevator came to a halt, and Callum led the way out and down a brightly lit hallway.

Ezra kept up as best he could, trying not to get distracted by, well, everything. His ears kept picking up noises he shouldn't have been able to hear, like the tap of Callum's shoelaces and the buzz of mechanical equipment in the far reaches of the building. Some of the rooms off the hallway were glassed in, and there were people moving around behind the windows, dressed in lab coats and goggles and doing mysterious science things. "I didn't know the CDC had a building in Missoula."

Callum grunted. "That's because it's classified."

Obviously. Wait. "So the government knows about you, then? About us, I mean? Werewolves?"

Callum stopped in front of the last door in the hallway and pressed his thumb to a pad beside the door. A light on the adjacent panel flashed green, and he pulled the door open. "It's lycanthropes. And certain branches of the government have some knowledge of us, yes. Each pack has a government-appointed liaison officer." He held the door for Ezra to precede him into the office. "Basically their job is to bring the concerns of the pack to the Natural Resources Committee of the U.S. Fish and Wildlife Service and vice versa."

Ha! That was kind of funny. Maybe Callum *did* have a sense of humor buried somewhere under that brusque exterior. Ezra smiled. "Fish and Wildlife Service. Good one."

Callum shot him a sideways look. "I wasn't kidding."

Then again, maybe not. If Ezra got his foot any further down his throat he was going to need the Heimlich maneuver. "Right. So." Embarrassed, he cast his gaze around the office. It was a decently sized room, but it had no windows, so it felt a little claustrophobic. There were two doors, not counting the one they'd come in through, as well as what seemed to be a tall standing wardrobe in one corner. Ezra counted no fewer than four mugs of coffee in varying stages of consumption, though an accidental sniff with his apparently improved nose informed him that the contents were actually some kind of tea. File folders of varying shapes and colors littered the desk, by the door a tattered umbrella slouched in a beat-up old stand, and an overcoat hung from a hook on the back of the door. "It smells like microwave dinners in here."

"I like to work late." Callum didn't bother looking up as he rooted through the folders on his desk. He finally came up with a purple one and grabbed a pen out of an organizer next to his widescreen computer monitor. Then he looked up, just briefly, but Ezra counted the eye contact as progress. "Follow me."

Tamping down on the thread of anxiety, Ezra did as he was told—*again*—feeling as suggestible as he ever had after drinking too much. Maybe, Ezra thought as he trailed after Callum into a small, sterile-smelling room, his ability to reason had been compromised by the amount of blood flowing away from his brain and into his stupid dick.

Callum clipped his folder to a clipboard and hung it on a hook on a small cabinet. "I need to get a few things. Undress and get up on the table, and I'll be back in a few minutes."

Ezra stood stock-still until the door closed behind him. Then he let out a trembling breath and fisted both hands in his hair. The plain white walls were oppressive, and the smell of disinfectant invaded his nostrils, choking him. All at once Ezra was fifteen years old again, sitting in his mother's hospital room while the heart monitor sang a steady, unforgettable note.

Well, at least his hard-on was a pretty powerful distraction. Now that the shock had worn off, he was starting to find Callum's constant orders more than just compelling. Ezra didn't know if it was a temporary side effect of the bite, some kind of weird hormonal thing, or if it was just the fact that Callum never said "please," never acted for a second as if there were a possibility Ezra might not follow his commands to the letter. Either way, he found himself suddenly battling between the compulsion to disrobe and the need to maintain some shred of dignity. The last thing he needed was for Callum to think he got off on being ordered around.

Maybe it was because he was thinking about it—or maybe because Callum hadn't strictly told him he needed to be naked—but Ezra managed to keep his boxers on as he climbed up onto the cold metal table. He shoved his hands underneath his thighs to protect himself somewhat from the cold and stared down his long, pale legs at his toes.

Someday not too long from now, he'd have paws there.

Every tick of the clock was overloud, and he kept seeing his mother's chest rising and falling and then stilling as she lay there in that hospital bed, dying right in front of him.

When the door opened again, Ezra was still staring at his feet, watching as his toes slowly turned blue from the cold.

The door clicked closed, and there was the slide of metal on metal as something was deposited on the table beside him. "Ezra?" Callum's voice had gone quiet and gentle again, like it had at the apartment when Ezra had started panicking. "Are you okay?"

Ezra laughed a little hysterically, though it sounded more like a strangled sob. "Are you *nuts*? I'm going to be a freaking werewolf! A *monster*! No, I'm not okay!"

"Hey." The soft, calming tone washed over Ezra's frayed nerves like a gentle wave. "Relax."

Closing his eyes for a moment, Ezra let himself be soothed. It probably should have concerned him that being ordered to relax was actually *helping*, but damn it, he'd had a hell of a day. He was allowed to find comfort wherever he wanted. "Sorry. I promise I'm usually not this crazy."

"Forget it," Callum said dismissively. "You're going to be crazy for the next couple of weeks until your DNA settles down. You might as well get used to it."

Awesome. Well, at least he had carte blanche to freak out.

Ezra opened his eyes again and let them actually focus on Callum this time. He had changed into scrubs and a lab coat, and the difference in his appearance was almost as striking as the change in his demeanor. Though not nearly so foreboding, he was still every bit as attractive. "So," Ezra managed, suddenly self-conscious. "Doctor?"

"PhD, not MD." Callum's eyes flicked up to his, then down to his shoulder, and he snapped on a pair of latex gloves as he examined the quickly scarring tissue. "I need to take a picture of this to verify that it was the escaped lycan that bit you."

"Go nuts." Ezra held still while Callum took several digital photographs of the wound. "Don't tell me a lycanthrope's bite is like a fingerprint."

"It's not quite that specific." Callum set the camera aside and reached for the tray, coming up with a single-use iodine swab. "Hold out your left arm."

Mostly naked or not, when Ezra shivered, it had nothing to do with the cold. Callum rubbed the cold cotton vigorously over the skin of his inner arm. "I thought you weren't a medical doctor."

"I'm not." To Callum's credit, Ezra barely felt the needle slide into the vein in the crook of his elbow. "But I took an EMT course once."

"That's not very reassuring." Ezra was a handy enough programmer despite the fact that he'd dropped out of MIT halfway through his third year, but he was pretty sure medicine wasn't something you could pick up in your free time.

Callum pulled the needle out and capped the vial of blood before disposing of the rest in a biohazard container. "I need to make sure Teller didn't infect you with anything other than lycanthrope DNA."

"Teller." Ezra watched as Callum peeled his gloves off and disposed of them as well. "That's the name of the werewolf—the lycanthrope who attacked me?"

"It was his name, before he got sick," Callum explained, rolling over a tall stool and sitting.

Great, now Ezra was worried he had werewolf AIDS too. And how sick did someone have to be, if they didn't keep their name after they got infected? "Sick with what?" he asked with no small degree of trepidation.

"We're calling it ARD for 'alphatropin regulatory dysfunction'— alphatropin's a werewolf hormone—even though it could be a symptom of something else. We've only encountered the infected individuals, never the source, and the most obvious symptom is abnormally elevated hormone levels."

Ezra was not comforted. "And by infected you mean…."

Callum met his eyes evenly, all business. "Normally, the human side of a lycanthrope is in control at all times, even during the full moon. But throughout history there have been cases of lycanthropes losing control to the animal aspect, and not only during the full moon."

"So they turn into monsters," Ezra said flatly.

"If you like." Callum leaned forward then. "But there's no evidence to suggest that it is communicable at all, never mind via a single bite."

Okay. So he probably wasn't going to go nuts and kill someone. That was a load off his mind. "And when it happens, you, what, go find them and lock them up until they get better? Is that what this building is for?"

"That's part of it." Standing straight again, Callum crossed his arms across his chest. "While we're here, I might as well lay down the ground rules."

"Rules," Ezra echoed flatly. What was he, a naughty teenager?

Callum ignored him. "Until you change for the first time, you won't fully be in control of your body. Stay out of public places and keep an experienced lycan with you at all times."

Despite the pull to give in, to accept Callum's word as law, Ezra managed to grit out, "I don't need a babysitter." He was starting to get a major headache.

"You do if I say you do," Callum told him. "I'm pack Alpha. It's my job to do what's best for everyone. And you're going to come home with me and do as I say. It's for your own good."

"I don't even know you," Ezra protested with difficulty. He did not *want* to go home with Callum and do whatever he said, no matter what his hormones were telling him. "I'm just supposed to trust that you're not going to drug me and keep me locked in a basement somewhere?"

"I'd prefer not to. But that brings me to my next point."

"Oh, I see." Ezra had been vulnerable and off-balance earlier that morning, but he was bouncing back now. The more he stood up to Callum's bullying, the easier it got, and he wasn't about to start rolling over on command just because Callum seemed to expect it. However, his growing headache was making it more difficult to concentrate on his defiance. "House arrest wasn't enough."

Callum narrowed his eyes slightly but otherwise didn't react. "If you do need to go out sometime in the next three weeks—I mean life or death—avoid humans. They react unpredictably to lycans during the change."

"So much for freedom of association," Ezra muttered, shifting on the table. A few minutes ago he'd been freezing, but he was sure it was several degrees warmer now. Wasn't it?

"But the most important thing is that you abstain from sexual contact until the next full moon."

Ezra's jaw dropped, and he stared, speechless, gaping like a fish and determinedly ignoring the little throb of want from his dick at just the sound of Callum's voice saying "sex." "Excuse me, *what*?"

"The rules are the same for born lycans when they start to change. Like I said, it's for your own benefit. It's only for a couple of weeks." Callum flicked his eyes down to Ezra's waistline for a moment before returning them to his face and flashing a brief smirk. "I'll leave you to get changed."

When the door closed behind him, Ezra let out a long, unsteady groan. Fantastic. In the space of a few days, he'd lost his father and his job and, apparently, his humanity. Now, to top it all off, it seemed like he was going to lose his independence too. No matter how temporary that situation was supposed to be, it was still degrading.

He took a deep, shuddering breath. Okay. Time to face the music. Ezra bent his head and looked down at his lap, then buried his face in his hands. Granted, it could have been worse—at least he was wearing boxers with buttons, so his dick wasn't actually peeking out the slit or anything, but it was bad enough. Whether it was due to Callum's presence or the messed-up hormones he'd warned about or some combination of the two, Ezra didn't know, and it didn't really matter. He was twenty-two, not twelve; he should have been past the uncontrollable hard-on stage.

"Fuck," he muttered, finally mustering the energy to slide off the table and begin dressing. Three weeks, Callum had said.

God, this was going to suck.

CALLUM waited until the door was shut behind him to run a hand over his mouth worriedly. He knew he'd been hot and cold, all over the place, with the new wolf today, and that wasn't really fair to him. Ezra needed stability right now, something he could count on—but Callum couldn't help it. He was drawn to the new lycan, to what he'd seen of the natural tendency to submit coupled, almost paradoxically, with the need to know, to question. So much so that he was finding it difficult to control himself and had to keep stepping back in order to maintain the proper distance. He had accidentally blasted the poor kid with pheromones more than once. Callum hadn't done that since long before he'd come to Montana to be pack Alpha.

But he didn't have time to worry about it now. Not with a rogue wolf on the loose and only three weeks to track Callum down before he'd attack again. He'd just have to grit his teeth and bear it. After all, it was only for three weeks.

He let out a breath and paged a tech to come collect Ezra's blood sample. Yeah, this was going to suck.

Chapter Two

Dog in the Manger

WITH a frustrated sigh, Ezra sat down on Callum's front steps. He was pretty sure that they wouldn't let him go anywhere. God, how had his life turned into this?

Suddenly a large ceramic mug appeared in front of his face. He sniffed. Was that…?

"I thought you might like some coffee," said a soft voice. Ezra looked up to see a petite, sweet-faced woman attached to the hand. She had long dark hair that fell around her face in a mess of waves and curls and a pair of dark, warm brown eyes.

"Thanks," he said, reaching for the life-giving brew. The first sip was heavenly.

"I was in the kitchen… anyway, we didn't really get the chance to meet yet. I'm Bronwyn. People call me Wyn for short."

Damn! It seemed he had once again forgotten his manners while in a coffee haze. Ezra flinched and tried to swallow more quickly. "Hi, I'm—"

"Ezra," she finished with him. "I know. You've caused a bit of a stir."

"Oh." Ezra didn't know what to say to that. He drank more of his coffee. When in doubt: coffee.

"They can forget sometimes, the strong alphas," Bronwyn said suddenly.

Ezra blinked in surprise and tried to make sense of what she'd just said. "What?"

"How overwhelming they can be, especially when you're still trying to figure out your place in the pack."

Ezra frowned at her. "I don't…."

Bronwyn gave him a soft smile. "You have the irresistible urge to do whatever he wants, right? Callum, I mean. You just want to do what he says. And you don't know where to start."

Ezra stared at her in surprise. Okay, so apparently she did know how he felt. He wondered if the other things were the same for her as well, if Callum's scent drew her in the way it did him, if she could sense his power like an electrical charge in the air, if even the thought of one of those proprietary touches made her skin flush like it did his.

"I felt the same way the first time Mom took me to a pack gathering after I wolfed out. I wanted to obey her, and the pack Alphas, and every other alpha in between."

"But... why?"

She shrugged. "I'm a beta. Dominance and hierarchies are some of the wolf traits our human selves can't let go of. There's no shame in it. A wolf is either alpha or beta, and the pack chooses two of the stronger alphas to lead it."

Very wolf-like. Then again, what Ezra knew about real wolves wouldn't top off his half-empty coffee mug.

Still, something else was bothering him. Sure, he got that there was a hierarchy in the group, but what about him? "But why do I...?" He didn't finish the question.

Fortunately, Bronwyn understood anyway. "Hormones, pheromones. The hormone balance is what determines alpha or beta. That tingly urge that makes you think even jumping off a cliff would be a good idea if Callum asked you to? That's the pheromones. The desire to be told, on the other hand...."

"Oh."

There was silence. Ezra didn't know how to respond to the implication that he wanted to be the slave to someone else's master. He considered denying it but worried he'd just look all the guiltier. Besides, he wasn't sure she'd listen to a denial.

Wyn sighed. "I'm not sure I'm saying all this right. Look. Callum's a great Alpha, but he's still an alpha. And sometimes alphas get caught up in being bossy, and they forget that being bossed around is intense at first."

They were quiet for a moment. Ezra didn't know what to say to that, other than to vehemently agree.

"The point is, you're allowed to tell him if it feels like too much."

"Right." The snort that followed was completely involuntary and totally unstoppable. Honest. "All he's done since we've met is boss me around no matter what I say to him."

Bronwyn gave a small laugh. "He's pack Alpha—he's used to having even other alphas do what he says."

"Oh."

"I'll tell you a secret." Bronwyn scooted closer and laid a hand on his arm. She looked like a conspiratorial schoolgirl. "They want to protect us as much as they want to boss us around. You just have to know how to ask." The statement was topped off with a wink that sent Ezra into laughter.

The two of them were still laughing on the steps when a shadow appeared in the doorway. "Ezra, there you are." Callum sounded displeased and annoyed. "Come back inside." The order was clear. And so was the dismissal—he turned and walked away. The air seemed to carry a hint of that sort of woodsy scent, only sharper this time.

It wasn't until he'd opened the door and stepped inside that Ezra realized he was once again doing exactly as Callum said—and that certain parts of his anatomy were once again reacting predictably. Yeah, this was getting old fast.

BLAISE was watching him with a smirk when Callum got back to the kitchen. His eyes were knowing and his lips curving and Callum couldn't help the growl that escaped. Blaise was a bastard, and he proved it further by smiling even wider.

Of course, Ezra and Bronwyn's arrival in the kitchen prevented Callum from properly responding. Bronwyn headed straight for the sink and washed Ezra's empty mug while Ezra stood just inside the door, waiting for further instructions.

God damn it. This kid was going to kill him. Never before had Callum met a turned human with such natural beta instincts. Or a guy who was as attractive as his obviously submissive desires were strong. Every time Callum gave an order, he could literally smell Ezra's arousal ratcheting up a notch. It was driving him crazy and making it all the more difficult to keep his own pheromones in check.

"What now?" Ezra looked a bit more relaxed now; it seemed that Bronwyn was good for him.

"We need to find you a place to sleep." A place other than Callum's bed.

Brows furrowed, Ezra asked, "I'm not staying here?" He said it almost like it mattered to him.

"No!" Callum said, too quickly. Yes, he had insisted Ezra come home with him, but he'd meant to the lycan community. He could *not* have Ezra staying here, in his *house*. Never mind that he made it a general rule not to keep guests—as Alpha he had to be careful not to show favoritism—but breaking that unofficial rule to have a newly turned and obviously submissive wolf stay in his house would have the gossip tongues wagging at a never-before-seen speed. The old wolves would have a field day.

Besides, there was no way Callum would be able to keep his hands to himself for three weeks.

The sound of Ezra's body shifting snapped Callum from his thoughts: the small current of air brought him a fresh wave of Ezra's scent. The rumors would have just cause. Ezra already smelled like fruit begging to be plucked. Callum would not survive resisting this temptation. That was, of course, if he could actually resist Ezra for any length of time.

"Where will I be staying, then?"

"With another wolf. All the houses in the neighborhood belong to pack members."

"Oh." Ezra looked thoughtful again.

"He could stay with me," Bronwyn cut in, her voice soft. She was leaning back against the sink and offered a shy, submissive smile when Callum turned to her.

"Great idea!" The words rushed out before Callum could give them proper consideration. By the time his brain caught up enough to think, *bad idea*, Bronwyn was already smiling at Ezra and explaining how she lived alone, next door. Key word being *alone*, Callum thought, dismayed.

"Boss?" So Blaise saw the problem too. They didn't know where Teller was, why he'd decided to attack Ezra, or whether he would come looking for him. Bronwyn was not a good choice for bodyguard. In fact, if Callum let Ezra stay with her, he could be putting her in danger. At the very least, it was a bad idea to leave a newly transformed wolf of Ezra's size alone in the care of a girl Bronwyn's size. There was no telling what damage Ezra might accidentally cause while under the influence of his new senses or out-of-control emotions.

Damn. How was he going to get out of this one?

"Maybe I should stay with them?" Blaise offered.

Callum felt an overwhelming sense of gratitude. "That could work. Thanks." He offered a grateful smile and then turned to Bronwyn, who was staring at them, surprised.

"What?" she said faintly.

"Blaise is right," Callum said, trying to sound like a self-assured leader and not a horny idiot. "It would be a good idea for both of you to have backup around."

"Why?" Ezra was looking worried again.

Callum licked his lips and considered. How could he say this without upsetting either of them? "Look, turning is supposed to be a pretty intense time, and since I don't know for sure what will happen, I'll feel better knowing there are more people around to help."

Ezra seemed thoughtful at that, Bronwyn relieved.

"If you're so worried, why aren't you keeping me here?"

"Because as Alpha, I don't have houseguests—it implies favoritism." *And I don't trust myself not to order you to your knees or to push you onto the bed and take you until you're begging and* mine. Callum was pretty sure he hadn't said that last part aloud. A quick check of faces and expressions confirmed he hadn't. Good.

The frown lines were disappearing from Ezra's forehead, Callum was pleased to note. Apparently that explanation had been sufficient.

Before anyone else could say anything, the front door slammed open.

"Dawson, what's this I hear about you bringing home delicious hunky men? Don't you remember what I told you about those one-night stands you bring home? You can't hide these things in this neighborhood!" Jax's voice came floating down the hall, gaining volume until she finally entered in the kitchen.

Callum just held in the groan of annoyance. Jax wasn't for the faint of heart. One look in Ezra's direction confirmed it: his eyes were wide, and he was staring at Jax, who was standing in the doorway.

Callum turned and tried to take in his partner as a stranger might. She was quite the dazzling sight: six feet of gorgeous blonde with bright blue eyes and what she called "awesome breasts, seriously, Dawson, these things get me everything!" She was loud, brash, and unapologetic and walked into every room like she knew that all the boys and girls would bow at her queenly feet. She also had a tendency to run at the mouth even when you gave every indication of ignoring her. To put it simply, she was kind of awe-inspiring.

"Yum, yum! Oh, Dawson, I approve!" She also lacked a filter for her mouth.

"Jax, please stop terrifying new pack members. This is Ezra Jones. He was bitten last night. Ezra, meet Jacqueline LaPorte, otherwise known as Jax or my annoying co-Alpha."

Despite the fact that his eyes were still wide as he stared at Jax, Ezra smiled and held his hand out. "Nice to meet you."

"Likewise, kiddo," said Jax as she stepped forward and took Ezra's hand in a firm handshake.

"So... you're the other Alpha?" Ezra looked adorably befuddled.

It seemed that Jax agreed; the grin she gave was shark-like. "Aren't you just the cutest new wolf? Can we keep him? Please, Dawson? I promise to walk and feed him every day!"

"We are keeping him." Blaise's voice was dry, though his lips were curled with brotherly affection.

"Really?" Jax asked with an arched brow.

Callum rolled his eyes. "Yes. As I said, Ezra was bitten last night; I've invited him to join our pack. And yes, Ezra, Jax is the other Alpha. Having two of us helps to keep things balanced."

"Also to lighten the workload, which is a good thing, because Dawson here can't balance the books, and I'm terrible at holding family meetings."

"Oh." Ezra still seemed a bit overwhelmed. Callum suspected Jax was to blame.

"Bronwyn, how about you take Ezra next door and get him settled in? Jax and I should talk pack business." With a nod of his head, Callum sent Bronwyn and Ezra out of the house. Blaise gave his own nod before following them out—probably to go pack some essentials for his stay at Wyn's.

Jax waited until the front door shut behind them before she turned wicked eyes on Callum. "Well, well, Dawson." Her smirk was very telling. "I leave you alone for a day, and you go and find yourself a pretty little pet."

Callum groaned. "Blaise and I were hunting down Teller. We found Ezra instead."

The smirk disappeared at this news. Jax knew just as well as Callum what was at stake. "So... you tested the bite?"

"Yeah. I brought him to my lab, drew some blood. I'll let you know what turns up, but I'm not counting on much." Actually, he was counting on nothing. If it turned out ARD *was* transmissible by bite, that was bad news for Ezra.

It was bad news for *everyone*.

"Still no sign of Teller?" She frowned, worried.

Callum let out a deep, frustrated sigh in response. "Yeah."

"So you found Ezra and decided to take him home?"

"What else could I do? The bite was fresh, and the guy reeks of unclaimed wolf." Callum had a lot of self-control, but not biting Ezra and securing his allegiance for himself had been a struggle. A less principled or disciplined Alpha—or even a rogue—might not think twice about it. "Besides, with Teller at large, I couldn't leave Ezra behind."

"*Ri-i-ight*. And this has nothing to do with the fact that he's absolutely gorgeous. Also, don't think I didn't notice his submissive little head tilts."

With narrowed eyes, Callum replied tersely, "You know that doesn't mean much—not until he's used to being a wolf, especially not when he's frightened and unsure about his new circumstances." Though—God, he wanted it to mean something. He was pretty sure it did. But there was no sense in giving Jax more ammunition.

"You say that like I don't know he's your type! Especially if he always plays such a good little beta." She paused. "Maybe this one will hold your interest for more than twenty minutes," she mused.

Color rose high in Callum's cheeks at that. She knew him way too well. "Get your mind out of the gutter, Jax. I couldn't leave him behind no matter what he looks like."

"I know. Obviously you couldn't do anything else. Still, doesn't mean you can't enjoy the view while you're being a Good Samaritan."

Callum closed his eyes. There was no arguing with Jax. And she was going to have a field day with the request that he was about to make. "I, uh, need to talk to you about something." He tried to meet her eyes so as to give her less fodder. "I brought Ezra to stay with us, but since he was bitten by Teller...."

The fine brow that she arched at Callum was very expressive. "Yes?"

Damn her, she was going to make him say it. "Someone's got to make him pack. Ezra needs to be bitten." Ezra's allegiance to the pack wouldn't be solid until he had been bitten by an Alpha, nor would other wolves respect Ezra's ties to the Missoula pack, not without a bite to prove he had the pack's backing. Any Alpha wolf could be tempted to bite Ezra themselves and force his allegiance to them. And given the way Ezra tended to display submission, that seemed like too much of a risk.

Jax nodded and waved a hand for him to continue.

"So you should get on that."

"*I* should get on that? You're the one who found him, Dawson. Why don't you do it?"

And here it was. Time to get to the reason why Callum was having this awkward conversation in the first place. "I'd rather you took care of it. I'm not sure...." He ran both hands through his hair, frustrated. "Look, you were right. He's just my type and hits all my... buttons."

Jax's grin was pure evil. "*Buttons*? I'm pretty sure that it's not your *buttons* that he's pushing."

"Jax! The point is, my inner wolf is sitting up and taking notice, and I'm not sure it will listen to me when I tell it to keep things light. I'm pretty sure it'll want more than is reasonable." Callum hated to admit it, but it was true. Ezra was... intoxicating to his wolf. Between his looks, scent, and behavior, Ezra might as well have walked out of one of Callum's fantasies; Callum was pretty certain that if he ever tried to bite Ezra, he wouldn't be satisfied with something as impersonal as a bite of formal pack submission. No, Callum's wolf would want something much more intimate than that, and that was definitely out of the question. *That* kind of bite was a social taboo—he couldn't have that even if he did eventually get to bend Ezra over the way he wanted.

Of course, Jax's response was less than comforting. "Don't be such a wuss. Man up and bite the boy."

"Thank you, Jax, for being such a kind and understanding friend."

"I am an awesome friend! I am encouraging you to go and bite the pretty toy."

"Jax...." It wasn't about being afraid, it was about common sense. He couldn't bite Ezra and not make it personal. He just couldn't.

"Fine! I'll bite him. Just so long as you understand that this is under protest." She poked him in the chest. "*You* need to let go a little. You're too uptight."

"I am not!"

"Are too!" Then, before the conversation could devolve further, Jax left with one last parting shot. "Now if you'll excuse me, there's a pretty little beta that I need to go bite."

WYN'S house was smaller and more pedestrian than Callum's, but there was something about it that Ezra found immediately comforting, welcoming. The small living area that the front door opened into was cozy, painted a rich purple, and there was a gas fireplace along the left wall that lent just the right amount of warm light.

"Sorry to just, you know...." Ezra gestured meaninglessly. "Impose on you like this."

"Oh!" Wyn said, shaking her head. "I volunteered, didn't I? I don't mind having some company."

"Well, I'm sure you didn't count on the babysitter." Ezra sighed and bent to untie his shoes. "Blaise isn't as bad as Callum, at least."

Wyn waited for him to stand again, then took his coat and hung it on one of the knobs on the back of the door. She had to stand on tiptoe to do so, even though it was her own house, and Ezra smiled a little at that. "He's distracted," she explained, leading him further into the house. "The rogue wolf that bit you is part of a larger problem he's been working on for almost a year. He gets very focused."

Now there was an understatement. Half the time, Ezra felt that Callum didn't even see him at all. He picked up his duffel bag and followed Wyn up the stairs. "Am I really going to be so dangerous you need Blaise to protect you?"

Wyn didn't answer at first, just pushed open one of three doors at the top of the stairs. "This one's you. The one in the middle is the bathroom, and the other one is mine."

Ezra nodded, settling his duffel bag on the floor and taking in a room that was just as tastefully decorated as the room downstairs, though the small space was almost completely dominated by the queen-sized four-poster bed. The fact that she'd avoided answering his question didn't fill him with confidence. "Thanks."

"As for your question…." Wyn sat down on the bed and gave Ezra a gentle smile before patting the space next to her, and Ezra breathed a small sigh of relief. It seemed that not every lycanthrope was going to be as stingy with details as the pack leader. "It's going to sound kind of awful."

"I've got a lot of experience with that lately," he reminded her ruefully.

"I can only imagine." Wyn shifted a little, looking down at her sock-clad feet, which dangled a good eighteen inches off the floor. "The wolf who bit you, Teller—he was infected with what they used to call Lyssavirus A, because at first they thought it was a lycanthrope-specific strain of rabies. The symptoms are similar: disorientation, anxiety, agitation, fever. But that's not what it is. When they caught Teller, they got a sample of his blood, and there's no virus in it. That's why they're calling it ARD now. It's something else."

"What does that have to do with the security detail Callum wants to put me under?"

"Because one of the effects of—whatever ARD really is—is to stimulate production of the signal pheromone specific to alpha wolves that makes betas want to do whatever they say."

Okay, Wyn was right, that sounded bad. At least it explained why Ezra was completely helpless when it came to disobeying commands from Callum. "Oh," he said quietly. "And this—pheromone, or whatever—it doesn't work on alpha wolves?"

"Right," Wyn answered. "Though don't forget that there are regular alphas and capital-A Alphas—the elected leaders. They usually end up being the strongest lowercase alpha wolves." She shot him a sideways glance. "Sorry, this is really confusing, isn't it?"

"I don't think that's your fault." Ezra tried to smile.

"Okay, so in the wild, most wolf packs are small, only consisting of one breeding pair and their offspring, but sometimes you get bigger packs, and they usually have a dominant pair."

"Callum called Jax his partner," Ezra recalled aloud.

Wyn nodded. "Exactly. In a lot of lycan packs, the Alphas do end up together—sort of a tradition, if you like. You spend a lot of time together, I guess. But a lot of the time it doesn't work out because they're, uh...." She stopped and blushed a little, and Ezra realized he could literally *smell* her embarrassment. That was just *weird*. "Because they start fighting about which of them should have *more* control."

Ezra figured it was probably a pretty safe guess that she didn't just mean in pack situations, either. Of *course* werewolves were into kinky sex. For years Ezra hadn't given those kinds of games much thought, but all of a sudden he couldn't seem to *stop* imagining them. "So are Callum and Jax...?"

"They're cousins, actually," Wyn supplied. "Callum was raised in another pack, but both he and his twin brother showed high levels of alpha behavior and signal pheromones when they started to change, so their pack Alphas trained them both. Then, about six years ago, both of our Alphas died in a car accident. They'd been mentoring Jax, so we had one spot covered, and then we sort of sent out an open call for any Alphas who might be at loose ends."

"On what?" Ezra asked. "The Twilight Bark?"

Wyn nudged him with her shoulder. "On the Internet, smarty pants. We have thumbs most of the time, you know. Anyway, so we had a couple of applicants, had an election, and now Callum's our Alpha. Jax had veto power, of course."

"Of course," Ezra echoed. "Okay, so alphas—no capital—are biologically predetermined to be dominant, and Alphas—capital A—are no-capital alphas who happen to be pack leaders."

"Sort of. We're not sure how much of it is nature and how much is nurture—the human brain is pretty complicated—but the rest is right."

That wasn't quite as confusing as it could have been. He swallowed. "And then there's us."

"Then there's us," Wyn said. "Sometimes it's difficult to tell who'll be alpha and who'll be beta until their first change, but...." She looked sort of apologetic. "Sometimes it's really obvious."

Great. Even as a freaking werewolf he was going to be at the bottom of the food chain. Ezra covered his eyes with his hands. "Awesome."

"Hey." Wyn nudged him again, then again and again until he finally looked up at her. "There's no shame in it, Ezra. The betas are the strength of the pack. Without us, there would *be* no pack."

Ezra let out a long breath. "I guess if it were all alphas, there would be a lot of fighting."

"Exactly!" Wyn beamed. Then she leaned in conspiratorially. "And between you and me, half of them are so headstrong they'd be completely lost without us to look after them and talk sense into them."

There was the click of a latch from downstairs, and both of them raised their heads. Wyn, Ezra noticed, tipped her head to one side to listen just like he was doing, an act that seemed completely instinctive even though he'd never have been able to hear anything when he was human.

"Speaking of Alphas," Wyn said, standing. "That's Jax. She's going to want to talk to you."

Ezra didn't ask how she knew, just nodded, putting his hands in his lap as Wyn went downstairs to greet her guest.

Chapter Three
Worse Than Its Bite

A FEW minutes later the door to the bedroom opened again and Jax was there, smiling vaguely. She had a ratty-looking towel in one hand, which she left on the bookshelf by the door. "Hey, new kid. Sorry if I embarrassed you earlier."

Ezra blinked. This Jax was so different from the one he'd met just half an hour before. "I... okay."

"I'm going to sit, okay?"

Wait, she was asking for *his* permission? Ezra frowned but nodded anyway, and Jax took Wyn's vacated spot on the bed.

"The thing is, Callum has been working way too hard lately. It makes him cranky and inattentive. Frankly, he needs to get laid, and how."

Okay, there was the Jax he'd thought he'd met. A strangled sound attempted to escape Ezra's throat. "Um, should you be talking about him like that?"

"All part of my apology." Jax waved an explanatory hand. "Besides, I'm Alpha too. I'm just trying to plant the idea in his brain, that's all. I didn't do it to be mean to you. I'm sure you have enough going on in your head right now without adding romantic entanglements with our fearless leader to the list."

Actually, if Ezra could get all thoughts of romantic—okay, basely sexual, but never mind—entanglements with Callum out of his head, that would be really awesome. "Okay. Apology accepted, I guess?" He wasn't actually sure he *had* been apologized to, technically, but he wasn't really in a position to belabor the point.

"Good! Now, on to pack affairs." Jax stood again, suddenly all business. "This is normally Callum's job, but as I said, he's busy. Now, you've been taken under the protection of this pack—the Missoula one; we're the largest pack in the state—for your own good, but we won't always be able to protect you. What we can do is make sure all the other lycans—other packs and lone wolves alike—recognize that you're affiliated with us. Signal pheromones from other packs don't have quite the same effect, so you should be reasonably safe as long as you don't let any other wolves bite you."

Ezra wasn't quite sure what other lycan packs would want with him anyway. He hadn't even changed once yet. "Wait, did you say—"

"The bite is the way we proclaim pack allegiance," Jax explained. "It shouldn't hurt. Just a quick nip and the exchange of some yummy pheromones. Right now you're susceptible to Teller's influence, and that could be dangerous to you as well as to this pack."

"You want to bite me," Ezra clarified for his own sanity.

"Exactly! But before I do, you have to take the pack oath."

Ezra narrowed his eyes at her, trying to gauge whether she was joking. He didn't think she was. "There's an oath?"

"Only for people who weren't born into the pack," Jax explained. "And for Alphas, when they're being sworn in. It's really long, but I'll give you the short version, okay?"

Like Ezra had any choice. He shrugged. "Go for it."

"Excellent. Do you, Ezra Jones, promise to uphold the ideals of the pack, to consider its needs above your own, to respect its leaders even when they are giant balls of frustrated sexual urges, and to keep it safe to the best of your ability?"

God, it was like marrying an entire *group* of people. Messed up, occasionally canine, *totally psychotic* people. "I do," he said a little hesitantly. What the hell was he letting himself in for?

"Great. Take off your shirt if you don't want it to get bloody."

Ezra sighed. "This is a disturbing trend with you guys, you know that?" At least Jax didn't seem to be using the signal pheromone on him. He was pretty sure he was taking off his shirt under his own power; there was no overwhelming rush of pleasure as he did so. Or maybe that was specific to Callum.

"Callum wasted no time ordering you out of your clothes, huh? Not surprising. You are just his type." Jax leaned down so she could examine the scar tissue on Ezra's shoulder and touched the skin lightly, her blasé demeanor becoming serious. "Teller really got you good. You're lucky to be alive."

Blinking, Ezra looked down at where her fingertips met his arm and realized she was right. He must have lost a lot of blood, and he had no idea how he'd even gotten into his apartment building. Had his attacker had a sudden moment of clarity and brought him up there to heal? Or had Teller merely been planning to turn him from the beginning? "I'm not feeling all that lucky," he confessed.

Jax straightened up and gave him a small smile. "That's understandable." Turning, she closed the bedroom door behind her, took the rag from the bookshelf, then made her way back to the bedside and tilted her head, considering. "Hmm. Okay, why don't you lie down on the bed? That will probably be easiest."

Again, there was no rush to do as she'd said, but Ezra complied anyway. Then, when he didn't get that happy buzz for a job well done, he decided he might as well ask about it. "When Callum tells me to do something, it's different, like I have to do what he says. I can't help it. But it's not like that with you."

"Like I said, he's been distracted." Jax leaned down over him and tucked her towel under his head, pulling it down so that the ends were just under his bare shoulders. "He's probably not zapping you with it on purpose. Still, that's not an excuse. I'll talk to him about it, ask him to scale it back."

"So you can control that? The, what did Wyn call it, signal pheromones?"

Jax patted his leg. "Some of us are better at it than others, but yeah, it's a skill alphas learn. Normally Callum is meticulous, but I don't think he's been sleeping well. Exhaustion can lead to a loss of control." Obviously considering the subject closed, she went on, "So, are you ready?"

"As I'll ever be," Ezra muttered. He had a hell of a lot more answers now than he'd had from Callum, so he supposed he had to be satisfied with them, at least for the time being.

"Great."

Then, without warning, Jax was on the bed with him, straddling his hips. Ezra froze, his eyes going wide, feeling more uncomfortable than he had ever been in his life. "Um, what—"

Jax put a finger on his chin, tilting his head to the desired angle. "I need to get as good a grip as possible. It's going to be a little weird, sorry."

It was already a little weird. A lot weird. Incredibly, excruciatingly weird. Ezra squirmed. "Could we maybe—"

Jax sighed and gathered up his wrists, pinning them in one hand. She was surprisingly strong for someone so slender. "Sorry about this, but it's for your own good. I'm likely to hurt you otherwise." Then Ezra felt it, the seductive lull of what must be the signal pheromones. He wanted to jerk away, but it was too late. "Hold still," Jax commanded, and he froze as he was: spine stiff, arms limp against the pillows, neck bared.

This time the rush of pleasure at having obeyed was coupled with a sudden sharp pain low on his neck. Ezra whined briefly before silencing himself, pressing his lips together in a hard line as Jax flooded his senses with what must have been the pack's signature pheromone, something spicy and wild that smelled of belonging, coming home. Apparently it wasn't only Callum's orders that went right to Ezra's dick.

Then the strength of Jax's command wore off and Ezra twitched, embarrassed.

Luckily, Jax seemed to have anticipated this, because she went with the motion, keeping her fangs from tearing a jagged hole in his flesh. There was a low warning growl that reverberated throughout Ezra's entire body, and he went limp again.

Well, *almost* limp, Ezra amended mentally, mortified. Jax had shifted her stance over his body, and there was no way she didn't feel his erection, pressed as it was to the inside of her thigh. Flushing hard enough to burst a vessel, he kept his eyes closed until the nightmare was over.

Finally Jax eased off of him and sat back, wiping at a trickle of blood in the corner of her mouth, her expression creased with distaste. "Ugh." She slid off to one side and wiped the skin of his neck with the towel. "Now I remember why I make Callum do this part."

Ezra trembled in shame at the touch, barely resisting the urge to curl into a ball. What the hell was wrong with him? Never in his life had a woman, no matter how beautiful, elicited that kind of response from him. He just wasn't wired for it—guys did it for him, end of story. Until now, apparently. "God, I'm so sorry, that's never...."

Jax patted him on the shoulder roughly. "I meant the taste of blood, kid. Not my thing."

Well, at least she wasn't offended. "I can't believe that happened," Ezra whispered. Like this day could get any worse.

Jax shrugged. "I can. If it helps, it doesn't have anything to do with me, and I don't take it personally. The same thing would have happened if Callum had bitten you."

Ezra doubted that. If Callum had bitten him, Ezra would have had to put his entire arm down his own throat to stop himself from begging Callum to fuck him. "So this always happens when you bite someone?"

"Not always." Jax pulled him into a sitting position. "Not usually with the alphas, and only sometimes with betas. We're not really sure why, but some wolves react to the signal pheromone sexually and some don't."

"But I'm not a freak."

"I can see you're going to take some convincing." Jax flashed him a quick, humorless smile. "In my years as Alpha, we've bitten fifteen people to bring them into the pack."

We. Wait—was she going to talk about this with Callum? Because that would be awful.

Ezra's eyes must have widened, because Jax went on, "You have to remember that most of them are just people moving around with their jobs, like regular people do. Most turned humans end up as lone wolves because they're not good at adhering to our social structure. You're *special*," Jax stressed like she didn't mean "a freak." "Anyway, of those fifteen people, four of them reacted like you—one woman and three men."

Ezra frowned. "How…?"

Jax tapped her nose.

"Oh God." He was *never* going to get used to being able to smell… *that*. Never.

"Anyway, one of them was an alpha. The others were betas. It's not as cut-and-dried as you might think."

Ezra sighed. "Nothing ever is."

With one last hearty pat on the shoulder, Jax rose off the bed and stretched. "Well, now that most of the trauma is over, I think I'll leave you to your rest. You're probably going to need it."

THE sound of the front door slamming shut heralded Callum's arrival home. Fortunately, there was no one in the house to give him attitude for it.

Callum knew that slamming the door was childish, but it had been a long, frustrating day. The CDC's video surveillance recordings had failed to meet even Callum's lowest expectations. Not only had they not provided any useful answers, but they had left Callum with more questions.

The footage had showed Teller talking to a guard, and the guard had approached the door as if drugged. Callum had recognized the look of a man under the influence of signal pheromones—a highly unwelcome surprise. Teller had been put under human guard for a reason. Pheromones didn't work across species; an alpha lycanthrope couldn't get a regular human to do their bidding like they could a beta. At least not by using *pheromones* to force a compulsion. So how had Teller managed to get the guard to unlock his cell door?

The rest of the escape had been accomplished through the use of teeth and claws. Teller had scratched and ripped, crushed and torn anyone who had tried to stop him. So Callum had focused on the only abnormal thing about the video: the guard susceptible to wolf pheromones.

Callum had asked the security officer manning the surveillance cameras where he could find the guard. She had informed him that he was working down on the main floor, guarding files and not people.

Entering room 116, Callum had found Phil Taylor sitting behind a desk, looking bored. The sign on the door read ARCHIVES: Patient Files, and behind it was a wide counter that stretched nearly the width of the room and separated visitors from the numerous filing cabinets.

"Are you Phil Taylor?"

Taylor had looked relieved to see someone interrupting his solitude. Hopeful his eagerness for company would translate into an eagerness to talk, Callum had approached with a friendly face.

It had worked. Taylor had answered all of Callum's questions about the experience. Callum had left the interview knowing two things: Taylor definitely wasn't a wolf, but his description of being under the influence had sounded very accurate. Unless Taylor had been well coached by a wolf, he was telling the truth.

It left Callum with a very frustrating clue. Teller had managed to compel a human, though how he had crossed the species line, Callum had no idea. Callum would have to try to solve that puzzle as well, though without having Teller close at hand, he was unlikely to get anywhere. At the moment, his best guess was that ARD somehow changed the chemical makeup of the signal pheromones so that they were potent for humans as well as lycans.

Callum made his way toward the kitchen. It was well past noon, and he hadn't yet had lunch.

By the time Jax came strolling into the room, Callum was scraping his plate clean. He was still craving more meat, like he always did when he was angry, but he felt somewhat sated and much calmer. Of course, Jax's arrival managed to undo that.

"Hello, Dawson, how's it hanging today?" The innuendo was obvious in her tone. She wore a form-hugging knee-length dress and knee-high black leather hooker boots. Callum felt a familiar wave of sympathy for the poor beta that Jax would one day set her sights on.

Callum pushed his plate away and sighed. "You'd better sit down," he told her, and he proceeded to update her on his findings at the CDC.

Jax sighed and ran her fingers through her hair. "So not only does Teller have super lycanthrope strength, but he can get humans to do what he wants. Great, just what I like to hear."

Callum nodded. "I know. No answers and more questions."

They sat in silence for a moment.

"Well, this wasn't why I came over. I wanted to talk to you about your new toy."

The groan was unavoidable. "He's not a toy. Or *my* anything."

"Sure he is! Anyway, I don't want to argue about that. What I wanted to tell you was that thanks to yours truly, the boy is now officially part of the pack. *Which* I deserve lots of treats for, because blood is gross."

"Yes, yes, you deserve a whole box of Milk-Bones." Callum was used to this. Jax was pretty vocal about how much she hated biting new pack members.

"Also, you need to give the kid a break. Based on what he said, you've been blasting him with enough pheromones to bamboozle even a seasoned wolf."

Busted. He covered his face with his hands. "I know," he mumbled into his palms. He scrubbed his face before letting his hands fall away with a sigh. "I wasn't doing it on purpose. It kept catching me off guard, though. It's like… the inner wolf wants to turn every interaction into a power play." He sat back and looked at Jax. "I'll do a better job of policing myself. I don't know how, but I'll do it."

Jax snorted. "You could start by getting some sleep. Or laid. Either would do your stress levels and your control a world of wonder."

Not this again. "Jax, I told you before—"

"Yes, yes, finding one-night stands is *so* difficult, and you get as much sleep as your job allows."

"I was going to say that I don't want you sticking your nose in my business."

"Tough. You joined my pack, so I get to stick my nose in your business all I want."

Despite the glare that he sent in Jax's direction, Callum couldn't help but feel somewhat relieved that she cared so much. Still, he didn't want to say as much to her. The expression "give her an inch, and she'll take a mile" might as well have been coined for Jax.

Fortunately, Callum was saved from having to repeat himself or agree with her when his phone rang. "Callum Dawson."

"Callum, it's Ryan Jackson." Ryan was a smart and capable young lycan that Callum trusted to do whatever was asked of him. He was also a police officer. "We just got a lead on Teller."

Callum's heart beat a little faster. Finally, some good news! "Where?" he barked out, grabbing a pen and paper to write down notes.

Ryan's response was succinct. Soon, Callum and Jax were out the door and heading to one of the seedier motels in town.

The motel was depressing. The exterior walls were water stained and covered in faded, peeling paint. The parking lot asphalt was crumbling into numerous pot holes, and the yellow demarcation lines were all but nonexistent. The lawns were dry and dreary, matched by the solemn door and window of the front office.

Callum and Jax shared a brief look. Though cheerless, the motel did offer a great deal of anonymity. No one here was likely to care who you were.

Ryan was waiting for Callum and Jax in the parking lot. He was standing next to his SUV, leaning back against the dark-green door. He nodded in greeting.

"So, anything else to tell me?" Callum didn't want to waste time.

"Not much. He's in room five. He checked in sometime during the night, and the clerk's certain he hasn't left his room since he got here. I've been here for thirty minutes, and I haven't seen hide nor hair of him."

Callum frowned as he took in the motel, the parking lot, and the street beyond. He could see Jax doing the same thing. "You get a key off the clerk?"

"Yup. Told him I was calling backup and he should stay quiet in his office."

Good. This might work.

They were cautious as they entered. Ryan had his sidearm out and cocked. Jax gave her telescoping baton one last twirl before she settled it into the palm of her hand.

Their weapons proved to be unnecessary. The room was dark and poorly lit, but there was enough light streaming through the half-closed blinds for Callum to make out Teller's huddled form. He was pressed into the far corner of the room, hiding behind one of the bedside tables.

He seemed quiet and calm, unmoving as he stared into space. Callum took a step into the room, Jax and Ryan close behind.

The inside, Callum thought as he took in his surroundings, was just as depressing as the outside. Here, too, the paint was faded and the walls marked, though he doubted the decor would have been anything but drab and weary even if it had been new. The smells of old sweat and sex, mold, and dirt were pervasive, but they failed to mask the stomach-churning scent of dried blood.

"Teller?" he asked as he took a step closer.

The reaction was immediate and violent. Teller's right arm flew out, and he smacked the wall with his closed fist. The drywall cracked, and Teller made a wounded noise.

"Don't say that name. He's not here."

"Are you not Adam Teller?"

"No." Teller shifted and brought one arm up to curve over his head protectively.

Callum took another cautious step. "Who are you, then?"

"Don't know. Someone… something bad." Callum could see his eyes shining from beneath his arm, two points of shimmery reflected light among dark shadows.

"Why do you think that?"

"I had a dream…. I stalked a man. Pounced." His body jerked in remembrance, and both arms flew forward to curl in the air. "Tore into his flesh and bit him. Bite, bite, bite…." The words trailed off, and Teller seemed to get lost in his own thoughts. His arms flopped to the ground like overcooked spaghetti, and Callum got his first glimpse of Teller's clothes. There was dry blood caked in the weave of his T-shirt, a deep rust color disfiguring the pattern painted onto the cloth. *That's Ezra's blood.* Callum's stomach twisted painfully at the sight.

"Blood like sweet wine all over my tongue and all over me. Blood, blood, blood. Everywhere!" Teller's elbow jerked back to hit the wall with force. When he continued, his voice was soft once more. "Then I woke up from the nightmare… but the blood… the blood was still everywhere." Teller looked down at the stains then and let out a long piteous moan.

"I dreamt I was a soldier and marched the streets of Bir— Billings." Teller hit his head against the wall. "The indolent town where the barkers call the moon down."

Suddenly he was a blur of motion, his limbs jerking around, fingers scrabbling at his shirt and pulling. "*Get it off!* There's blood, *blood everywhere*! It's trying to choke me. It wants me *dead*!" Teller tore the shirt to pieces in his haste to remove it from his body, but he kept screaming about the blood. "The monster—the monster wants them all dead! Torn, ripped, shredded to pieces."

Making a rapid decision, Callum asked Ryan, "You got any tranqs in your kit?"

"Yes, sir, standard issue for wildlife that wanders into the city."

"Get them."

Ryan turned and dashed from the room.

Callum could feel his heart beating a fierce tattoo against his ribs. Teller's sudden violent outburst had Callum doubting that taking the madman in would be as easy as he'd hoped. No, using the tranquilizer would be best; Teller would travel better if he weren't conscious.

Sharp eyes turned on Callum. They were surprisingly clear and calm. "Alpha." Teller snarled. "You stink of Alpha." It was all the warning he gave before launching himself to his feet and straight for Callum.

Callum had just enough time to throw his arms up to defend himself before he heard the sound of a gun being fired.

Spinning on his toes, he searched out the source of the noise and found Ryan standing in the doorway with a rifle still braced against his shoulder. "Told you. It's standard issue for bears."

The breath Callum took next was deep but shaky.

"Son of a bitch," Jax cursed even as she took a few steps closer to Teller's body as he faded out of consciousness. She poked at the limp hand on the floor with the toe of her boot. The eyes she lifted to Callum were wide and a little fearful. "Callum, what the hell was that?"

"The rather unpleasant aftereffects of ARD, I'm assuming. I knew it would likely be bad, but I wasn't expecting…."

There was silence. No, none of them had been expecting *that*.

"Right, let's get this out of here. Ryan, can you transport Teller back to my lab? I need to run a battery of tests on him as soon as possible." It wouldn't be good for Teller's mental state, but without Callum's research, he didn't have a chance at all.

"Sure thing, Alpha."

In the end, it took all three of them to carry and navigate Teller out of the room and into Ryan's SUV. It was an awkward task, given that Teller was dead weight. It was also rather nerve-racking, as they were still in a public parking lot. Ryan might have local public authority, but fewer witnesses to pack business were always best.

It wasn't until both Callum and Jax were once again safely in his car and Ryan was out of hearing that Jax turned to him and said, "Shit, Dawson. Shit, shit, shit. We are so fucked."

Callum silently agreed.

Chapter Four
Of Wolf and Man

DAMN!

Davis pulled the sample from the centrifuge and tossed it aside. Still no change. The levels of alphatropin in the sample blood were still as random and unpredictable as ever.

Placing both hands on the lab table, Davis let his head fall forward with a sigh. He'd been working on the issue for weeks without much success. Though the serum had worked in every test subject so far, he had had little success at controlling the outcomes.

Pulling away from the table, Davis turned his back on his recent findings. He ignored the beast strapped to the table in the corner and instead headed for the coffee pot.

Not that caffeine would help much, judging by his lack of success for the past few weeks. The Boss wouldn't be happy. He had come to Davis a week ago, angry that the infected lycans refused any sort of direction. He had ordered Davis to find a way of making the infected more compliant. Unfortunately, whenever a new lycan succumbed to the drug, it became a loose cannon. Not that loose cannons weren't useful, especially if you wanted to create terror through randomized attacks—the infected were nothing if not random—but they were useless at targeting specific people. And the Boss *had* a list of people to target.

Davis had hoped that by refining the serum he could find a way to control the size of the spike in the hormone levels so that the infected wouldn't be so wildly unpredictable. He hadn't had any success so far, and the lack of progress was making the Boss extra cranky. Davis was beginning to think he'd have to give up his current efforts to refocus in a totally new direction. It was possible that there was another way of making them more biddable, but Davis had thought that regulating the alphatropin levels would be their best bet.

With a sigh, Davis turned back to the lycan and picked up a tray of syringes before walking back across the room. It was time to get back to work. The Boss would be by for a check-in tomorrow, and Davis really didn't have time to waste. Maybe he'd make a breakthrough before then.

THE next morning Ezra woke up to discover that not only was the usual delicious spread already laid out, but that Wyn was standing over her large standing mixer hard at work. Arranged on the counter next to her was a large collection of raw ingredients, packages of cheese, and several boxes of... Ezra tilted his head to read the label. Ladies' fingers?

Grabbing some pancakes, Ezra took a seat on a bar stool before filling a coffee mug from the carafe. Then he settled in to eat and watch Wyn work.

Ezra tended to be fairly nonverbal before consuming his first cup of coffee. Both Wyn and Blaise had learned to accept this.

While pouring his second cup, Ezra finally asked, "So what's with the early morning baking?" Seriously, Wyn must've been up for hours already.

"Tiramisu needs a good two hours in the fridge, and I want it to be ready before we leave," Wyn said rather unhelpfully, though the way she wrinkled her nose as she contemplated the refrigeration time was adorable.

"You're *making* tiramisu?" Even though Ezra had been waking up to Wyn's delicious culinary skills for a week and a half, this impressed him.

"Yes, I'm making tiramisu. You do realize that it was made by home cooks long before it was served in restaurants."

Ezra just rolled his eyes at that. "Yes. I've just never known anyone who had that kind of skill."

Wyn wrinkled her nose again. "At least wait to taste it before you decide that."

"I'll get to taste it?" He hadn't figured he was included in Wyn's "we" earlier.

Wyn mirrored his surprise. She blinked a few times in his direction before saying, "Of course you will."

Sometimes Wyn was adorably slow. "So… where are *we* going today?"

The look she gave him was still baffled. "To family dinner, of course. Didn't—didn't Callum tell you about it?"

That would be a big fat no. Ezra said as much, and Wyn suddenly looked very uncertain.

"Oh, well, every Sunday afternoon the pack gets together for an early dinner. We let you sleep through it last week because you were so tired."

Oh. Oh God. The pack had a family dinner? It struck Ezra now that he had been lucky to get sick the week before—his new digestive system didn't like chocolate, and between that and his body's exhaustion from the genetic changes, he had spent most of the weekend in bed. Now Wyn, and likely Callum, too, thought Ezra was ready to be thrown right into the middle of this free-for-all? According to Callum, there were over fifty members in the pack, which hadn't sounded that big to Ezra when Callum had first told him, but he hadn't planned on meeting them all at once. Maybe he could get more chocolate…. "Um. Are you sure that's a good idea? Maybe I should just stay home?"

"Of course it is. Everyone will be very disappointed if you don't show up."

Ezra swallowed hard.

"Besides, Callum promised to bring you. Everyone started calling and knocking on his door when you didn't show up last week. Callum made the deal so that they'd leave you alone at first and give you time to settle in."

Ezra stared. Oh God, Callum promised to *bring* him? Like he was a new puppy or something? And damn, but that metaphor was too close to the truth for comfort. But if Callum had promised, then no way was Ezra getting out it. If he tried to stay home, Callum would just show up and order him to go. And Ezra really didn't want to show up to meet the rest of the pack coming down from a positive reinforcement kick.

"Okay. So, if I'm going to go to this shindig, why don't you give me the rundown?"

DESPITE the fact that Wyn was very forthcoming when it came to providing details about this afternoon, Ezra wasn't feeling very well prepared by the time they reached the "community center." Callum had rolled his eyes to hear Wyn call it that, but he had failed to come up with a better name.

"It might look like a bungalow from the outside, but inside it's a sprawling open concept design with a large kitchen and plenty of space. It's where we always get together for pack gatherings," Wyn had told Ezra. He had to agree with her: that sounded like a community center to him.

He hesitated on the front step, trying to gear himself up to go inside. On the other side: fifty people who wanted to meet him, because he was a rarity and a bit of a freak show. *Awesome.*

"By now, everyone will know all the important information about you," Wyn had explained. And when Ezra had hazarded to wonder what she deemed important, Wyn had wrinkled her nose and shrugged apologetically. "That you've recently been turned, that you're a beta, and that you're staying with me."

Ezra had groaned. Great, they all knew the most embarrassing fact about him.

"Are you sure I have to go?" Ezra had asked her and then, later, Callum, when he had arrived to escort them to the meeting. Callum had looked equally apologetic but as expected had refused to back down.

"Think positive. If you let them stare all they want now, then there's less chance of them peeking in your window later." To say that Ezra hadn't been comforted by that would be an understatement.

Still, Callum refused to let him off the hook. "Every week it will get easier," he told Ezra as they were walking over, and Ezra barely contained the groan as he contemplated the prospect of having to do this every week.

Callum went in first. Ezra was too relieved at not having to be in front to feel insulted. Still, despite the fact that he waved Wyn to go in second, when Ezra walked through the front door, everyone went silent, watching.

Wyn's description of the building had been fairly accurate. The front door led to a large main room filled with seats. In the center was a large colorful rug covered in children and toys and surrounded by parents and other minders, including Jax. At the other end of the room, there was a large kitchen that was separated from the rest of the room by a long half wall. To the left was a wide doorway, and Ezra caught a glimpse of a table and chairs. All in all it looked like the perfect setup for the family get-together that was clearly in progress.

A large group of teens and pre-teens sprawled across two couches, a window seat, and the floor in between. The guilty flush on the cheeks of one young girl at the window suggested she had been unofficial lookout. Small groups of adults stood and sat all around the room, and several waist-high children bobbed and weaved between them. The last group to notice Ezra's arrival was the small army of mostly women that was working in the kitchen. Their laughter had been the last to go quiet. Ezra felt the blush rise in his cheeks at the knowledge that they were *all* staring at him.

"Well," was Callum's opening gambit. "It looks like everyone is here. Perfect, that means I can go ahead and introduce the newest member of our pack. By now I'm sure you've all heard the rumors, so I'd like to get some facts straight. Ezra was bitten without permission, but he has pledged allegiance to our pack." Callum held up his hand to forestall the comment of a middle-aged man. "No, Matt, Jax and I haven't forgotten about procedure. However, given the circumstances, we feel it best to welcome Ezra into our pack. So, everyone, I would like you to meet Ezra Jones." Callum pulled Ezra forward with one hand on his arm, and there was a chorus of fifty strangers saying, "Hello, Ezra."

Ezra wished the floor would swallow him up, but when it didn't, he just lifted one hand to give an awkward wave.

Then Callum more or less told everyone to back off and let Ezra meet them in smaller groups, and slowly people let their attentions drift.

Wyn began weaving her way toward the kitchen, Blaise following happily behind her. Callum shifted forward, and Ezra's hand shot out to grip his forearm without any input from his brain. The desperate whisper of "Don't leave me!" that followed was similarly involuntary. Wow, could he get more pathetic?

Fortunately, Callum only gave a reassuring smile before promising not to leave Ezra alone before he was ready.

The warm happy feeling hadn't yet faded when Callum wrapped one hand around his forearm—there it was, back again—and pulled Ezra away from the group. Ezra was all too happy to go.

The dining room was unoccupied, but it was filled with chairs, and Ezra and Callum settled into neighboring ones at the end of the large table, limiting the number of people who could ambush them at once. Ezra sighed in relief.

"Relax. They're good people, and they don't *want* to frighten you. I promise." Callum's eyes were warm and comforting.

"So… what happens now?"

"We wait for someone to be bold enough to be the first to come join us. They'll meet you, talk to you, and then wander off so someone else can have a turn."

"I feel like the guest speaker at some kind of awkward fancy dinner… thing." The exact word he was looking for escaped him.

"Well, I don't know about fancy, but you certainly are the guest of honor," said an amused voice from the doorway.

Ezra spun to see a large man with an arm wrapped around a petite woman's shoulders. While he was tall and broad with pale skin, blond hair, and ice-blue eyes, she was short and slim with skin the color of dark chocolate and hair and eyes black as night. They were rather striking together.

"Ah, Ezra, I'd like you to meet Sebastien and Emma LaPorte, Blaise and Jax's parents."

Ezra couldn't help the way he stared at the biracial couple with his mouth open. When he had been told that Jax and Blaise were brother and sister, he had just assumed they were step or half siblings, but… well, the similarity in facial features between Jax and this Emma woman was too startling to ignore, and Blaise had certainly not gotten his height from her. "Uh."

The grins that Emma and Sebastien gave Ezra were nothing but cheeky. "Yes, we know, Blaise and Jax are both actually our children," Sebastien said.

Ezra blushed hotly and looked away, mortified. Damn, he didn't want the LaPortes' first impression of him to be that he was rude and slack-jawed. Underneath the table, Callum pressed their knees together, offering comfort.

"Oh, he's adorable," said Sebastien as he pulled out a chair first for his wife and then for himself. "I can see why Jax likes him so much already."

"Ignore my husband, Ezra, he's just being an ass. Now stop blushing, you'd be silly to think that you are the first person to be surprised by our family's biological roulette. Genetics are a strange and wonderful thing, we know."

Despite himself, Ezra lifted his head to get a better look at this new stranger. He liked her already.

"So, Ezra, Jax tells us that you've been living at Wyn's house." Emma smiled encouragingly. "How are you finding it?"

He started nodding straight away. "Good. Wyn's great. She's been the perfect hostess. And to be honest, I think she likes having two men with healthy appetites to feed."

Emma and Sebastien both laughed. "Yes, Blaise can eat and always did appreciate fine cooking," Emma said.

Sebastien gave a wink as he added, "And Wyn is, perhaps, the finest baker in the pack."

Without thought, Ezra gave an answering smile. "Best waffles I ever tasted. Makes me glad to get out of bed in the morning."

That made Sebastien laugh. "Too right, son, delicious breakfasts are certainly a great way of getting a man out of bed."

That was probably a blush heating up his face. Sebastien hadn't winked or leered to suggest anything that might keep a man in or out of bed, but somehow he had made the subtext of the comment clear. "Um." Ezra licked his lips, uncertain what to say next.

"Are you thirsty, dear?" Emma looked as if she might stand up and fetch him something to drink.

Callum shifted. "Sit, Emma, let me fetch us some water." Then he stood up and moved away toward the kitchen. Ezra couldn't help but watch after him longingly. He wasn't sure he was ready to deal with even these two nice strangers on his own.

There was a long awkward silence that followed Callum's departure, and Ezra let his gaze flicker around the room.

"So," said Sebastien in a tone of voice that reminded Ezra of Jax and made him very nervous. When Jax sounded like that, she usually said something to make Ezra cringe. "My daughter tells me that she bit you into the pack."

There was nothing to say to that, though Ezra tried, for a moment, to come up with something. "Uh…."

"What?" Ezra turned his head at Emma's surprised outburst to see that he was being regarded with a suspicious look. "Jax didn't tell me that."

It was Sebastien who answered her. "Didn't she? She said something a few days ago—something about helping Callum out."

"Really?" Emma turned away from her husband to look back at Ezra again. "Jax bit you?"

"Um… yes? Is that—is this very odd? I mean, I know that Jax said Callum usually bites new members, but…."

Sebastien nodded. "Jax hates biting people. She hasn't bitten anyone into the pack in years," he explained.

"Oh." Ezra wasn't sure how to respond to that.

"So why did she bite you?" Emma tilted her head and eyed Ezra in a manner that was all too knowing.

"I don't…." *Know why? Know what to tell you?* Ezra really had no idea what to say to the woman. How did you respond to someone giving you such an eagle-eyed look when you didn't know what they wanted?

"Here we are. Water for everyone." Callum had arrived, saving Ezra from having to answer. He was carrying four glasses between his two large hands and set them down on the table. "Emma, Sebastien," he murmured as he passed them each a glass. Then he passed one to Ezra and resumed his seat.

For a moment there was an awkward pause; Emma seemed unwilling to pick up where she had left off, and the men were reluctant to change the subject. Finally, Callum broke the silence. "So, it's been some time since I've last seen you. How have you two been?"

Sebastien gave a small smile and easily took up the obvious subject change. After a time, Emma joined the conversation once again, and soon the subject turned to the antics of young Blaise and Jax.

"She stopped answering to Jacqueline when she was five. She'd glare at you with her hands on her hips if you called her name. Kept insisting on Jax—with an X when she realized that was easier to spell." The smile that Emma gave him was the same shark smile that Jax favored.

"You telling stories again?" All of them turned to see Jax standing in the doorway. "You know you've got to stop hogging Ezra."

She gave her parents a teasing grin as she slid into the room. Sebastien rose to hug his daughter.

"Hey, Ez, hope these two aren't giving you a hard time." Jax's smile was genuine, and Ezra returned it.

"Your parents are much nicer than you are," Ezra found himself saying, and both Jax and Sebastien tossed their heads back and laughed.

Unfortunately, Jax was right, and others were waiting to meet him. Once Jax led her parents away, someone else took their place. The next few hours were a bit overwhelming, as people flowed in and out of the room in groups of two to four, all staring at him and asking questions. All in all, it was probably the most awkward time of Ezra's life, and he was so glad that Callum was there, a warm presence at his side.

Still, the afternoon did have enjoyable moments. For the most part, the lycans were kind, and some of them were actually fun to talk to. And of course the food was fantastic—though it might have tasted all the better because once the meal began, the focus was taken off Ezra, to some extent.

"Hey, Uncle Ezra, I got a joke for you!"

Ezra turned to stare down the table to find one of the five-year-olds staring at him with a gleeful grin. "Okay," he hedged.

"What did the lycan say when he got back from rehab?" The boy waited a half a beat before continuing, "I used to be a werewolf, but I'm a' right *noooooooooooooooow*!"

The gaggle of kids broke out into giggles, muffling their laughter in sticky palms, while the joke-teller grinned even wider. Suddenly one of the girls with blond pigtails was shouting that she too had a joke, and the kids all fell over themselves to share their favorites.

Unfortunately, not all of the lycans were as inviting or sweet as the children. Like in any other situation in life, Ezra found himself confronted by the surly unwelcoming one. Lucien was a young beta who greeted Ezra with a cool smile and regarded him with sneers. He shot Ezra barely veiled glares throughout the meal and made a few comments that weren't entirely nasty but weren't very kind either, like when he looked down the table and told Ezra that it must be nice to have found people who accepted him. There was something about the way he said it that made Ezra feel the double edge of the comment—

acknowledging the way the wolves had accepted him but implying effortlessly that no one else had or could.

Lucien didn't show his true colors until after dinner, when Ezra went to find the bathroom. After emptying his bladder, he exited the room and found himself face to face with Lucien.

Ezra froze under the onslaught of lazy, contemptuous elevator eyes. He had a feeling he was in for something unpleasant, but Lucien seemed to want to *talk*—there was no obvious way around him without brushing against him or asking him to move.

Finally, Lucien spoke, his words a lazy drawl. "You know, the way everyone's talking, I expected a little more Abercrombie. To be honest, I'm not sure what the fuss is about. It's not like Callum hasn't had... *interests* before. They never last. The boy—gets around." Lucien's lips quirked as he eyed Ezra. The challenge was clear in his every look, even his posture.

Ezra licked his lips and stared at Lucien. What was this guy's angle? "Well, anyone new is an oddity, no matter where you go," Ezra said with a modest shrug before trying to move around Lucien.

As he was passing him, Lucien reached out and poked at the bite mark on Ezra's neck. "We all heard about that too. Jax bit you. Strange, Callum usually marks his *territory*." He said "territory" with a sneer, as if to suggest that it was just code for something else, something filthy.

Unsure of how to respond to that, Ezra kept his mouth shut. He was just grateful right then that the other lycan was a beta—pushing him to the side and walking away was doable. It was hard to say, but Ezra suspected he'd have a hard time dismissing an alpha like that.

Despite the hiccup that was Lucien, as Ezra left the community center ("It's not a community center!" Callum protested), he felt remarkably good about being the new pack interest. Meeting the family hadn't been nearly as terrible as he had thought it was going to be.

THE psychiatrist that Callum sent him to was nothing like what Ezra had expected. Ezra had pictured a man or woman well into their fifties; however, he was sure that Robin Hertz was no more than thirty-five. He was thin and somewhat handsome and bore an uncanny resemblance to a young Alan Alda. The thought of getting a psych profile from Hawkeye Pierce made Ezra's lips twitch.

"So, has Callum explained to you exactly what's going to happen here?" Call-Me-Robin said after introductions were made.

"You're going to decide if I'm crazy?" Despite his best efforts to crack a joke, the sentence came out sounding mostly uncertain.

Robin smiled. "Not quite. You're a stranger, and you've been put through quite the ordeal, so my purpose is twofold. First, I'm here to make sure that you're coping well during this stressful time. Second, I'm to make sure that you're not a threat to the pack. It's why I asked you to fill out those questionnaires before you came in."

Ezra had been asked to sit down at a computer and rate dozens of statements about himself. Each question had seemed more ridiculous and random than the last, and Ezra had been obliged to say if he strongly agreed, somewhat agreed, felt ambivalent, disagreed, or strongly disagreed. The task had been boring but apparently not useless.

"Such tests, if you did your best to answer them truthfully, offer me insight into your mind and character. I use them in conjunction with this interview to create a profile for you."

"A profile?"

"Yes, one that will help us determine how best you'll fit into the pack."

"Wait, so you're also a lycan?"

"Would it make a difference if I was?"

"Yes. No." Ezra paused and actually thought about the question for a moment. It was probably a good idea to actually think before speaking to a psychiatrist. "I think that it would help knowing how much I can say and how much you'd understand from firsthand experience. I mean, the whole hyper-senses thing is a bit overwhelming, and I'm not sure anyone who hasn't experienced it could truly understand."

Robin nodded sympathetically and made a note on his pad. "Overwhelming? Are they too difficult to manage?"

There was silence as Ezra considered this. "No, not too difficult, just…. Well, it's not very fun."

"Hm. Other than hyperactive senses, how are you settling into life in the lycan community?"

"Okay, I guess." Robin was silent, as if waiting for Ezra to say more. God, he felt like he was fucking this up. In a bid to fill the uncomfortable silence, Ezra tossed out, "I've been staying with Wyn. She's really nice... welcoming."

"Hm, yes, Bronwyn. She's also a fantastic cook, I believe."

Ezra nodded. Relieved to have something to say, he might have gone overboard with his enthusiasm for her cooking. "And she makes the best waffles I've ever tasted." Ezra stopped to laugh along with Robin.

"You sound very passionate about this. Are you interested in culinary arts?"

"Not really." A shrug. "Just like to eat."

"So you have a healthy appetite?"

Ezra was suddenly reminded that he was talking to a psychiatrist, a doctor, and once again felt uncomfortable and uncertain. "Sure. I mean, who doesn't?" he asked, and then winced. He sounded like an idiot.

"Ezra, you should relax." The smile Robin offered was warm and soothing. "I'm not judging you, or at least not in the way that you imagine. True, I listen carefully to what you say to give it some sort of value, meaning, but not so that I can then lay judgment on you. I simply want to understand you better."

Ezra tried to smile.

"How about we start with something easy. Why don't you tell me about your hobbies?"

"Well, I do yoga and go camping—one of the benefits of living in Montana."

"Very true. When was the last time you were camping?"

"The weekend before my father passed away. I went up to Mt. Baker National Forest."

"What's it like there?"

"Gorgeous, as it's protected. And they have some pretty decent hiking trails."

"Did you ever go camping as a kid?"

"All the time. Dad used to take me up to Lolo or Beaverhead Forest for camping. We made the drive up to Greenough Lake more than once—it was my favorite. We'd hike to the lake and then drop a worm in the water. There are no motors allowed on the lake, so it's a beautiful spot." Ezra spent the next ten minutes telling Robin about his experiences camping as a child. It was easy to get lost in the familiar stories about sleeping in tents and building campfires and fishing in lakes and going on nature hikes.

Then Robin wanted to know how Ezra got into yoga—an embarrassing story that involved a rather bendy ex-boyfriend—which was followed by how Ezra had tried judo and tai chi and then tales about learning about computers and how he sometimes still wrote programs in his spare time. By then Ezra was feeling much more comfortable about talking with Robin, and he barely flinched when Robin turned the conversation to more serious topics.

"I'd like to talk about your recent transformation. Could you tell me about the experience of getting bitten?"

"I don't remember it. I was walking home drunk, and then I was waking up in my apartment and Callum and Blaise were knocking on the door." Ezra really didn't want to remember the first few hours as a werewolf. He hoped Robin would change the subject.

"What happened then?"

Not that lucky today, apparently. "They took me to the community, asked a lot of questions, set out a lot of rules, and then told me I had to stay at Wyn's." Ezra tried to give a nonchalant shrug.

After making another note, Robin regarded him for a long moment, then asked, "What did you first think of Callum?"

"First?"

"When you first saw him standing on your door step."

His very first impression? "That he looked like he was someone with power—someone used to having respect and control and used to using it."

"You let him into your house?"

"He asked." Another shrug. "Callum is kind of bossy and… well, I've learned since then that these new instincts have me wanting to do whatever he says."

"Oh?"

"Yeah. They say I'm a beta, and my body's all for this positive reinforcement bullshit. I keep getting this happy feeling whenever I do what Callum says."

"How does that make you feel?"

A slight blush warmed Ezra's cheeks. "Awkward. Uncomfortable. Callum tells me to do something and I just do it. I don't even think to question it until afterwards…."

"This makes you unhappy?"

"I don't—I'm just so unused to it. But I guess I'm going to have to *get* used to it."

"That seems like a fairly pragmatic approach."

"Well. I can't change it…."

"Would you like to?"

"… yes."

"You don't sound very sure about that."

"I don't mind getting directions or doing as asked. I just would like to have the choice is all."

More notes were made, and then Robin wanted to know about Ezra's schooling. After that topic was exhausted, he asked, "You mentioned a boyfriend earlier; do you identify as homosexual?"

"Yes."

"How long?"

"Uh, since my freshman year of high school. Like a lot of other teenage boys, I got initiated into gay desire while in PE locker rooms. Not the nicest time of a gay man's life, but…." Ezra shrugged.

"Why don't you tell me about your first boyfriend?"

"Adam Langley." At Robin's silent encouragement, Ezra continued. "He was quite handsome. Adam went to college for engineering. It was how we met. I was a freshman; he was a TA in one of my classes."

"So he was older?"

"Much. I was eighteen, nineteen, and Adam was twenty-four."

"And in a position of authority," Robin pointed out with one raised brow.

Ezra smirked a little. "That just made it hotter."

"Hm…. Who seduced who?"

Ezra recalled how Adam had looked those first few meetings. The way he had brought Ezra to his office, summoning him with an e-mail… how he had pressed Ezra up against the bookshelf, invading his space and making tantalizing promises. Ezra cleared his throat, uncomfortable with the flash of arousal that now filled him. "Adam seduced me."

Robin nodded, looking unsurprised. "How long did the relationship last?"

"Not very. We started sleeping together during second term, and Adam defended his master's thesis that August. Then he was off to another college for his PhD. He—we broke it off before he left. Seemed stupid to continue."

"Did you want to?"

Frowning deeply, Ezra said, "I just told you—"

"You told me that it 'seemed stupid to continue.' I'd like to know how you *felt* about your relationship, what you *desired*."

Once, Ezra had been in love with Adam Langley—or at least, he had thought himself in love. He had wanted to spend the rest of his life with Adam and had thought that Adam had felt the same way. He had had no idea that Adam was moving away to get his PhD or that he would break up with Ezra before he did so—at least, not until Adam had arrived at Ezra's apartment to tell him that he was leaving the state in two days. Ezra had been so angered by the news that he had tossed Adam out and ignored his offers for goodbye sex and his sneering insistence that Ezra surely hadn't thought that they would be *staying together*.

Ezra had cried himself to sleep that night and called in sick to work the next morning. When he had gone back to his day-to-day life, he had told himself that he was better off without Adam anyway. Now, three years later, it was easier to remember only the good times with Adam.

"I wanted to stay together, but Adam was dead set against it. What could I do?" Another nonchalant shrug.

"You could have made attempts to go after him, to seduce him."

He could have, he supposed, but… something had stopped Ezra then from pushing at Adam to keep him, and it had also kept Ezra from lingering on any *if only*s. "He said he didn't want me. He told me we were through and ended the relationship. It seems silly for me to have tried to ignore his vehemence."

"Hm." There was another long pause as Robin made more notes. "You've had other boyfriends since then, I'm assuming."

Ezra's nod was one of relief. He would happily talk about the other boyfriends he had had in the past three years. He hadn't loved any of *them*—most of them, in fact, had been more fuck buddy than boyfriend—and they had all parted ways with Ezra amicably. He was quite happy about the subject change and answered all of Robin's following questions with enthusiasm. Anything to get through this interview and on with the rest of his life.

BY THE time Ezra stumbled out of the psychiatrist's office, he was tired in a way that he hadn't been for some time. He was so emotionally wrung out that even his body felt tired. It wasn't as if the afternoon had been particularly exhausting, so he wasn't sure why, exactly, he felt that way—maybe the hormones? Still, Ezra was longing to get back to Wyn's house; he was sure that she would feed him something tasty and maybe give him something comforting to drink. Coffee, maybe, or a beer....

Ezra was surprised to find Blaise waiting for him outside Robin's office building. "Hello...?"

"Hey. How'd it go?"

"Uh, all right, I think."

"Not crazy?"

"No, I don't think so. Er, at least not today." He offered a tentative smile.

One corner of Blaise's mouth tilted upward in a quiet smirk before he led Ezra toward his car. Ezra got in, buckled up, and settled himself back in the seat. "So... you going to tell me why you're here to pick me up?"

Blaise made a noncommittal grunt.

"Where are we going? Can you tell me that?"

Blaise just glanced at him and arched an eyebrow.

"Fine, have your secrets."

"It's not a secret. You're the one trying to make this sound mysterious."

"It is! You show up and won't tell me why."

"Callum wanted me to bring you back to his house."

Which was where they were heading, Ezra realized. Blaise had just turned off the main drag and onto the first side street that would bring them home.

Or, rather, back to the lycan neighborhood.

Blaise slid his SUV smoothly into Callum's driveway.

It wasn't until Ezra was sitting at Callum's kitchen table and taking his first sip of his drink that he began to feel suspicious. It was as he was savoring the delicious flavors on his tongue that he looked down and truly took note of his drink. It was a pumpkin spice latte with extra whipped cream—his favorite seasonal guilty pleasure… and somewhat unusual coming from Callum. Especially since Ezra knew for certain that Callum could barely make a cup of black coffee. Callum would have had to buy this drink or have Wyn make it, and since it wasn't in a paper cup….

"Did you bring Wyn over just to make me a latte?" The drink was piping hot in his hands. Ezra looked around. "And then send her away?"

A shifty-eyed look was all Ezra got in response for several long moments. "She offered" was the eventual, and very lame, reply. It was kind of sweet in a very bizarre and weird way.

"Uh-huh. So. Why are you bribing me?"

"I'm not—"

"You clearly are, since you bothered to make sure that my favorite drink was ready and waiting for me when I arrived, *after* you sent Blaise to pick me up and bring me straight here. So what's the deal? This can't just be guilt over the therapy session this morning."

"I don't feel guilty about that! That's standard procedure, and I'm sure that you're not—"

Ezra smirked and took another drink of his latte. So, not guilt about this morning—there was definitely something else going on here. He took another long drink, ready to wait Callum out.

With a deep sigh, Callum leaned his elbows forward on the table and ran his hands through his hair. Ezra watched in amusement as a few curls stayed in disarray. "I'm not trying to bribe you. I just… wanted you to be comfortable when I gave you some news."

"Oh?" He looked down at his latte and then back up at Callum. "What news is that?" He wondered what could be so bad that Callum thought he had to get Wyn to make Ezra coffee. Especially after the past few days.

"Last week I... *we* got a call, a lead on where we might find Teller. We brought him in. He was the lycan that bit you," Callum explained, but Ezra didn't need the reminder. As if he could ever forget that name.

They brought him in? What did that mean? And why hadn't they told Ezra earlier? "Brought him where? Is he... I mean, where is he?" Ezra licked his lips. "So I can go home? I mean, it's safe now, right?"

"He's back in our custody. He's been put in a facility best suited to his needs. He's not...." Callum let loose another frustrated sigh and notably did not address Ezra's last question. Then he leaned forward and laid a hand on top of Ezra's on the table. The unexpected contact sent a spark through Ezra's system, the news of his would-be killer be damned. "He's not exactly sane right now. Whatever's causing the ARD has messed with his head. But we're doing what we can to make sure that he stays put and to get him healthy again."

Ezra licked his lips and tried not to stare at the hand covering his. But raising his gaze to Callum's didn't do anything to calm his pounding heart. "Oh."

"In the meantime...." Callum still looked uncomfortable. Hell, he *smelled* uncomfortable. Kind of salt-sour. Ezra was getting better at deciphering the extra-sensory information from his nose. "No, Teller isn't a danger to you anymore, but it's still best for you to stay here. Just for two and a half more weeks. The lycan DNA won't settle completely until the full moon, and if something goes wrong, well, a human doctor isn't going to know what to do with you."

Yeah, that was pretty much what Ezra had thought when he hadn't gotten a straight answer to that question right away. Just a few more weeks, he reminded himself. And then he could go back to his life... if he still wanted to. If he even wanted to *now*.

Ezra stared down into his coffee, taking in the information. His fingers clenched, and he realized that at some point, he had turned his hand so that he could grip Callum back. He stared at their tangled fingers. How had he got here?

"Ezra, you're never going to have to see him again. There's no trial or anything because he's sick." Now Callum was squeezing his fingers. "It's just not going to happen. You don't have to worry about him."

"Oh."

Silence filled the room. Ezra would never again have to see the animal that had attacked him and turned him into a monster. Not that Ezra thought that lycans were *monster* monsters, but they were still the stuff of legend and horror flicks. And Ezra would never again see the face of the man who had done this to him.

Not that he really knew what the man looked like when he *was* a man. Or even when he wasn't.

"Well, that's… good, I guess."

Callum squeezed his hand again. "I'm sorry I didn't tell you sooner. I didn't want to upset you, but I thought that you should know that it's over."

Over. It was over. Right.

"Over." Ezra tested the word on his tongue, nodding while he spoke. Because it was the truth, right? It was over.

Chapter Five
Old Dog and New Tricks

THE lycan was curled up in the corner of the lab. He had both arms wrapped around himself and was staring out around one limb with wide, frightened eyes. He was younger than his predecessors had been, probably only eighteen.

Davis sighed with annoyance and disgust as he took in the trembling form. God, these betas were pathetic, but fortunately, they were not useless.

It had been during the Boss's last visit that they had come up with the current line of experimentation: if increased alphatropin levels made alphas less tractable, then why not start with someone more obedient? The Boss's lip had curled as he recounted how spineless all betas were: "A bunch of submissive women and eunuchs. Maybe that will actually prove to be useful for once. Just let me know how many bitch boys you need."

The first beta had arrived the following day. He had been different from the lycans that had come to Davis's lab before him. Instead of raving and threatening Davis, the man had simply cowered in front of the Boss. And then he had climbed onto the table, his shoulders hunched forward, when the Boss had told him to. It had been a rather disgusting display of weakness. Davis hadn't hesitated to strap the man down and attach the IV so that he could start administering the drug.

The tests had proved to be very successful. While violent behaviors had increased, the tendency to become more prone to dominant behavior wasn't as strong as it was with the alpha test subjects. True, Davis was still working at figuring out how to *ensure* that every beta was still eager to please, but most of them were.

Naturally there were other issues. Two of the betas so far, including the last one, had been unable to cope with their new urges and had clawed their own arms open. Davis still wasn't sure if they had been deliberate suicides or accidental deaths from self-harm. Still, the preliminaries were promising.

"Get him on the table," Davis told the guard acting as the beta's handler. He was large, with a gap-toothed grin and a bald head, and he was smiling a wicked smile. He walked over to the beta and gripped him by the upper arms before pulling him to his feet. The beta whimpered; Gap-tooth just grinned wider. He was human, if you could call it that, but he'd taken some charming etiquette lessons from the hopped-up alphas.

The long sniff he took of the boy was accompanied by a satisfied growling groan. "You subs always smell so nice when you're afraid." The boy's trembling worsened, which only made Gap-tooth laugh dirtily as he hoisted the boy onto the table and locked him down. "But you smell even better after the doc is done with you—all desperate for a fight... or a fuck."

Which was rather unfortunately true. The betas had shown a disappointing tendency to look to that other avenue of release. Still, just last week they had found and cleaned up a homeless man to shove into the room with one young beta who was more interested in humping the furniture than taking it apart. The way he had clawed the man to death in his desperation had not been disappointing.

Gap-tooth took another long sniff of the boy as he attached the cuff around the neck. By the time he finished, the boy was whimpering, soft, but constant.

Davis shook his head at the ridiculous display but didn't bother to comment.

There were tears glistening in the boy's eyes when Davis approached. With quick, efficient movements, he attached the leads for the heart and oxygen saturation monitors. Once his machines were recording the beta's vitals, Davis pulled out a tourniquet and needle. Tying the rubber length around the boy's arm made him whine louder.

Davis ignored him. He knew from experience that the betas wouldn't listen to his commands, and the Boss wasn't likely to waste his time making Davis's life easier. Besides, he would shut up soon.

Davis inserted the needle, attached the line, and administered the first injections. Then in went the serum. It usually took a few minutes for the drug to take—for some reason the betas' reaction was much slower than the alphas'—so Davis set up a saline drip and turned away from the lycan. He tried to ignore the continued whines but found that this one was particularly persistent in his frightened simpering. With a sigh, Davis went for the radio and turned it on. Then he cranked the volume up until it drowned out the beta.

There was nothing to do with the boy right now but to continue monitoring his vitals while they waited for the alphatropin to spike. And then Davis would be able to collect all the data he needed.

Until then, he could go over the results from the last beta. He had a few minutes to kill.

IT WAS a dream.

Callum knew that he was dreaming, because the whole thing had that bizarre, disconnected feeling that all dreams had. Still, just because he knew it was a dream didn't mean that he couldn't take a minute to appreciate the sight of Ezra naked in his bed. God, he was beautiful, hard and begging.

"Callum, please! I need you."

This right here was easily one of Callum's top ten fantasies: a beautiful man just waiting to be had.

Then Ezra tilted his head back with a whimper and a whine and said, "Please, Alpha," and the dream shot to the top of the fantasy list. This was everything that Callum had ever wanted and never had: a gorgeous male beta wolf begging to be dominated, to be Callum's.

His dream self wasn't an idiot—Callum was suddenly in bed with Ezra, his hips cradled by strong thighs and his lips welcomed by a swollen mouth.

"Alpha," Ezra whined over and over again. He kept widening the splay of his legs and clutching at Callum's shoulders and the sheets. "Please! Take me, fuck me, make me yours!"

Another sign it was a dream, Callum thought distantly: the cheesy porn dialogue was making him hornier. Horny enough, apparently, to be suddenly sliding his cock into Ezra's body, no preparation or warning necessary. Ezra tossed his head back and groaned out his desire. He sounded exultant. And positively indecent.

Callum's eyes shot open, and he gasped with the shock. His hips, still receiving directions from his dream self, shot up into the air, trying to bury his cock into something that wasn't there.

He fell back to the bed with a groan and threw one arm over his eyes, frustrated. Thoughts of Ezra might not be new, but that damned psych eval had certainly fueled them. Callum had had a handle on his desires (and those early Ezra dreams) until he had read that damned file. With phrases like "a natural beta" and "extremely accommodating," the thing had read like a personals ad—no, worse, like a how-to guide for seducing Ezra.

Since sleep was out of the question—besides, it was 6:00 a.m., technically daytime—Callum untangled himself from the sheets. He needed a shower, preferably one that was ice-cold.

Clean and cooled down, Callum searched out coffee next. But even after the caffeine had been ingested, Callum's clearer mind failed to pick a safe topic to dwell on.

It didn't help, he supposed, that he had left the folder on the kitchen counter last night, and so it was sitting out in plain sight, mocking him.

The real problem now was not that Callum was attracted to Ezra (he had been from the start), nor was it that Callum could seduce Ezra (a fairly easy task, given that Ezra was a new lycan). The problem was that Callum now had all the insight he needed into wooing Ezra Jones. And the damned eval had said nothing to deter Callum from wanting to do so very badly.

Sighing, Callum flipped the folder open. He wasn't sure why he felt compelled to read it again, but he couldn't seem to resist.

"EJ shows high levels of interdependence…. He is likely to form attachments quickly and unreservedly." The words sounded encouraging at first, but Callum reminded himself that there were other parts that were less so. He easily found the lines that began hinting that any attachment Ezra had to Callum was simply because he had been there during a stressful time. Given that Ezra likely had "poor coping mechanisms," sleeping with Ezra would be taking advantage of those feelings, wouldn't it?

Then again…. He had noticed Ezra because of his vulnerability that first day, but that wasn't why he wanted him now. Maybe, if Ezra were settled—that was, once he was used to being a lycan, after the first moon—it wouldn't be an issue anymore.

Callum couldn't stop his eyes from finding and reading the most thrilling part. "EJ is likely to be self-sacrificing. A natural beta, with strong tendencies to seek out alpha control, EJ may be almost too accommodating toward an alpha he desires, especially during sexual interactions…. Highly sexual, EJ may have promiscuous and or fetishist tendencies."

And there they were. The "Callum, he's ready for the taking" lines. All Callum needed do was *be* that alpha. Ezra wanted a man to take charge, to be his support and his possibly kinky lover. All Callum need do was be sure that Ezra knew he wanted to and could fill the role, and it would likely be his.

Callum wondered how inevitable it was. Ezra was staying here, after all. According to this—Callum glanced at the paper—Ezra had already "formed strong attachments to the pack and both Alphas." It didn't sound like he was likely to leave or join another pack after the full moon. Callum and Ezra would be stuck knowing and associating with one another, just like before, but not. Because now Callum knew exactly what Ezra wanted in a man and that he fit the bill.

Callum was so fucked.

BETWEEN his seemingly uncontrollable new super-senses, the sudden appearance of fifty long-lost family members, and the unforeseen urge to eat a lot of red meat, Ezra's first days as a bona fide lycanthrope had been strange, to say the least.

And, if he were perfectly honest, kind of boring.

Like he had for the past eleven days, Ezra got out of bed, made a brief detour to the bathroom, and descended the stairs to find Wyn and Blaise (who had been sleeping on the couch since Ezra's unexpected arrival) already at the breakfast table in what he was starting to recognize as their characteristic silence. Wyn gazed determinedly at her plate, picking at her eggs. Every once in a while she would glance up from under her eyelashes at Blaise, who was staring into his coffee mug like it held the answers to all the world's questions.

Ezra didn't need to be able to smell sexual tension to figure out what was going on. He cleared his throat. "Good morning."

Blaise grunted a hello, but Wyn pasted on a smile. "Good morning, Ezra. Did you sleep well?"

About as well as a fledgling lycanthrope in a house with an alpha and beta lycan who wanted to fuck each other's brains out could sleep. But it would have been rude to say so aloud, so Ezra faked a smile right back. "Well enough, thanks. Do I smell coffee?"

"Help yourself."

By now Ezra had been left here alone and bored with Blaise enough times that he could find just about anything in Wyn's cupboards—including hot chocolate, which had made him violently ill, though Blaise had laughingly assured him that the allergy was probably temporary. He immediately located the second-largest mug—the largest having been appropriated, likely by Wyn, for use by Blaise—and filled it to the brim. "Thanks."

Like the past eleven mornings, he was forced to sit between the two of them at the table. Unlike the past eleven mornings, today he was not content to sit in awkward silence and wait for Wyn to leave for her job at the nursing home. Or sit around watching television while Blaise whittled pieces of wood into increasingly more threatening-looking phallic-shaped objects in an obvious display of sexual frustration. "So," he said with forced cheer, "Blaise. Not that I don't appreciate the company, but don't you have anything better to do than sit around and listen to me breathe all day? You have a job, right?"

"Yes," Blaise said. He shoveled a forkful of eggs into his mouth.

Right. "Exactly. Doesn't your boss need protecting?"

Blaise shrugged. "Callum can take care of himself. There's security at the office."

Security so good an insane caged lycanthrope had escaped from it without a trace. "The office." It wasn't exactly Ezra's first choice of destinations, containing as it did the Alpha lycanthrope he hadn't been able to stop thinking about for most of the past week and a half, but if Ezra had to spend another day cooped up with Blaise in Wyn's tiny house, he was going to lose his mind. "They found the lycan who bit me, right?"

Blaise and Wyn exchanged a glance. It was the first time Ezra had seen their eyes meet in a week. Then Wyn looked away with a flush and began clearing her breakfast dishes.

"I want to see him."

Out of the corner of his eye, Ezra saw Wyn freeze with her back to the table. Blaise slowly lowered his fork down to his plate. "Why?"

Ezra stared. "Because I'd like to know why he bit me?"

"He bit you because he's out of his mind and you smelled like a tasty snack."

Ezra shuddered. "I want to see him," he insisted again, not nearly as confident about it as he sounded. "I need to see for myself."

There was a sharp clatter as Wyn deposited her dishes in the sink. "I need to get ready for work," she said quietly, and she disappeared from the kitchen without another sound.

Ezra turned back to Blaise. "Look, we no longer have to worry about the guy you were afraid was after me, right? So you can go back to your day job, whatever that is, and in the meantime you can drop me off at the lab." He paused. "I really need to talk to this guy, okay? If something happens before I get a chance...." He shrugged helplessly.

Ezra was nearly sure that was what persuaded him. He had only been part of the pack for a few days, but he already understood that the low thrum at the back of his brain was the wolf, that part of him that responded to Callum's presence and, to a lesser extent, the presence of every other lycan in the pack. The part of him that sang with the feeling of belonging. And under the steady throbbing awareness of *family home pack*—odd enough in itself for someone who'd been on his own for the past four years, give or take—was a thread of... something. A compulsion to protect the pack. Ezra imagined that instinct would be even stronger in Blaise.

"Fine." Blaise got up too, leaving his empty coffee mug on the table. Ezra wondered absently if that was an alpha thing, or if Blaise was just a crappy houseguest. "You have twenty minutes. Then I'm leaving."

IF THE guards recognized him, they gave no indication. Blaise flashed his ID and signed Ezra in, then borrowed the desk phone at reception to buzz Callum's office. He let it ring four or five times before replacing the handset on the receiver and nodding at the receptionist. "He must be in the med lab. Let's go."

Ezra could do nothing but steel himself and follow.

Before he knew it, they were stepping out of the elevator into the bowels of the building, but instead of taking a left and heading toward Callum's office, Blaise led him right and through some double-thick metal doors with a key-swipe lock mechanism and a retinal scanner, and another set of locking doors operated by an intense-looking security guard.

"Jesus," Ezra muttered. "It's not easy to get into this place."

Blaise barely flicked him a glance. "Right now we're more concerned about people getting out."

There was an unpleasant buzz and the click of an electronic lock as the second set of doors opened, and Blaise pushed through them into a small observation room.

For Ezra, everything went still. The world narrowed down to the tiny whitewashed room on the other side of the glass and the wild-haired, hollow-eyed man sitting at the table. His hands were bruised, several fingernails bloody and torn. For the life of him, Ezra could not understand how this beaten, bruised, half-mad thing had almost killed him.

Ezra was so fixated on the man in the room that he almost didn't hear the doors buzz open a second time.

"Blaise." Callum's voice held a hint of question and a whole lot of suspicion. His scent was even more complicated—anxiety, exhaustion, power—and something Ezra was starting to think of as possessiveness. "Ezra. What are you doing here?"

Sensing this question was directed more toward Blaise than toward him, Ezra ignored it and took another step closer to the glass. Either it was a two-way mirror, or Teller was even more messed up than Ezra had thought, because he kept his gaze low, to the left of Ezra's right elbow.

"Ezra wanted to check this guy out for himself." Blaise's low-pitched rumble soothed Ezra's frazzled nerves. "He's one of us now. He needs to know what we're up against."

That sounded ominous, but Ezra didn't have time to think on it further. "You should have called me first." Callum's voice was tight. When Ezra tore his eyes away from Teller and caught Callum's reflection in the glass, he could see a muscle twitching in his jaw.

Blaise shrugged. "You weren't in your office." Ezra noticed that he didn't bother to mention that they hadn't called until they were in the building.

"I want to talk to him," Ezra interrupted, raising his fingers absently to touch the cool glass.

"That's not a good idea," Callum said firmly. "Ezra, this guy is seriously messed up. You're not going to get any answers from him."

"Well I'm sure as hell not getting them from anyone else," Ezra snapped, going for the door.

"He's dangerous!" Callum warned. Suddenly his scent had a whole bunch more layers, most of which Ezra couldn't identify. "There's no telling what he might do. Ezra, he already tried to kill you."

Well, at least he wasn't ordering him not to go in. Not yet, anyway. Ezra hit the panel for the electronic lock and yanked open the door before he could.

When the door closed behind him he stopped short and took a few uneasy, shallow breaths. The air smelled of rank sweat and blood and pain and despair. Ezra recoiled at the stench, then somehow managed to stop smelling it in self-defense. The sense reverted to the shadow it had been when he was human, and he was able to breathe clearly, even if it still wasn't pleasant. God, what should he say? "Mr. Teller?" That seemed an awfully formal way to address the man who'd tried to kill him. He hardened his heart. "Do you know who I am?"

Teller wrapped his arms around himself without looking up, still murmuring steadily under his breath.

Ezra leaned closer, wanting to get a look at his face. "Teller?"

"Ezra," Callum broke in over an intercom system Ezra hadn't known existed. "That's close enough—"

He was right up in the other lycan's space when Teller raised his head, showing inhuman yellow eyes and teeth that protruded below his lips as if he were still partially shifted. Teller's gaze went from Ezra's eyes to the scar on his neck and then to his shoulder. His nostrils flared. "No, no, no," he whispered, spittle coating his lips. "Rabbit hole, little girl. The red queen caught the gardeners painting roses and Alice tried to save them." He backed away clumsily, toppling his chair behind him, and he went crashing over it into the corner while Ezra watched in horror. "But when the queen caught them she made them into mock turtle soup!"

Ezra glanced back to the window, but from this side all he could see was his own reflection and Teller's where he was huddled in the corner, his arms wrapped tightly around his body. Wasn't Callum going to help? He was a scientist, right? This Teller person was obviously in serious distress; there had to be something that could be done. Tentatively, Ezra took another step forward.

"No, no, no!" Teller screamed this time, twitching in his corner and hiding his face with his forearm. "No, it can't be. I didn't kill the Jabberwock! I didn't kill it! I didn't!"

The hair stood up on the back of Ezra's neck, and he backed away, suddenly overwhelmed by the stench of sweat and fear and urine so strong it seemed to claw its way down his throat. Bile rose in his throat, and he bolted for the door, hearing the lock click open just as he slammed into it. "Where—?" he managed to gasp out as his vision blurred, and someone put Ezra's arm around his shoulder and half-dragged him in front of a toilet.

Ezra's knees hit the tile at the same time his hands touched cool enamel, and he didn't even have time to take another full breath—piss and chlorine smell of public washroom—before his stomach revolted and he leaned forward over the bowl, retching furiously, tears leaking from his eyes.

When the tremors finally subsided, Ezra reached up with a shaking arm and flushed, then sat back until he felt a wall behind him to support his weight while he recovered. After a few more deep breaths, he opened his eyes again.

White tile walls, white porcelain sink, white floor, white halogen lights that were already giving Ezra a headache. Blaise stood in the doorway, holding up a bottle of water. "You should drink this."

Ezra shuddered before pulling himself up off the floor, running the cold water in the tap, and splashing his face. Catching a glimpse of his reflection in the mirror, he thought morosely that he looked even worse than he felt. "Thanks," he finally said, cracked the bottle open and rinsed his mouth out. "Ugh."

"Don't mention it." Blaise stepped back from the doorway. "Callum wants to talk to you when you're done."

Ezra sighed. "Of course he does."

FIRST, though, Ezra got to take a shower. The water pressure kind of sucked, and there wasn't any of privacy; the hotel-sized soap he'd been given was harsh, and the towel was thin and tiny. But it was a shower, and Ezra had been so soaked with nervous, sympathetic sweat that he'd choked at his own smell. He didn't know how Callum and Blaise had been able to stand it.

Someone had scrounged up a set of scrubs for him from somewhere, and he slipped into them. The thin material left him feeling exposed, almost naked, but he definitely couldn't put his own clothes back on, so this would have to do. He deposited the towel in a rolling laundry bin and navigated his way back to Callum's office.

The door was open a crack when he got there, so he just knocked once and pushed it open. He found Callum sitting at his desk, leaning on one elbow and tapping a ballpoint pen against his chin. "You wanted to see me?"

"Hmm," Callum said without looking up from his computer screen. After a moment he put down his pen and turned his attention to Ezra. "I'm sorry you didn't get the answers you were looking for."

Ezra, who had been expecting an "I told you so," shrugged uncomfortably. "It's not your fault."

Callum sighed. "Frankly, it might be. If we'd done a few more tests, learned sooner the modified signal pheromone was effective on humans…. He could've killed you."

Ezra was getting really tired of hearing that. Did Callum think he was going to forget? "You were trying to help him," he pointed out. *You are helping me*, he didn't add—he wasn't sure it was true. He was pretty sure Callum was trying, but sometimes being around him was more of a headache than it was worth.

"That doesn't excuse it." Callum shook his head. "Never mind. There's nothing either of us can do about it now." He stopped for a moment and then leaned forward. "So what happened in there?"

So much for the compassionate host. "You were right there! He saw me and freaked out." Ezra spread his hands helplessly. "It was like he was afraid of me or something." Which made no sense whatsoever. Ezra was a lycanthrope, but not a particularly threatening one—especially next to Callum or Blaise.

Callum looked thoughtful. "You may not be far off. Teller is severely unbalanced, but before he became infected, he was a normal lycan. Somewhere inside, he was probably hoping he'd just imagined attacking you. Seeing you again with Jax's bite on your neck proves his nightmare was real."

Ezra touched the scar on his neck that Jax had left behind. She had explained that other wolves would be able to scent his pack allegiance. He was beginning to regret demanding to see the poor man. Clearly he was no criminal. "I didn't think it would upset him to see me." He'd been envisioning the Hyde-ish monster who'd bitten him, not the milder-mannered, damaged Dr. Jekyll version.

"It's a good sign, actually. Until now, it's been hard to tell if the infected are capable of understanding the world around them once the worst of the sickness is past. I doubt he'll ever recover fully, but he might make enough progress that he doesn't need to be permanently hospitalized. It's a slim chance, but it's more hope than we had before."

God, that was an optimistic prognosis? No wonder Callum was strung out all the time. "How many more of them are there?"

"We're not actually sure." More than a note of frustration crept into Callum's voice. "We know there have been a few scattered reports across Montana, Wyoming, and Idaho, but until someone finds or reports the infected parties, there's no way to get an accurate count."

"One lycan could be responsible for more than one incident," Ezra interpreted.

"Right. Not to mention that they're not easy to identify unless you know what you're looking for."

Ezra frowned. "Identify?" Didn't he mean "find"?

Callum winced.

Oh, Ezra thought. *That "identify."*

"It's very difficult to tell if someone's a lycan once they're already dead," Callum explained haltingly. "Especially if they pass away while transformed, since they don't change back. And of course most humans don't even know we exist, so there's no avenue for them to contact the NFWS, who could then contact us. And if they *are* human form, sometimes they just get tagged as John or Jane Doe."

Ezra suppressed a shudder. "Well, that's horrible."

"The human-form bodies can still be IDed through conventional methods as long as someone reports them missing."

"There's no government infrastructure to support this? Shouldn't there be some kind of flagging mechanism when somebody finds something, uh, weird?"

"Unfortunately not." Callum ran a hand through his hair, mussing the curls further. Ezra fought back the urge to reach out and smooth them. "We're trying to implement something, but the branches of government that are officially allowed to know about us are limited, and it's making jurisdiction painfully difficult."

"And there's nothing you can do about the ones who die as wolves at all." No wonder this outbreak or whatever had Callum tied up in knots. He didn't even have a way to identify all of the victims.

Actually, now that Ezra was thinking about it, Callum looked dreadful. He was still hot, but his skin was pallid, and there were dark circles under his eyes. And he'd clearly missed a spot shaving, right at the edge of his jaw. Ezra was having a hard time pulling his eyes away from it now that he'd noticed. "This is really getting to you, isn't it? Have you been sleeping?"

Callum huffed out a breath. "It's my job to fix it, both in my position here and as Alpha of the pack. What I really need is a dedicated research assistant, but approval for hiring somebody new goes to Director Abrams, and there's a limited number of qualified people who know about lycans, and Abrams.... Well, anyway, everyone else is up to their eyeballs in other important aspects of the project." He stopped and looked away, up at the clock on the wall, before turning back to Ezra, adding almost sheepishly, "And no, not really."

"Maybe I can help with that," Ezra said without processing what he was saying. Callum's eyes widened. "I mean with the research thing!" he backtracked. "I used to write computer programs in my spare time." It had helped him pay the bills until his computer had died. "I can start by looking up animal attacks and deaths and go from there."

"I don't know if that's such a good idea," Callum began. Ezra opened his mouth to interrupt, but Callum raised a hand, and he found himself swallowing his objection without thinking about it, that warm rush going through him and settling between his legs. He gritted his teeth. "Sorry," Callum said, making a face. Ezra didn't know if he meant for the pheromone slip or the refusal. "You don't even know what you're looking for, and you'd have to do it here to avoid compromising security."

"God, you mean I'll have somewhere to be and something to do all day? That sounds awful, I take it back." Ezra rolled his eyes and shifted in his seat. *Please let this erection go away before I have to stand up.* "I can get a ride in with you in the morning. Just tell me what I'm looking for."

For a long moment, Callum just looked at him. Then he nodded once, decisively, and stood up, motioning toward the door. "Come with me."

No such luck. Ezra had to hurry to keep up as he followed Callum down the sterile corridors. "Where are we going?"

"You want to help, you can start today," Callum told him brusquely, glancing back over his shoulder. "That means you have things to learn."

Ezra quickened his steps again. "I'm listening."

"First things first." Callum stopped dead and turned around, and suddenly the *scent* of him hit Ezra like a two-by-four to the face. That scent, the one he'd been trying to work out, that warm, inviting, musky scent he always seemed to get from Callum—that was *arousal*. Ezra's dick hardened a little more.

Then Callum said, "You have got to learn to control *this*," and he reached out and tapped Ezra on the nose.

Ezra flushed. Damn it. Being a lycanthrope was fucking *embarrassing*. It wasn't enough that the slightest hint of a pheromone suggestion from an alpha carried a weight and a buzz that made him comply without thinking. Oh, no. No, he had to be so damn sensitive to it—or at least to Callum—that it made him react physically. But that wasn't enough either. The worst part was that any other lycan could *tell*.

While Ezra had been busy dying of mortification, Callum had continued down the hallway, and now Ezra had to catch up again as the implications set in. "Wait, you mean I can turn that off?" If there was any way to save himself the embarrassment, he was all ears.

"With practice," Callum answered. "Most natural wolves learn during puberty." He shot Ezra a wry sideways glance. His cheeks were pink. "If you thought human pubescent boners were embarrassing…."

Seriously. At least humans could try to hide theirs. "I thought it was just me." Ezra cleared his throat. Awkward.

"The rest of us just have more practice dealing with it," Callum assured him stiltedly. "But actually I don't need you to fight that part. Just the nasty headache you get for disobeying."

"You think there are more of these super-alphas hanging around?"

"It's our job to find out, but I'm not taking any chances." Callum pushed open the door to an airy room filled with metal picnic benches. A few vending machines dotted the far wall, and in one corner, a small kitchenette contained a microwave, sink, kettle, coffee maker, and other essentials. "Have a seat."

Ezra slid onto the bench before he could think better of it, then caught himself and looked up to see Callum smirking at him slightly.

"That's lesson one."

"I think I missed the point."

"The point is you have to be aware you're being manipulated to stop it from happening."

Ezra chewed on that for a minute. "Okay." Great, now he was going to have to spend the rest of his life *actively listening*. Oh, if his high school psychology teacher could see him now. "I think I can handle that."

"Good. Okay, I'm going to give you a series of commands, and I want you to fight me. I'll keep the signal pheromones low at first so you can get the hang of refusing before I crank it up."

"Fantastic." At least he was getting fair warning this time. "All right, I guess. Go for it."

Callum gave him a sheepish smile. "Start with the obvious. Stand up."

Ezra felt the command filter through his ears and nose and set up like an itch in the base of his brain. His toes twitched in his shoes, and the muscles in the backs of his legs tensed, but he fought the urge to stand, and after a minute, it passed. He winced a little as his head throbbed gently in response to the ignored command, but there didn't seem to be any other immediate consequences. "That wasn't so bad."

"Good!" Callum nodded. "Very good."

"Mind you, it doesn't exactly feel nice," Ezra noted. Still, his relief at having been able to refuse at all ameliorated most of his discomfort. He wondered if that was chemical or just some kind of psychological placebo effect.

"What does it feel like? Be specific; don't leave anything out."

Ezra huffed in consideration. "It's hard to say. It's like having an itch, I guess? The more you try to ignore it, the harder it gets." His lips twisted in amusement at his own phrasing. That wasn't quite how it worked in this case, but in some? There was definitely some hardness involved. "At this level, it's not compulsive, just annoying. Ignoring it gives me a headache, but it's not too bad."

Callum raised his eyebrows knowingly, and Ezra felt his mouth drop open as his nerves sang with pleasure. "Oh, son of a bitch." He gritted his teeth as the headache dissipated only to be replaced by a low heat in his belly. "You tricked me."

"I'm one of the bad guys for this exercise, remember?" Callum pointed out. Ezra wondered a little at the glaze he seemed to blink away from his eyes and the color that was creeping up in his cheeks again. That scent was back, heady and distracting, but like always, Callum made no reference to it. "I'm not just going to come right out with a brute-force attack. I might try to finesse you a little. You need to be able to recognize when someone tries to use your brain chemistry against you."

Ezra let out a long breath. "Okay," he said, steeling himself. "Try it again."

"One thing at a time." Callum pushed back from the table and walked over to the kitchenette set up in the corner, throwing Ezra a look back over his shoulder. "You're going to want something in your stomach. It helps with the headaches, or so I've been told, anyway."

Deciding Callum was probably right, even if he never did have to deal with the headaches himself, Ezra pulled himself up out of his chair and followed him over. "Why couldn't I just be an alpha," he muttered to himself as he took a paper cup from a stack and poured himself some water from the cooler.

"We alphas have our own crosses to bear," Callum reminded him as he opened the small bar fridge that was tucked up under the counter top and pulled out a package of Dad's Oatmeal Cookies. "At least those of us who are born lycans do. It's possible the wires get crossed a bit with the new recruits." He reached into the fridge again and withdrew a box of Oreos.

"Yeah, well, at least you don't get a boner when someone asks you to pass the salt." Ezra took a few sips of the water and found that he really did feel better, so he refilled the cup.

When he turned around again, Callum had added an individual serving package of Chipits to the pile. "What are you doing?"

"Getting your blood sugar up," Callum said somewhat apologetically. "This exercise could get painful otherwise. Like I was saying—we all have our crosses to bear. Preference?"

Ezra ignored the incongruous image of Callum being sheepish and concentrated on the choice. The Oreos and chocolate chips were tempting, but after the experience he'd had with chocolate right after he'd been bitten, he wasn't sure he wanted to risk it. "I'll take the oatmeal, I guess."

"Good choice." Callum put the rejected cookies back in the refrigerator and led the way back to their table. "Ready to try again?"

"If I say no, will you let me out of it?"

"You're the one who said he wanted to help."

Taking that as a firm no, Ezra shrugged. "Okay, then. Let's do it."

The next hour and a half was possibly the most trying of his life. By the time Callum decided Ezra had had enough of attempting to resist his charms, Ezra was good and ready for a long, hot shower and some Internet porn.

Unfortunately, that was not to be. "Finish your water," Callum suggested, no alpha mojo backing it at all, and it had only taken Ezra the first forty minutes to be able to tell the difference. He was on his fifth glass of water and had the feeling he was going to be spending most of the evening making trips to the bathroom, but since following Callum's advice had so far precluded him from getting a migraine, he knocked back the last few swallows. "We've got more work to do."

Fantastic.

Instead of heading back to Callum's office, though, they moved deeper into the labyrinth of sterile rooms and hallways until finally there was nowhere else to turn. A small silver placard on the right side of the double doors read MORGUE. "You're sure you want to do this?" Callum asked.

"Is there a dead lycan in there?"

"Not at the moment."

Ezra nodded his assent, and Callum pushed open the door.

The room was cold, which Ezra had been expecting, and smelled of formaldehyde rather than decay, which he hadn't. A stainless steel refrigeration unit was situated at the far end of the long, narrow room; two stainless steel autopsy tables dominated the remainder of space on that side. On the near side, a long countertop of sinks and various scientific equipment—microscopes, test tubes and beakers, Bunsen burners, centrifuges—ran nearly the width of the room. The wall to the right of the door was a light board illuminating a few scattered X-rays and MRIs.

"Why are we doing this in the morgue if there aren't any dead bodies here?" Ezra asked.

"Because this is where we keep the specimens." Callum gestured to a shelving unit along the opposite wall. "And the files."

Specimens? Ezra suppressed a shudder. "Okay. Where do we start?"

They sat on a couple of stools at the counter, and Callum pulled a thick binder from under the counter top. "There's not exactly an official textbook on lycanthrope physiology for obvious reasons." He flipped the binder open to the first page. "But for all intents and purposes, this will be your textbook."

Eyes wide, Ezra stared at the book. There had to be five or six hundred pages in that binder; it was huge. "Jesus. That's a hell of a starting point." He was starting to feel like he was back in college again.

"That's just your homework." Callum pushed the book across the counter, then withdrew a notepad and pen to go with it. "We're actually starting with Myth Debunking 101. You must have some questions."

Oh, sure. *Now* Callum decided he wanted to answer Ezra's questions. "Um, I'll start with the obvious, I guess. The whole fire and silver thing?"

"If someone sets you on fire or stabs you in the heart with a silver knife, you're gonna die," Callum said bluntly. "Same as if you drink poison or get in a car accident or ski into a tree. Sorry, no convenient immortality clause."

"I'm shockingly okay with that." Relieved, actually—Ezra's life was lonely enough as it was; he didn't need it to go on forever just to top it all off.

"That said, you will find that you heal a lot faster from injuries that don't kill you. You already saw that to some extent when you were bitten, and you'll heal faster the closer it is to the full moon. As for the silver thing—it's actually a myth based in truth. You're going to be hypersensitive to nickel around that time, too, so if you have a cheap watch, you might want to ditch it."

Ezra's mouth dropped open, and he hazarded a guess. "Chocolate too?"

Callum dimpled, and when he spoke, his voice was halfway between amused and apologetic. "Chocolate's pretty safe for the two weeks around the new moon. Some lycans never have any trouble with it; some are sick for three days if they eat it when the moon is near full. It just depends."

After what had happened the last time, Ezra thought he might just avoid it rather than take his chances. He tried to ignore the part of his brain that was insisting Callum would be a more than adequate substitute. "Okay, so that's that covered. What about the half man, half beast rumors?"

"Well, if you caught the whole transformation on a time-lapsed camera, it would be pretty horrifying. But no, we're generic Canis lupus once the moon rises."

"Crazed, slobbering, predatory beasts?"

Callum grinned. The easy expression just made him that much more ridiculously attractive. "Most of us just curl up and sleep in front of the fire. We do have to work the next day, you know."

That was so incongruous that it drew Ezra up short for a few seconds. Of course he knew Callum was a *werewolf*—hell, *Ezra* was a werewolf!—but he couldn't quite imagine him as anything other than human-shaped just yet. And the idea of him curled up on a carpet with his nose on his tail was frankly ridiculous. "Seriously?"

"No. The bed is much more comfortable, though in the morning you sometimes have to vacuum the sheets."

In the morning. That raised another interesting question. "So— when the transformation happens." He paused. "I'm assuming there's some shredding of clothes."

"Nudity can be a factor," Callum said, eyes twinkling in amusement.

"Right. Good to know." And now to stop himself from thinking about *that* for the rest of the day. Awesome. *Good luck with that*, Ezra thought to himself. Callum was just so hot when he was being competent. Or, you know, breathing. "This sickness, or whatever," he began. "What are you calling it again?"

"Acute alphatropin regulatory dysfunction," Callum reminded him.

"Right. How long has it been going on?" Something clicked into place in his brain. "Hey, that rabies thing, Lyssavirus A—that's got to be what's behind the popular slavering beast myth, right?"

Callum nodded seriously, sitting forward and lacing his big hands together on the countertop. "Probably," he hedged. "The symptoms fit. Originally, that's what we thought this outbreak was. Until very recently, we only saw one or two cases of that a generation, and that was worldwide. But there have been at least three incidents in the last three months just here in Montana, so we started looking at alternatives. We found Teller, ran a couple tests, and it turned out he doesn't have Lyssavirus or anything like it in his system. Something else is going on. So we named it after the symptom: acute alphatropin regulatory dysfunction. And now we're trying to figure out if we've got some environmental risk factors."

A sudden chill shook down Ezra's spine. "What do you mean?"

"We couldn't identify a virus in Teller's blood. Whatever ARD is, it's not contagious." Callum spread his hands in explanation. "Like I told you when you were bitten, there's a backward unscientific contingent that thinks anyone turned by a mad werewolf will start showing the symptoms, too, but it never happened with Lyssavirus A as far as anyone can tell, and no one who was in contact with Teller and ARD got sick either. Even if it were contagious, I doubt you'd be at risk."

Ezra frowned. That sounded like a good thing, but for some reason it just made him nervous. "Why not?"

"There has never been a documented case of a beta with lunar madness. Same with ARD, though of course it's a much newer disease. All of the infected—right back to the first known case of Lyssavirus in 1500 or so—have been alpha lycans. That's why we think the two are related somehow." Callum looked grim. "We're not sure why alphas yet, but we think it's something to do with the differences in brain chemistry. Some weakness we have that you don't. It's been hard to study because there's no way to test it in a lab without a live subject."

Well, that was horrible to think about. Ezra shuddered again. "Okay. So say a victim of this Lyssavirus or ARD or whatever died in human form. There must be a way to tell if they were a lycan."

Callum nodded encouragingly. "There are a few. Unfortunately, most of them are useless unless you're able to see the body in person. Smell is the easiest, though you probably haven't mastered that yet."

"You are hell-bent on making this difficult, aren't you?" Ezra sighed. "I can't exactly go around sniffing every suspicious dead body. Not that I'd want to." Yeah, no. That was disgusting *and* inefficient. He needed something he could put through some kind of computerized information filter. "What else?"

"Stomach contents. Raw meat is a pretty solid indicator of a sick lycan. Most healthy ones won't touch it even when transformed. And it's usually a heart attack that gets them, whether it's Lyssavirus or ARD—something about the adrenaline overload."

Now they were getting somewhere. Ezra made a note on the scratch pad. "Stomach contents and heart disease. Okay. What about if no autopsy was done? Are there any external signs a layman could pick up on?"

Nodding, Callum began ticking off items on his fingers. "Dehydration. Look for cracked, drying skin on the hands and lips. Blown pupils—infected wolves have heightened light sensitivity. Blood or bruising on the hands—they get violent." Callum watched him write that down. "How do you plan on getting all of this information, anyway? You can't just go around telling people you're investigating werewolf deaths."

Ezra shrugged. "I work for the CDC now," he said. "Unofficially and unpaid, sure, but I can draft a memo for you to send to heads of police departments saying we're investigating a possible unknown contagion and that they should forward any unknown cases matching the description to me. Honestly, I can't believe you didn't put something like this into place a long time ago."

"Yeah, well." Callum visibly deflated. "It's not that we haven't tried. But we're notoriously understaffed. Maybe if one of the lycan agents working at the FBI gets infected they'll allocate some resources, but for now...." He shrugged, then smirked a little. "Help us, Ezra-Wan Kenobi. You're our only hope."

Oh God, he was a geek! A geeky, lab-coat-wearing, science-talking alpha lycanthrope with a killer body and eyes deep enough to drown in. Ezra was doomed. "Some problems are universal, apparently," he croaked out before clearing his throat and tossing down his pen. "Okay, now what if one of us dies as a wolf?"

"That's both trickier and easier. It really depends. If they find the body in a national or state park, there's always a necropsy and a full genetic workup, so if it's a lycan, we find out about it."

"And if the body is found anywhere else...?"

Callum gave him a tight-lipped smile. "That's where it gets complicated. Disposal usually falls to animal control, and depending on whether they're contractors or employees of the municipality, they may not even have a documentation system. If it's an urban area, they usually get flagged because there aren't a lot of wolves in the city, but if it's rural, it's kind of a crapshoot. We found one once because she'd painted her toenails."

"Not a lot of wolves going for pedicures these days," Ezra said, wincing a little. It was awfully macabre to attempt to find humor in the situation, but not finding any would've been far worse for his mental health. He raised his eyes to the light board across from him. "Are you going to tell me about that?"

Nodding to Ezra's notebook, Callum said, "Pick that up and come over here." He pushed out his chair and walked over to the wall, finding a switch under a chalkboard-like ledge, and flicking it so that the wall lit the images on it. "Too much to hope that you're an *ER* fan?"

Ezra made a face at him. "*ER*? Really?" He turned his attention back to the wall. "What am I looking at? I mean, I can see that's a hand, obviously."

"This is what a lycanthrope's bones look like within sixty seconds of the moon setting," Callum explained. "Do you notice anything unusual?"

Ezra squinted at the image, trying to make out any errant details. "Um. It's a really big hand?"

Callum snorted. "Try again."

So he did, stepping closer, following the lines of the delicate bones with his eyes. Was it supposed to look more like a paw? It was completely human-hand shaped as far as he could tell. There were no claws or anything. Although—"Are those fractures?" he asked in horror.

"Healing ones," Callum said, not very reassuringly as far as Ezra was concerned.

"I need to start buying my aspirin at Costco," Ezra muttered.

"Like I said, that stage only lasts a very short period of time because the proximity of the full moon promotes faster healing. It's most noticeable in hands and feet—or paws, as the case may be—and shoulders, hips, and knees."

"Knees?" Ezra echoed in dread.

Grimacing, Callum pointed out, "Human knees bend the wrong way."

Okay, *ow*. How many days until the full moon again? "I don't get it. How does anyone function? In the wolf form, I mean? It seems like you'd hardly be transformed long enough to heal."

"The healing factor is extremely accelerated when you're wolf-shaped. Maybe it's because that's when the effects of the moon are strongest, or maybe it has something to do with how fast wolves age in relation to humans—again, it's a tough thing to research."

Ezra nodded. Every time Callum answered a question, three more sprung up in its place. It was like fighting the hydra. "Okay. And what about those? Brain scans, right?"

"Side-by-side MRIs. Mine and Jax's and Blaise's. The last one is Teller's."

Ezra was no neurosurgeon, but there was definitely something funky going on with the MRIs. Where Callum and Jax and Blaise were elliptical maps of seemingly random blues and purples and oranges spread haphazardly across the landscape of their brains, Teller was a concentrated red and orange cyclone almost dead center. It didn't look *right*.

"What does that mean?"

Callum exhaled loudly. "In a nutshell, his hormone production is out of control, there's very little activity in the portion of his brain that controls reason, and he may be having auditory hallucinations."

Ezra stared at the MRI. "That sounds like a really bad combination."

"Tell me about it." Callum gestured back to the stools, and they sat back down again. "So what's the plan? You haven't exactly shared with the class."

Ezra thought that was pretty rich, coming from Callum, but he took his time formulating a reply that didn't sound snarky. "I'm going to write a computer program," Ezra told him. "Well—several computer programs. One to scan through any information I get from police departments about Jane and John Does presenting symptoms like you described. One to trawl the web for any reports of unusually vicious animal attacks and crosscheck it with the phase of the moon. One to take all the resulting data and plot it on a map and sort it by date and e-mail me the results."

Callum stared for a few long seconds, then blinked. "Wouldn't it be easier to just check the results on the program?"

"Sure, if you can find me a computer with ten gigabytes of RAM!" Ezra said cheerfully. "Seriously, I'm going to need two fast machines and a lot of bandwidth to begin with. Otherwise we have no chance of figuring out anything by the next full moon."

Nodding, Callum made his way toward the door, stopping only long enough for Ezra to gather his books and catch up. "Come on, then. We have work to do."

Chapter Six
Barking Up the Wrong Tree

EZRA'S day had definitely taken a turn for the better. He was finally doing something useful instead of whiling away time at Wyn's, and he had managed to get a good start on designing the programs he'd need to find lycan victims. All in all, he had been feeling pretty pleased with the general state of the world—until he had found Callum when it was time to go home.

Callum had informed Ezra that he would be working late and that security would drive Ezra home. Ezra had not been pleased by either announcement, so he had argued that he was perfectly capable of going home without a bodyguard.

"After the morning you had? You're not going anywhere alone." Which was completely unfair, and all the goodwill Callum had earned that afternoon by actually answering Ezra's questions evaporated in a hurry. Ezra had stomped out of the room and managed to leave before Callum could call anyone to stop him. The bitching headache was totally worth ignoring his commands to come back.

The encounter had left Ezra cranky, to say the least. Between that and the morning's events, his head was a constant swirl of emotion.

He rolled his shoulders as he went through Wyn's front door, trying to ease the tension in his neck. God. He needed a beer and a bath. And a massage. His shoulder twinged. Yeah, definitely needed a massage. Too bad he wouldn't find one here.

He was so intent on getting his beer that it took him a while to notice the change. It wasn't until he had popped the cap and was taking a sip that the heavy smell of pheromones registered.

Ezra frowned as he lowered the bottle. There was something different yet familiar about the scent. A deep breath offered no answers.

Curious, he crossed the kitchen and headed toward the stairs. Maybe Wyn would have an idea about what was going on.

Halfway up the stairs, the pheromones became a thick fog that nearly had him choking. They also had his pulse racing and his libido taking notice. Fuck. What the hell? By the top of the stairs, his cock was hard in his jeans, and the desire to find someone to get off with was stronger than it had been since he was sixteen. Even Callum hadn't done this to him.

"Wy—?"

He found her sitting on the bathroom counter, her head tossed back as she panted and moaned, both legs wrapped around Blaise's hips. Blaise was holding her in his huge hands and kissing her neck possessively, snapping his hips in time with Wyn's moans.

Ezra was going to need to wash out his eyes. And his brain.

Blaise pulled his mouth from Wyn's so that he could turn and lock eyes with Ezra. God, he'd been spotted, but apparently Blaise had no intention of being embarrassed by it. Or of stopping, either.

After turning away, Ezra stumbled back down the stairs, though this time the increased distance from the amorous couple seemed to do little to alleviate the effects of the pheromones. It was like hearing, smelling, and tasting sex—sex that other people were having—and the hunger was now unbearable.

Living with Wyn and Blaise the past few days had been like living above a bakery and being on a gluten-free diet. He could smell all the delicious treats but wasn't allowed to have anything to sate the hunger they inspired.

But this… this was too much. This was like floating in fresh coffee and being told not to taste.

Screw this. Ezra had spent the last days feeling off balance and horny and his life was a mess and Callum had this list of rules that he was supposed to follow. He had had enough of this, and Ezra wanted… Ezra wanted to get laid.

Setting his beer down on the entry table, Ezra grabbed his coat and shot out the door.

It had been several years since Ezra had wanted to find a one-night stand in Missoula, but he still knew where to go. There were some things you didn't forget, and how to get to the only gay bar in town was definitely one of them.

Walking through the front doors of The Barnyard brought back a lot of memories. Memories of a misspent youth, nights of drinking and sex.

Ezra rolled up his shirtsleeves and undid the top buttons and then made his way to the bar. Tonight he was getting drunk and he was getting laid. It had been ages since Ezra had been properly fucked. The last time had been weeks before he got the news about his father's death, and Ezra wasn't the type to fuck away his grief. But now... now the urge to find himself a strong man with a big cock and an attitude to match was stronger than ever before. Strong enough to drown out any reservations he had about one-night stands.

The bar was crowded, but Ezra managed to battle his way to the front. A wave and a nod got him the bartender's ear, and he ordered three vodka shots. Ezra wasn't out to get blind drunk, but he was not spending another second sober. Besides, after seeing straight sex starring *Wyn,* his new favorite girl, Ezra needed the alcohol to cope. Even if each shot burned on its way down.

The man he found, or rather who found Ezra, was gorgeous. He was taller than Ezra and probably several years older, with dark hair and eyes that promised a night of sin.

He was also sweet. He bought Ezra a beer and then offered to take him home. In a place like The Barnyard, a man who gave you free alcohol and offered to fuck you someplace soft was a gentleman.

A last glance at the man's hips and thighs—both framed in strong muscle—had Ezra nodding his head. Yes, please.

EZRA ignored the knowing looks that the cabbie kept giving him via the rearview mirror. It wasn't like he hadn't known to expect this when he called for a cab at two in the morning. There weren't a lot of reasons for getting a cab ride from one residence to another at this time of night, and considering Ezra reeked of sex, there was no way to misinterpret his cab ride of shame.

Still, Ezra tried not to be bothered by the cabbie knowing. He could think whatever he wanted. Ezra wasn't going to start being ashamed of his sex life now. Besides, he wasn't likely to see this stranger again. Let him think as poorly about Ezra as he wanted.

With a sigh, Ezra tilted his head back against the headrest and then shifted his hips, trying to find a more comfortable position. This was the downside to a really good fucking: the leftover achy feeling. Which, despite being kind of nice—it was a not unpleasant way of being reminded of how thoroughly he had been had—it was damned uncomfortable when trying to sit for a car ride home.

At least the discomfort was usually worth it. And boy had it been worth it tonight.

Nick had been an awesome lay. He hadn't wasted any time getting Ezra back to his apartment, nor had he hesitated to shove Ezra down on the bed before doing filthy things with his mouth and his cock. And he was good at them too. Oh boy, had he been good with his cock. This walk of shame was totally worth it for the time spent on the end of that dick.

Except that while the actual fucking had been amazing, the aftermath....

Ezra had found himself restless and itchy once the afterglow had faded. Nick had fallen into a deep sleep, and Ezra had thought he would do the same, but he had lain awake for several minutes, staring at a stranger's bedroom ceiling. When the clock gave a mild beep to indicate the beginning of a new hour, he had decided that enough was enough. He got up, got dressed, and called a cab. Obviously he wasn't going to be sleeping there.

So here he was, taking a cab back to Wyn's at 2:08 a.m., and though his body was sated and happily drifting along on wonderful sex hormones, his mind was racing with an unnamable itch.

The cab came to a halt, and the driver demanded ten dollars for his trouble. Ezra handed over fifteen and got out of the car.

He was nearly all the way up the drive before he noticed that there was someone on the porch, waiting. He slowed his pace and took a few deep breaths through his nose, trying to ascertain who it was that was between him and the safe haven of Wyn's home.

The scent was strong and masculine. Callum.

Fuck a duck. Ezra did not want to deal with Callum and his domineering bullshit right now. Not when he was still a little drunk, and really tired, and, oh yeah, smelling of sex. No, no way was this conversation happening now.

Ezra walked up the steps to the front door. Fortunately, Callum wasn't standing before it but rather right in front of the deck chair that he had been sitting in not thirty seconds ago.

"Ezra." Callum's voice gave nothing away, but the deep resonance made Ezra shiver.

"Callum." A long silence followed this exchange. Ezra was the first to fill it. "Well, nice talking to you. I'm going to bed. Night."

"Do not move." The command was laced with tension and came with a veritable wave of pheromones that had Ezra stopping midstep. His hand was reaching for the door handle and most of his weight was on one leg, and yet despite all his practice, Ezra couldn't muster up any resistance. Callum had said not to move, and so Ezra would not be moving. Any good Nick might have done him evaporated as his cock decided it really wasn't all that tired after all.

"Where have you been?"

"Out." Oh, great. Now Ezra was going to relive his rebellious teenage years with Callum cast as his anxious and disapproving father. With bonus sexual tension.

"Out where?" Callum came closer, and Ezra could see his nose twitch as he took in a deep breath. He could also see the way his eyes went wide and then dark as he took in the scents of alcohol and sex. A fine tremor ran through Callum's body, and he clenched his fists. His eyes were bright with anger and looked almost golden in the porchlight. Arousal lay thick over undertones of jealousy and worry in his scent. Then he said, voice very calm, "Go to my house. Now."

Ezra spun and began to walk, unable to disobey. He was pretty sure that if he tried to ignore that command, he would end up with a migraine. Ezra was beginning to suspect that alcohol seriously impaired a man's ability to say no.

He was supremely aware of Callum walking behind him; he could almost feel the heat of his body. He heard a rustle and then the sound of buttons on a cell phone. "Tell Wyn he's home and he's fine. For now. She's to stop worrying and to go to sleep." Then Callum hung up, presumably on Blaise—a man who was likely to be very unhappy with him, if Ezra had indeed kept Wyn awake with worry. Damn, Ezra hadn't thought about that when he had left without a word.

Reaching Callum's front door, Ezra found that the command hadn't been enough to force him into walking through it. Callum hadn't told him he needed to be *inside* the house, and Ezra's trepidation about what would happen next was enough to keep his feet firmly on this side of the door.

"Inside." Well, there went that self-defense. Callum's arm came reaching past him and opened the door; he was standing very close.

Obeying the command, Ezra suppressed the pleased shiver as he walked through the door that Callum held open. Inside, he braced himself for the lecture that was surely to come.

"Where did you go?" The question came with more pheromones, and Ezra found he was too tired to even try to fight it.

"The Barnyard." His brain gave him another happy fuzzy feeling for his obedience. He could smell his own arousal now, too, so there was no way Callum could miss it. The knowledge made him brazen.

"The only gay bar in town? So you went out to find sex." It wasn't a question.

"And? So what if I did?" Great. He really sounded like a petulant teenager.

"I told you that you weren't to have sexual contact with anyone until the full moon."

Bitter resentment filled him at that. Callum had been very clear about that, but it wasn't like he'd offered any sort of explanation. "*Ri-i-ight*. I forgot, Callum said no sex, and I have to listen to Callum!"

That made Callum's face go tight. He looked even angrier. "The rules exist for a reason, Ezra! Do you have any idea what could have happened?"

Ezra knew the risks of having one-night stands and of going home with strange men, he wasn't stupid, but he suspected that wasn't what Callum was talking about. And those risks, the new lycanthrope-specific ones, were not ones he was familiar with, because *Callum* hadn't told him those. "*No*! But I'm sure the great Callum will enlighten me about how I nearly ruined everything!"

"Your brain is in a state of flux, Ezra. This isn't some controlled lab experiment. This is your life, your brain. You've got more hormones running loose in there than a locker room full of tenth graders. Even if that wasn't compromising your judgment, your brain literally cannot handle the overstimulation. You could've had a fucking stroke!"

Ezra's stomach turned at that. God, that would have been awful. Now he felt queasy. And why hadn't Callum told him this before? That Callum would only warn him after the fact, and that Ezra was letting himself be manipulated by it, made him all the angrier. "But what a way to go! Having a stroke midcoitus couldn't possibly make my month any worse!"

Callum, whose features had been softening as they stood in brief silence while Ezra tried to tell his stomach it was not upset, went cold again. "This is not a fucking *joke*, Ezra! Nothing about this is funny!"

At least on that they could agree. "No, it's really not. But if I want to risk a stroke by getting off, I don't see how it's any business of yours."

"That's where you're wrong." Was Ezra going crazy, or was that genuine sadness and concern flashing briefly in Callum's eyes? "Everything that affects the well-being of this pack is my business, and that includes you and your poor decision making."

That forced a strangled-sounding bark of a laugh out of Ezra's throat. "*My* poor decision making? Fine, you want to talk about poor decision making. Let's talk about sticking me in a house with Wyn and Blaise. Living with those two is like popping Viagra every morning. So yeah, I went out to get laid."

"I don't care what—" Callum paused midsentence and frowned, his features turning from anger into confusion. "Wait, what? Wyn and Blaise?"

Callum's apparently genuine confusion only made Ezra feel bewildered himself. "How have you not noticed the insane amount of pheromones those two emit?" Ezra crossed his arms, recalling how Wyn seemed to give out a constant buzz of "Take me!" that Blaise always answered with a "Yes, please!" Living with them had been unbearably awkward. "Christ, Blaise's a veritable leaky faucet of want, and Wyn isn't any better. Though at least I don't want to respond to her," he couldn't stop himself from mumbling. Embarrassed to have admitted as much out loud, he continued on. "And then tonight! Don't get me started on tonight."

"Jesus." Callum lifted one hand to cover his face. "Sorry. Jesus. I haven't spent a lot of time with the two of them together in the past couple months. I wouldn't have put you in that position if I'd known, I swear."

"Oh." And Ezra hadn't known that. He had had no idea that if he just *told* Callum that Wyn and Blaise wanted to bang each other that Callum might have rescued him from the agonizing sexual tension.

"Wait, what did you mean by 'tonight'?"

That brought the blush in full force. "Um, when I got home, they were... in the bathroom. And I saw—which was *awful*, but the pheromones were…." Ezra was having a hard time finding the words to express himself.

Fortunately, Callum seemed to understand. He let out a long groan and put both hands over his face. The curses he uttered were not made entirely unintelligible by the muffling of his palms. When he pulled his hands away, he looked very tired. "Blaise should know better."

Now Ezra felt unaccountably like he'd accidentally ratted out one of his friends to the teacher. The urge to defend him was kind of surprising. "Well, Wyn's kind of been walking around with a 'take me, big boy' sign around her neck the last few days."

"That doesn't excuse losing control and putting a new lycan in that situation. That's unacceptable."

"Look, I forgive them both. It's no big deal: I'm fine, they're fine. Why don't we just forget about this? Just… don't send me back there."

Callum let out a deep, tired-sounding sigh. For the first time tonight, Ezra took a good look at him. He looked tired and worn, like he wasn't just suffering from the lack of sleep tonight. "Ezra, it's not that simple. Usually, with new wolves, you have to worry about the stimulation overload. We start changing when we're in our young teens, and the increase in unsteady hormones is intense. But there is another concern that's not as pressing, but just as dangerous."

Okay, what was Callum talking about? Ezra grunted his confusion.

"Having sex with a human can be dangerous for a lycan if they're not careful. A lot of wolves like it rougher than most humans can handle, but sex with a human when changing can be even more dangerous. Young changing wolves often get confused about their desire for pack hierarchy, and so even those who will eventually have no want for power play will crave it during the change. Alphas have a tendency to get overexcited and domineering, which at best frightens the human, at worst does permanent physical damage."

"Well, that's not exactly something I have to worry about, so…." Ezra couldn't hide the bitterness in his tone.

"Betas come with their own issue. Some have a tendency to become frustrated with their partner's lack of… domination. Sometimes they'll push in an attempt to get their partner to take control, which isn't a problem if the partner is willing and knows their limits—because changing wolves *don't*."

With shocking clarity, Ezra was suddenly brought back to that moment when he had been on his knees, pushing back into Nick and feeling suddenly wild with want. He had thrust back hard and taunted, "That the best you can do?"

Nick had let out a breathless laugh before placing a hand on the top of his spine and pushing him down face-first into the bed. Ezra had whined and pushed his hips up for more, but he wondered now what might have happened if Nick hadn't been so obliging—or if he'd taken it too far.

Sitting down would probably be a good idea, because Ezra's knees felt a little weak.

"Shit." Then Callum was there, guiding him into a chair and looking worried. "Damn it, Ezra, I'm not trying to frighten you. But you've got to understand that the next two weeks are going to be intense for good reason. Sex is a dangerous proposition for everyone involved right now, but I promise it's only for a few weeks. After your first change, everything will get easier."

"So… then I can go and get laid?" Ezra's mocking smile was a little shaky. He still felt like he might throw up.

The answering frown was deep and conflicted. "Uh. Well, sex with humans is still tricky for some wolves. But yes, in a couple weeks you can start to… explore that side of yourself."

"You say that like I'm a virgin."

"Well, you will be, to having sex as a lycan. The new genetic makeup sometimes changes the way you approach sex."

Oh. So in other words, Ezra was going to relive puberty for the next couple of months. Wasn't life just fantastic?

Actually, maybe if Callum were willing to fuck him through it….

"Are you okay?" Despite the fact that the voice sounded strained and uncomfortable, the warm hand that rested on his thigh was reassuring. Also, kind of crazily hot. Ezra was suddenly keenly aware of two things: one, Callum was really, really close, and two, Ezra was discussing his future sex life with Callum. Also, three, Callum really was extremely close.

"Well. I think I'm done being mortified for tonight. I'm going to bed."

"Right." Callum nodded and stood. He shifted, and then he sniffed slightly and froze for a second before continuing as if nothing had happened.

Oh. Right. Ezra blushed hotly again. He probably still smelled like sex.

"Bed. And a shower first." He stood with purpose and turned to go... he didn't know where. "Uh. Should I go back to Wyn's?" He winced. That sounded so pathetic, but Ezra really wasn't sure he could take the lingering scent of their pheromones. Not tonight.

"No. I think we've learned how disastrously that ends." There was a long pause, and then Callum sighed. "Look, it's three in the morning. Use my guest room. We'll figure something out tomorrow."

Right. Tomorrow they would have to figure out a new solution, because Ezra couldn't stay here. Not with Callum. He nodded and then followed Callum upstairs to the bathroom and guest bedroom. Christ, but was he ever ready to sleep.

EZRA woke from the dream in a sweat and had half a second to wonder where he was before his nose chimed in. Wherever it was, the place smelled like Callum, or like whatever laundry detergent Callum used, anyway. That was probably at least partially responsible for his current state.

For a moment, Ezra barely resisted the urge to roll over and hump the mattress. The desire for simple but messy was part frustration, part desperation, and part very pointed payback at Callum for showing up in his dream and getting him all hot and bothered in the first place. But... it wasn't like Ezra wouldn't end up washing the sheets himself. He did have a tiny scrap of pride left, so he sucked it up and closed his eyes as he wrapped a too-familiar hand around himself and let his mind wander back to the dream.

It wasn't that he was surprised to be dreaming about Callum. Between the amount of time they spent together and Ezra's seemingly uncontrollable attraction to him, it would have been a miracle *not* to wake up with a hard-on or a wet spot on the sheets. It wasn't even that he was surprised at the kinds of things his unconscious (and now subconscious and conscious as well, damn it) mind imagined Callum doing to him. It was the *way* he did it.

Ezra had known Callum just long enough to figure out that this was a man who knew exactly what he wanted. And how he wanted it. And in Ezra's dreams, whether it was a byproduct of his new beta lycan DNA or a heretofore repressed fantasy or just a result of his knowledge of the man he wanted to fuck him blind, well…. Dream Callum made sure he got exactly what he wanted, using just the right combination of physical force and explicitly worded demands to make Ezra consider the possibility that he had some seriously repressed kink issues.

Ezra barely contained a little groan as he thought back to this most recent dream. It had been especially vivid and realistic. Ezra hadn't quite thought it was possible to have such an intense dream the night after getting thoroughly pounded, but apparently normal rules did not apply to Callum in that respect either.

In the dream, it wasn't Nick Ezra encountered at the bar last night. It was Callum. *Ezra was dancing by himself, lost in the pounding baseline of a song so loud he couldn't hear the lyrics, when a warm body had slid into place behind him. Then a hand came to rest between his pectorals. A brief flash of tongue just below his ear and then a deep, appreciative sniff, followed by a low rumble: "Let's go."*

The pheromone compunction had to be part of the dream, but that didn't make it any less effective. *Ezra had let Callum herd him toward the bathroom, already buzzing with anticipation.*

The door of the bathroom led to Ezra's father's apartment.

Here, now, in Callum's guest bedroom, Ezra heard the shower start down the hall. Callum was in there. Naked. Wet. Maybe Ezra should have felt bad for jerking off in his house, but the idea that Callum might catch him just made it that much better.

Fuck.

Callum was wearing the suit again, the one he'd worn the first time Ezra had met him. When the apartment door closed behind them, he removed his jacket and loosened his tie. By the time he looked up again and fixed his eyes on Ezra, his expression was smoldering. "Go stand behind the couch."

When Ezra obeyed, his unconscious mind provided him with the same positive reinforcement the pheromones provided when he was awake. Even the memory of it was powerful.

"Brace yourself."

Ezra kicked the sheets down and swallowed a whine.

Callum put a hand in the center of his back and pushed until Ezra was leaning at an angle, arms supported on the back of the couch. At some point in the past few seconds his clothes had disappeared.

A finger traced its way down Ezra's spine. "I told you no one was to touch you."

A rough squeeze, and then Ezra bucked up into his hand. This was so twisted. Ezra didn't like being told what to do. He *didn't*. But this? God, apparently he got off on this.

"But you couldn't keep it in your pants." Callum brought his hand up to Ezra's mouth, and Ezra opened for the fingers automatically, drawing them in, making them wet. Callum's hot breath rasped in his ear and his lips were micrometers away from Ezra's flesh when he whispered, "And now I'm going to remind you who you belong to."

The fingers disappeared, but Callum's mouth only got closer to Ezra's skin, and his tongue flicked across the bite scar. A teasing scrape of teeth, then the lightest of touches of wet fingers gliding across Ezra's hole—

Callum's fingers pushed inside at the same time his teeth closed over the bite.

Ezra came silently, open-mouthed, hard enough that he needed time afterward to catch his breath.

Then he remembered that Callum's house only had the one shower.

Fuck.

Last night, Callum had caught him coming home from the bar smelling like he'd been rolled over and thoroughly fucked. And now he reeked of sex *again*. Honestly, he knew his hormones were out of control right now, but it would have been nice to have a little privacy about it.

He really didn't want to face Callum this morning. God.

But he had a job now, and he couldn't stay in bed all day, much as he wanted to, so he swung his legs over the side and headed for the kitchen.

The house was quiet apart from the background hiss of water from Callum's shower, and even that thought was enough that Ezra had to firmly steer his thoughts in another direction, because his dick was trying to get hard *again*. Putting all thoughts of hot, wet Alphas determinedly out of his brain—damn it—he moved to the coffee maker.

Two and a half years of college engineering courses had more than prepared him for the challenge set forth by Callum's coffee maker; afterward, he tackled the toaster. Maybe it was weird to go through Callum's kitchen, but it wasn't like a little more weird was going to be a big deal at this point. He'd spent the day before learning how not to get a boner every time he did something Callum asked of him and then essentially got caught with his pants down after getting some guy to fuck it out of him.

Besides, he was used to Wyn's epic breakfasts now, and he was hungry.

A quick glance at the front step revealed that either the newspaper hadn't arrived or Callum didn't have a subscription, so Ezra braved the perils of a trip next door to Wyn's—determinedly ignoring all input from his ears and nose—and collected his textbook. He was back in Callum's kitchen, immersed brain-deep in the exact reasons why his late-night tryst had been a spectacularly bad idea when Callum cleared his throat.

Startled, Ezra looked up, feeling a flush spread across his cheeks to the tips of his ears. Callum stood in the doorway of the kitchen, holding himself somewhat awkwardly. Instead of what Ezra thought of as his usual work attire—dress pants and a shirt and tie, though he knew Callum changed into scrubs and a lab coat occasionally—he was wearing a pair of bleach-stained blue jeans a vintage band T-shirt.

Ezra wasn't so much staring as he was attempting to eat Callum with his eyeballs. It wasn't that he looked *better* than he usually did, because Callum pretty much always looked like he'd just stepped off the pages of *GQ*. But the casual style made him seem so much more attainable.

Callum had obviously caught him staring, because he glanced down at himself self-consciously. "I'm running some tests today," he said by way of explanation. "They're not kind on dress pants."

Ezra nodded and made a concerted effort to close his mouth. "Right. Of course." He looked back down at his textbook. "I was just reading up."

When he raised his head again, he saw Callum's eyes flicker down at the book, and his mouth flattened. "About that." He blew out a breath, then poured himself a coffee and sat down across from Ezra at the table.

Then he inhaled. Deeply. His breath caught, and he froze where he was.

Ezra wondered if werewolves considered tandem blushing a sport.

It was another long moment before Callum met Ezra's gaze. His cheeks were still flushed pink. "I shouldn't have shouted at you yesterday. I should have made sure you knew why it was dangerous."

Ezra looked at him over the rim of his coffee mug and tried not to die of embarrassment. "I feel like we've had this conversation before."

Callum made a face as he reached for the stack of toast Ezra had left on the table. "Call me a slow learner." He sighed. "I'm making kind of a mess of your education, aren't I?"

That was an understatement. "If it's any consolation, I'm fairly sure you're not doing it on purpose."

"That's hardly an excuse. Maybe I should have contacted an Alpha with some experience with new lycanthropes."

Ezra scoffed. "So I'd have to move too? Yeah, that sounds awesome. I'll take my chances with you, if it's all the same."

Callum held his gaze for a moment, his lips slightly parted, and then he blinked and shook his head. "Thanks for making breakfast, by the way."

"Toast isn't exactly the haute cuisine I've been eating at Wyn's," Ezra pointed out. "But, uh, you're welcome?" Ezra was desperate to smooth things over between them, and he was willing to try anything to do it.

Callum tried to wave him off, though it looked uncomfortable. "Listen, about last night—forget about it. You didn't know."

"I'm not going to forget about it," Ezra protested. The dream part especially. Jesus. "And in fairness, I don't think you should either." He grimaced and pushed away his plate. This was going to suck. "Look— you had to know what you were doing to me with all the alpha stuff, right?"

Color suffused Callum's cheeks, and he averted his eyes. "It's not—uh—see, the thing is…."

What the hell? Since when did Callum stutter? "Yes?" Ezra prompted.

"Talking about it is taboo," Callum finished.

Oh for—seriously? The reason Ezra didn't have the information he needed to live his life safely was that talking about it was a lycanthrope faux pas? "What?" he exclaimed.

"When you're a member of an intelligent species closely related to humans and who can smell one another's arousal"—at the word "arousal," Callum flushed bright red again, and Ezra would have sworn his eyes dropped to Ezra's crotch for half a second—"it's the only way to maintain the illusion of privacy."

It made sense in a twisted, backward, Victorian way, but.... "Okay, well, you're just going to have to be uncomfortable for a minute." This situation could not continue. Ezra would lose his mind long before the next full moon.

"Ezra—"

"No, look, if we're going to work together, we need to have ground rules."

Callum looked away.

"You knew what you were doing to me. And I get that it was for my own good in the long run, that if I come up against some hopped-up alpha lycan who doesn't respect the rules about who's allowed to say what to whom, I'm going to need to be able to say no. But that stops now. From here on out, if you want me to do something, you ask me. No pheromone whammy, no authoritative tone of voice. That's not fair."

"I'm sorry," Callum said miserably. "I'm normally not this bad at keeping those under control. I've never had this problem before."

He really did sound sorry. At least if Ezra died of a penis hemorrhage he could count on Callum to feel bad about it. "What do you think changed?"

The expression of misery deepened, so obviously they were still in taboo territory.

"Just be straight with me and let's get it over with," Ezra told him, fighting the urge to just bury his head in his arms on the table until it was over. "Then we can go back to pretending this conversation never happened."

"You asked for it." Callum sighed. "It's you."

Ezra's mouth dropped open. "Excuse me?"

"*You*," Callum repeated. "When juvenile lycanthropes go through puberty, they aren't sexually mature enough to interest an adult lycan, okay? So their hormone and pheromone production goes nuts, but it only affects *them*. The only one who's going to screw them is another horny teenager. You're already grown."

Oh, fantastic. "So I'm giving off come-fuck-me vibes at everyone?" Just fucking typical.

"Not exactly."

Why did he think this was only going to get worse? "Well, while we're being honest…?"

"Pheromones are kind of without direction. They're just in the air. Part of life. Sure, if you walk in on two people going at it, you're going to react, but in normal circumstances, if you're not looking for them, they don't have much effect." Callum shrugged, looking up from his fingernails at last. "Until they're coupled with a physical signal from the lycan who's emitting them. It could be anything—a touch on the shoulder, eye contact—Ezra."

Ezra paused halfway through licking his lips and bit them instead, though it was probably too late for Callum. "Sorry!" he said hastily. "How do I stop?"

Callum took a deep breath. "You can't. That's why I wanted you to stay with Wyn. You can throw all the pheromones you want at her; she's a woman. Unless you're interested, they won't work. Historically, turned wolves would go into seclusion for the month before they turned until they got their pituitary glands under control, but I think that kind of thing's against the Geneva Convention now."

"So we're stuck like this until the full moon."

Callum gritted his teeth. "Yes."

Ezra swallowed and nodded grimly. "In that case, I'm definitely going to need my own office." Preferably one that was stocked with a healthy amount of lube and Kleenex.

SON-of-a-whoring-bitch!

Throwing the phone down, the man cursed Callum Dawson and the day he'd met him. No, the day Dawson was born. That little cocksucking faggot had long been a pain in the ass, and now he was asking questions. He had been working too long and too hard at this project to let a fucking pansy fuck things up.

He had first met Dawson shortly after being turned—they had both been aiming to be head Alpha of the Missoula pack. The pack had been fucking elitists, and had picked the lycan that had been born a werewolf. Fucking idiots didn't know what was important. Dawson might have been born a lycan, but he wasn't pure or interested in protecting lycan traditions. No, the faggot wasn't worried about the blight that was the so-called female alpha, and he didn't worry about how beta males were ruining their gender.

Swallowing two fingers of whiskey in one go, he conceded that Dawson would never want beta males to be removed. After all, if the rumors were true, the pervert was taking full advantage. An old bitch had been happy to gossip with him and tell him all about Dawson's new... pet. A newly changed lycan who was the biggest he-bitch ever. Couldn't wait to roll over for Dawson and play. To be his bitch in bed and out.

A knock came on the door, and he turned to see his young housemaid standing there, murmuring that lunch was served. Pretty and well curved, she was a real woman: quiet, submissive, and willing to please. She was what was worth keeping, worth breeding, not those women who fancied themselves alphas and who wanted to play above their stations. He had known it from the first moment he had joined lycan society, and he didn't know how others couldn't see it.

Of course, the biggest problem wasn't the women who wanted some power—that could be forgiven—it was the men who let them have it. The alphas who allowed it and the bitches who encouraged it. Those *betas* needed to be wiped from society: put down like the pathetic, defective dogs they were. And with selective breeding, things would get better.

Little matter, he didn't need to work at showing others the errors of their ways just yet. Once Davis had perfected the drug, he would be able to get to work at fixing things. Still... there was the matter of Dawson and his damned questions. Maybe…. No, it was too delicious! He couldn't—oh but he could, he was sure. There had to be a way of getting the he-bitch away from Dawson, and then he truly would be a sight: stressed and worried about his new toy and much too distracted to worry about a few missing bitches. Yes, the he-bitch was definitely the key to getting Dawson out of the way, and he was going to use it.

Satisfied, he downed the last of his whiskey and headed for the door, a smile on his face. It was lunchtime; the maid had said it was lamb.

Chapter Seven
A Wolf in Sheep's Clothing

HINDSIGHT was a remarkable thing. Take this afternoon—it had seemed like such a good idea when Wyn had stopped by to suggest it. Ezra sighed as he unfastened his pants. Wyn had played her cards well: she had appealed to his vanity.

"Don't you *want* to look good?" she had asked. "You could look stunning in the right suit. Don't you want to make the best impression?"

That had cinched it. Ezra was pretty nervous about being in a roomful of lycans, most of them Alphas, who had no allegiance to Callum. He wanted to make a good impression not only for himself—he wouldn't be seen as just some tag-along beta—but for Callum and the pack. He didn't want anyone to think that the man had made a mistake hiring Ezra on as his research assistant, especially Callum. And since his only suit predated his stint in college, Ezra had agreed to let Wyn take him shopping.

The experience wasn't his favorite. Wyn, though, was on a first-name basis with the clerk, Martin, who eyed Ezra in turn with something uncomfortably like lust, which just made it even more uncomfortable when he needed to measure Ezra for jacket sizes.

Ezra was, he reminded himself, doing this for a reason. He needed a suit if he wanted people to take him seriously.

When Callum had first told Ezra about the conference, Ezra had wanted to laugh at the absurdity—a conference of *werewolves*. And apparently it happened every year! The Alphas of the Midwest got together to share information: medical and scientific knowledge relating to lycans as well as social, legislative, or political changes that would affect their communities.

Callum said this year it was critical that he attend—he had to share what he knew about ARD—and it was only logical to take Ezra, his research assistant, with him.

To Ezra, the invite for the three-day business trip had felt more like marching orders than a request, but either way he needed a suit, because apparently the first night had an "event" with a dress code.

Ezra sighed again and pulled on the black slacks. Pants and shirt on, he stepped out of the dressing room.

Martin, of the wandering hands and the convenient fit-checking excuse, stood there holding up the jacket for Ezra to slip on.

Ezra turned to see himself in the mirror. "This looks good," he said.

Wyn hummed. "It's kind of boring. Black on white."

"It's classic," Ezra protested. The cut was flattering; there was no reason not to take it.

Wyn rolled her eyes. "The gray one next, I think," she said, looking at the clerk.

The clerk nodded his agreement before wandering off to find more suits.

Belaboring the point would have been useless, so Ezra meekly complied.

"So how goes living at Callum's?" Wyn called.

"It's interesting," Ezra said, swapping the black slacks for the gray.

"Interesting? Do tell."

"There is nothing to tell," Ezra said. He only felt a little bitter about that.

"Oh, come on, there's got to be something."

Ezra opened the curtain to find her red-faced.

"Not even burning sexual tension?" She looked half-mortified, half-naughtily pleased.

Ezra raised his eyebrows at her and swallowed his own embarrassment to say, "Well, there's always been that."

Wyn giggled and blushed, and Ezra smiled back. When she was under control again, she returned to her task of judging his outfit. "Not with the white shirt." She picked up a shirt from the pile next to her. "Try the green." She pushed him back into the changing room.

Ezra pulled on the new shirt and returned.

The clerk was back with another armload. "Hm," he said.

"Yes," said Wyn. "I think I agree."

"So the gray is a no." Ezra nodded, seeing an opportunity. "Good, let's take the black."

"Ezra! Martin has picked out a brown for you to try. And a green!" She watched the clerk hang the suits and then said, "I bet he'd look handsome in a pinstripe."

Martin unfortunately agreed.

The brown made his hair look dull, and the green wasn't cut right. The pinstripe made Wyn beam.

"I look like a gangster."

"No, you don't."

"All I need is a '30s hat and a machine gun."

She frowned at him like she wanted to argue but couldn't.

"I look ridiculous. I want these people to take me seriously." He added in an undertone, "I'm at enough of a disadvantage already."

"That's not true!" She shot a glance at Martin. "You know you're not going to be the only b-boyfriend there." She emphasized the B and raised her eyebrows to ensure her meaning was clear.

"Maybe, but I bet all the rest of the *boyfriends* will be scientists. Or husbands." Ezra fidgeted with the suit cuff and made a face at himself in the mirror.

Wyn looked appalled. "And you're Callum's assistant. He asked you to go for a *reason*, Ezra. And not because you look so pretty in a suit. Oh, all right, go change." She sighed a little in disappointment as the suit was returned to the rack, but made no further protests.

"That's the one," said Martin when Ezra walked out wearing a navy-blue suit.

Ezra had to admit that the cut was good, and Wyn did have a point when she started gushing about how the suit made his eyes pop.

"But I'm not sure about the shirt," said Martin.

"Hm. You're right."

Ezra looked down. It was charcoal gray and perfectly acceptable.

"Maybe...." Wyn reached into the pile of shirts and pulled one out; it was chocolate brown with blue stripes. They were narrow and evenly spaced about two inches apart. Ezra wasn't so sure, but he shrugged and took the shirt behind the curtain to change.

"So, you're surviving at Callum's?"

"I miss waking up to waffles every morning."

Wyn giggled. "But I'm not as cute as Callum, so trade-off, right?"

Ezra grinned. "He's also not as nice first thing in the morning."

She giggled again.

"I haven't had your cooking for… oh, five days now? That's too long."

"You know, I'm starting to think you only liked me for my food," Wyn said as he donned the jacket.

He slid the curtain back with a dramatic flair. "Never! I miss *you* too."

"Good." She grinned, then eyed the new shirt.

It was odd, he thought, not to see her for five days after seeing her every morning and night for a week and a half. Because he really *did* miss her, he asked, "So what have you been up to?"

Wyn turned beet red. "Oh, the usual."

"Yeah?"

"Yeah." She wouldn't look him in the eye. What—?

"Oh!" Ezra blushed. "I wasn't—I mean—"

Wyn was stammering now too. "Oh. I didn't—I'm sure you weren't—"

They stumbled into silence.

Fortunately, Martin broke it when he returned. "That is perfect! You were right, Wyn. That shirt looks fabulous. How about you hop up here and our tailor will check the fit."

Once again Ezra was subject to handsiness, though at least this time the one with the hands was a professional middle-aged man and not a young man who was obviously enjoying his job too much. Still, he was relieved when he was told he could step down off the pedestal and take the suit off again, even if he did have to "mind the pins."

Once again in his jeans and hoodie, Ezra paid for the suit and shirt with Callum's credit card. It was awkward, and he tried not to think of words like *sugar* or *daddy*, but he just couldn't afford to buy himself a suit. Also, Callum was taking him to this thing for business, so he could probably write it off.

The clerk also tried to sell them a tie, but Wyn, unsatisfied with the selection, told them to wrap up the shirt so they could use it to go tie shopping.

Out of the store, Ezra finally felt free to say, "You know, Wyn, I'm super happy for you, right? You and Blaise are perfect for each other."

She looked inordinately pleased to hear him say so. "Thanks."

"I mean, I wasn't thrilled about *how* I found out." She glared at his grin. "But you two should be together."

"I'm glad you think so. Also that you're not too mad at us."

"Hey, whoa, mad? I'm not mad. How could I be mad at my Wyn? Callum has had me super busy the last few days. I wasn't staying away on purpose."

"Good." She turned toward a shop called The Tie Rack. Right, this torture wasn't over yet.

"Though I might have thought it was best not to hurry over." He gave a suggestive eyebrow waggle. "I figured you and Blaise would want all the quality time you could get."

The look she gave him as he passed through the door totally made up for any hell that would follow.

CALLUM couldn't help but notice the way Ezra fussed with his cuffs once they got a good look at the hall. Chandeliers dripping with faux gems hung from the high ceiling of the spacious room, floor-to-ceiling windows taking up one wall. The place was filled with tables and chairs—and a lot of people. Most were lycans, some Alphas, some doctors, scientists, policymakers, and the like, but there were a few human scientists as well. Ezra appeared to be somewhat intimidated by the crowd.

Controlling the biological imperative to protect Ezra from the masses was going to be *awesome*. Callum tried to remind himself that Ezra's fidgeting was not adorable.

"Relax. There are fewer lycans here than in the pack. You handled *them* just fine."

The answering snort sounded desperate. "They weren't dressed in black tie."

"Neither are these people." Then, when Ezra opened his mouth to argue, "And you aren't exactly underdressed. Your suit fits in fine." Not to mention the fact that it was stunningly hot on Ezra. The pants and shirt fit as if they had been made for him, which was probably because Wyn had taken him shopping. Callum was having a hard time concentrating on anything but the way the fabric seemed to cling to Ezra's ass. He wasn't sure if he should kill Wyn or thank her. Maybe he'd wait on his credit card bill to decide.

"Now," Callum said, steeling himself for resistance and tearing his eyes away from the vision in front of him, "let's go mingle."

"Mingle?"

"Yes. And eat hors d'oeuvres." Callum was *starving*.

Ezra seemed swayed by the prospect of food, but unfortunately for him, they didn't make it to any. They were only a few feet into the room when a booming voice said, "Dawson!" and Callum turned to see Malcolm Shaw walking toward them. *Wonderful.*

"Malcolm, how are you?" Callum said politely.

"Fine, fine. Been keeping busy. Lots of work to run a pack, as you know, lots of work."

Callum nodded. "Yes, it is."

"Truth be told, I probably don't have time to be here, but we can't *always* do what we'd like. Can't say no to this lot." Malcolm waved one hand imperiously to indicate the group filling up the room.

Callum had never really cared for Malcolm.

"But we come, we come. And I see you didn't come alone. But why bring along this beta?"

And that was why.

Though clenched teeth, he managed to get out, "Ezra is my assistant. He's here to help with my speech and to help me take notes." Callum wasn't sure why he felt the need to justify Ezra's presence to Malcolm, except that it was at least in part to forestall the kind of assumption Malcolm let leak out his filthy mouth next.

"Ah, *assistant*, eh? If you needed one, why not pick that pretty little Wyn girl—now she was a beta worth asking for assistance!" Malcolm leered at them before his eyes suddenly cut to the left, and for a moment his focus slipped past Callum.

Callum took the moment to grab hold of Ezra's flexing arm and give him a warning look: *down, boy.* Though Callum agreed that talking about Wyn—or anyone—that way was disgusting, trying to change Malcolm Shaw was futile. And punching him in the face would only be a very temporary fix.

"I thought a math and science background would be much more useful when it came to a research assistant. Ezra is a whiz with computers."

Malcolm faltered. "Well, I suppose a *talent* might make up for looks," he said with the barest of glances in Ezra's direction. His gaze lingered instead over Callum's shoulder. He was getting increasingly distracted.

"Really, Malcolm, you would know best on the subject, I'm sure." Malcolm didn't react to the sarcasm, and Callum took a deep breath before asking, "How's the pack?"

"Good, good. No complaints," Malcolm muttered, and right then Callum knew just how distracted Malcolm was—he was never without a complaint.

Callum took a glance over his shoulder but saw nothing interesting. "Malcolm?"

"Hm? Oh, so I hear you'll be giving us a presentation. Some problem you think we've got?"

"Yes." Callum frowned but allowed the subject change. "The rising number of cases of lycan violence and increase in the number of disappearing lycans—"

"Hm, interesting, I'm sure." Malcolm clapped his hands together. "Well, must be off!" His gaze flicked back to Callum's face one last time. Then he said goodbye and dashed away.

Callum and Ezra both turned to watch where he was headed, but he left the hall.

"Odd," Ezra said.

"Very," Callum agreed.

"Is he always like that?"

"Like what? An arrogant, condescending pig? Sadly, yes. So distracted he ignores me completely?" Callum shrugged. "Sadly, no. We've never seen eye to eye, so he's never truly enjoyed face time with me."

"Douche," Ezra muttered.

Callum laughed.

"Well, he made his point loud and clear," Ezra pointed out stoutly. "He's a douche."

Malcolm's introduction was followed by many others. Now that attention had been drawn to their arrival, many old friends and acquaintances were eager to greet Callum—and get a closer look at

Ezra. Callum couldn't help but notice the way their gazes lingered as they took in Ezra's appearance.

Jealousy warmed Callum's belly and burned in his chest. He wanted to stake a claim. The wolf demanded he let these rivals know that Ezra was not free to mate, and if Callum couldn't have him, nobody could. It was irrational, given his own self-imposed rule about playing with lycans, never mind pack members, but the wolf was not prone to introspection. He was an Alpha with an interest, and they were Alphas with curiosity. While Callum could keep a lid on his baser urges, he didn't stop himself from letting his hand linger on Ezra's arm after Alpha Carter shook it, leaning closer when Alpha Harriett sized him up, or guiding Ezra away from the smirking scientists with his hand on the small of his back.

Eventually they made their way from the door and into the hall, finding themselves at the heart of the gathering. Ezra spotted the food first and made a beeline; Callum didn't argue.

Standing near the tables, munching on finger food and sipping champagne, Callum took stock of Ezra. He seemed fairly relaxed now, at least compared to earlier, and if he was still nervous, it wasn't affecting his appetite. "How are you doing?" Callum asked, wanting to be sure.

Ezra gave a grimace in response. "Fine. Would be feeling better if everyone had to wear nametags."

Callum jerked and laughed with surprise. "You're doing just fine."

"Thanks. I appreciate that you're willing to lie to make me feel better."

"Not a lie. Just stay relaxed. You're good with people, Ezra."

Callum didn't notice his rising hand until after it had settled on the other man's arm and given a gentle squeeze.

Fuck.

CALLUM and Ezra were in the middle of puzzling over a mysterious hors d'oeuvre when a deep voice said, "And who is this?"

Ezra's human form didn't technically have *hackles*, he reminded himself. But that didn't stop them from rising. He hated being snuck up on.

When he turned around, he found an older, but still very handsome, man standing behind him. He was cradling a wine glass in one large hand, and the other was tucked into his pocket. Like every other Alpha in the building, he seemed perfectly at home.

"Ezra, this is Darius Maulsby, Alpha of the Great Falls pack," Callum said through tight lips. "Darius, this is Ezra, the newest member of our pack."

The man was quite good-looking. Even the assessing look he gave Ezra shaped his features in a flattering way. "Ezra Jones, how good to finally meet you. The rumor mill has been relentless."

Ezra flushed with embarrassment and couldn't help but feel that it would have been easier if more people had simply talked about him as if he weren't there, like Malcolm had. "Surely I'm not that exciting."

Darius shook his head in that knowing older gentleman sort of way. Ezra imagined him with a top hat and cane, the top of which he would waggle at Ezra for emphasis. "It would seem many beg to differ."

Ezra licked his lips through the awkward pause, not sure what to say to that. He'd only been a lycan for a few weeks, had yet even to transform. What could possibly be so interesting about him? "Yes, well...."

"Ezra's here as my new assistant. You should hear our talk tomorrow," Callum said, his tone—Ezra hesitated to call it dismissive, but maybe cautious? There was definitely more going on than Ezra was privy to. Callum didn't like Darius, that much was obvious, but Ezra couldn't figure out why, unless it was some weird Alpha thing he was never going to understand anyway.

"Yes, of course," Maulsby said with a nod. "I'm sure everyone is very eager to hear what you and your assistant have to say."

Callum acknowledged the remark with a quick nod. "I see you're alone again. No luck on finding another Alpha?"

Darius shook his head. "Not yet, I'm afraid. There is still the chance that Diana will recover. I know it seems foolish...."

The older man did seem genuinely sad. Ezra wondered who this Diana person was.

"I'm sorry," Callum offered.

Darius brushed him off. "Never mind," he said stiffly. "If you'll excuse me, Doctor, I think I see Malcolm Shaw." He gave Ezra a cursory nod and then walked off, his gait swaying awkwardly.

When he was gone, Ezra said, "Who's Diana?"

Callum was watching Darius's retreating back, a thoughtful look on his face. "She's an old friend of mine, Darius's co-Alpha. She was in a car accident a couple months ago—she's been in a coma since. I always thought they didn't get along." He shook his head. "They must've been closer than I thought if he still hasn't started looking for another Alpha." Then he clapped Ezra on the shoulder. "Come on, I think I smell cheesecake."

IT WAS late, the party was over, and they were both tipsy. Time for bed.

It wasn't until they stumbled into the room that Callum remembered that they hadn't yet seen it. They had been late arriving, and so the receptionist had sent their luggage up with the bellhop. Now that he saw the room, Callum wished he had taken the time to pay attention despite being late. There was only one bed.

A very large and comfortable-looking bed—a king-size one—but still only *one*.

Double fuck.

"Huh." Ezra eyed the room, then turned to Callum. There was the faint air of suspicion about him. "One bed?"

"There must have been a mistake," Callum explained. He was not taking responsibility for this. He had definitely requested a room with two beds once he'd been informed that the suites were all booked up.

Ezra turned back to the bed. "To clarify, I'm not allowed to sleep with you."

"Sleeping is fine," Callum shot back. "I'm just not allowed to fuck you" *like I so dearly want to do right now.*

Ezra sighed, looked at Callum again lingeringly, and then groaned. "I should have had less to drink," he said mournfully. "What do you think the odds are of getting another room?"

Callum shook his head. "Not good. I overheard the people at the front desk talking. They've got three different conferences this weekend. No vacancy."

"Ugh." Ezra kicked off his dress shoes—Callum didn't want to think about what that was going to do to his chances of getting the laces untied—and flopped face-first on the bed. The movement sent a rush of warm, Ezra-scented air Callum's way, and he stepped back before it could draw him in. His mouth watered anyway, and he bit his lip, contemplating a cold shower.

Ezra rolled over on the bed, which didn't help matters. "So, any brilliant ideas?"

Callum shrugged and started taking off his own shoes. "We man up and keep it in our pants. I assume you can control yourself?"

Ezra didn't answer right away, and eventually Callum had to look up from his shoelaces—he was half a second away from taking a page out of Ezra's book—and say into Ezra's uncomfortable silence, "Really?"

"Remember when you compared the hormone production to being a teenager?"

Callum nodded mutely.

"I was *never* this horny as a teenager."

Oh. Damn, Ezra really should not have told him that. Callum finally defeated his shoelaces and sat carefully in the chair by the window. It was probably, he realized, at least partially his fault. He'd been... proprietary... all evening, and even though he'd been fairly conscious of his pheromone production—a necessity in a room full of fellow lycans, some as cutthroat as any politician—he knew his control slipped when he consumed alcohol. Not enough to affect a seasoned lycan, maybe, but Ezra hadn't been blooded. "So basically you're going to jump me if I get within touching distance."

"Probably? Maybe. I... I'm not sure." Ezra sounded surprisingly young just then.

"Why not?"

"Because it's not like I have precedent for this situation."

"Right."

"What about you?"

Did Callum have a precedent for this situation? No. No, he didn't. "No." He sighed. "So, any suggestions for how to get through the night?"

"Does our room have a minibar?"

Callum turned to stare at Ezra. "You're too drunk to control your libido, so you want to drink more?"

"Well… if I get drunk enough, my libido won't have anything to say."

"Right. I don't think that's a good idea." Getting more drunk had the risk of just removing the last of their inhibitions. And Callum wasn't sure there was enough liquor in the world to make his dick ignore the fact that it was within touching distance of Ezra's. "How about we both take a cold shower and then watch TV until we fall asleep. On opposite sides of the bed."

Ezra let out a groan. "I hate taking cold showers."

Who didn't? Callum arched an eyebrow.

"I like my showers scalding," Ezra pointed out with a pout… a pout that went straight to Callum's cock.

"Right. I'm going to go have that shower now." Callum stood and walked straight for the bathroom.

Unfortunately, the shower did little to get rid of his hard-on. Callum really wished that he could jerk off, but those kinds of sex pheromones were likely to just make Ezra's plight worse. Either they'd lure Ezra into the bathroom with him, or he'd go back to the main room to find Ezra humping the bed, and just—no. Callum didn't have that kind of willpower.

At least by the time he left the bathroom Callum's cock wasn't exactly hard. It wasn't completely soft, given Ezra's proximity and his sweet, intoxicating scent, but it was softer than before. It was something.

By the time Ezra stumbled out of the bathroom, Callum was tucked into bed. He thought that it might make things a little easier if they weren't climbing in at the same time. That was his theory, anyway, but the sight of Ezra climbing into bed in flannel pants and a tight T-shirt was enough to get Callum's blood pumping. He needed a distraction.

"What do you want to watch?"

Ezra shrugged. "I'm easy."

Callum fumbled the remote control. Oh God.

Once he regained control of the remote, he began flicking through channels. "Oh look, *CSI!*" The image flicked from a gruesome dead body to one of the infamous flashback scenes that showed a crime in gory detail. Disgusting. Callum honestly wasn't sure if his nausea or his relief would win out on this occasion.

With a satisfied sigh, Ezra wiggled himself into a slouched position. Definitely relief. "Awesome, I haven't seen this one yet."

Ezra must have been more drunk than Callum had thought, because he was snoring before the culprit was arrested.

Callum was not so lucky. He stayed awake through the whole episode and then finished off a hockey game before finally nodding off watching *M*A*S*H* reruns.

He woke up sometime in the wee hours to fumble for the remote and turn off the annoying sound of infomercials, but he quickly fell back asleep.

HE WATCHED them all night, his attention covert but persistent; he stayed aware of the Alpha and his new bitch. And the beta *was* his bitch. Sickening. Oh, Dawson hadn't laid *claim* to him, but everyone there knew what was going on. It was obvious—the way Dawson leaned toward him, the way he wouldn't let him out of his sight, the way his hand lingered in the small of his back. It wasn't the formal claim of a lover and a mate, but all the other alphas in the room knew better than to try to fuck *that* one. Not that many of them would want to.

Thank God that most alphas had no desire to fuck a pretty beta boy—they'd leave that up to a female alpha—even if they tended not to protest when a lycan claimed to be a fag. The indulgent smiles on the faces of many of the lycans watching the mating dance were almost as sickening as Dawson's display.

A display that was obvious to everyone but the bitch. The bitch who was obviously overwhelmed by so many strange wolves in one place and just as apparently oblivious to the way that his Alpha was telling everyone how much he wanted to fuck him.

He shuddered and pushed the disgusting thought away. He didn't need to ponder what Dawson and the bitch would do on their own time.

No, he was much more interested in Dawson's new behavior and the way he was so *distracted*.

The bitch let out a loud laugh that cut through the air and drew the attention of several wolves, many of whom took a moment to watch Dawson's new toy. Despite being six feet tall and well muscled, he was obviously no alpha. He automatically lowered his gaze when presented with new Alphas, he responded to Dawson's touch and followed his directions, and he never took the dominant position when standing next to him. He never even tried to do anything that might be considered aggressive—except perhaps for the few times he moved in a way that might have been a declaration if it wasn't so obvious that the bitch had *no idea* he was doing it. Like when he got so excited by something he saw that he stepped in front of Dawson. Dawson had just smiled and followed after the scampering idiot. It had been embarrassing to watch, to see an Alpha chase after tail like that.

Even the bitch's scent, when Dawson had introduced them, had been beta through and through. Disgusting.

So he watched Dawson and his bitch—not because he found them particularly fascinating, but because he couldn't tear his eyes away from their sickening display.

And because he suspected that someday soon, knowing as much as he could about the pair would be very, very important.

WHEN Ezra woke up, he had a few blissful moments to simply enjoy the feeling of being held close, to bask in the warmth of someone else's body, and even to revel in the feeling of a hard cock pressed up against his ass. Particularly the last one. Still foggy with sleep, he shifted his hips, rubbing his ass against the length. Hm, it was big, and Ezra could think of a really good use for it.

The soft moan and gusty sigh were what brought Ezra to awareness. Awareness being full knowledge of whom he was pressed against and why. It was also then that he became aware of a few pertinent facts: 1) Callum was still asleep, and 2) his left arm was curled around Ezra's waist, while the right was resting beneath his head.

Christ! This was going to be a bitch to get out of without waking Callum.

Callum let out a loud moan and began thrusting his hips.

Fuck! Ezra whimpered into his pillow and tried to shift away. Unfortunately, Callum followed. And then pushed against Ezra harder, managing to get his hard dick between Ezra's ass cheeks despite the two layers of fabric. Oh God! Another roll of those hips, and Ezra whimpered again. Fuck, that felt good.

It could feel better too. If only their clothes weren't in the way, then that hot erection could be sliding teasingly over his hole. And with just a little lube, it could be sliding inside. Ezra let out a loud moan.

The body behind him froze.

"Wha—?" Callum mumbled. He didn't yet sound fully awake, but he was getting there.

"I—uh. We woke up this way," Ezra managed to get out. He still couldn't make himself move away and wondered if that had something to do with the storm cloud of hormones and pheromones taking over his brain. *Damn it.*

Now that Callum was awake, Ezra kicked at the covers and made for the edge of the bed.

A deep grumble of displeasure vibrated against his back, and Callum's left arm tightened.

Shit. Ezra took a deep breath and wrapped his hands around Callum's forearm, trying to pry it away from his body. "Callum, wake up. We have to give a presentation today, and I can't help you if you *fry my brain before breakfast.*"

Callum jolted at that and seemed to come to full awareness, because he finally released Ezra and rolled over onto his back with a pitiful moan. "Sorry," he said to the ceiling. "You want the first cold shower this time?"

No, Ezra did not want to take a cold shower. He wanted Callum to roll him onto his stomach and apply his dick to Ezra's ass until a cold shower became a moot point. But he also wanted to keep his higher brain function, so he huffed and crawled out of bed. The sooner this presentation was over with, the sooner he could start avoiding Callum for their own good.

DESPITE the flashiness of the night before, the actual conference itself was low-key. Robbed of their black-tie finery, the hobnobbing Alphas filed into the room in twos, threes, or fours, slowly taking their seats in uncomfortable hotel chairs.

There were a few other talks slated for the conference—one about creating a virtual pack network so lycans living in less populated areas wouldn't feel so isolated, another about protecting pack investments in a recession—but those were later in the day. Callum and Ezra had the first event.

Well, at least Callum didn't have to worry about any unforeseen technical problems. Ezra had that aspect of things well in hand. He had hooked his laptop up to the projector and successfully tested it in less time than it usually took Callum to find the appropriate cable.

Maybe Callum could get him to set up his surround sound system.

Finally the clock ticked over to half past ten, and Callum figured just about everyone was present. He nodded to one of the event coordinators sitting in the back, and the woman stood and closed the door.

"Are you ready for this?" Callum asked, sotto voce.

Ezra looked a little green, staring out over the assembled crowd. "Well, at least I don't have to remember all their names this time," he muttered back. "Do your thing."

Figuring that was about as much as he could hope for, Callum flicked on his lapel mic. "Good morning, everyone. If you'll all take a seat, we'd like to get started as soon as possible."

The few stragglers still left standing migrated toward empty chairs, and a few seconds later, Callum continued. "As some of you may be aware, over the past few months, several alpha lycans in the Midwest have been observed to display erratic and even violent behavior." Behind him, the projector screen flicked to show a map of Ezra's creation pinpointing known incidents.

A sea of solemn faces stared back at him. That much wasn't news.

"Originally, the pack doctors and the CDC thought we were dealing with an outbreak of Lyssavirus A, but we've recently been able to study the subjects, and now we know that is not the case."

There were a few quiet murmurs at that.

Callum nodded at Ezra, and the screen behind him switched again, this time showing a closer view of the area that had been affected. "My assistant, Ezra, has written a computer program that monitors police and other reports that contain specific keywords that could indicate a lycan was involved in an attack. These were the initial results the program sent back. Of the suspicious animal attacks, most can be ruled out because they did not take place at the full moon."

Ezra clicked over to the next screen.

"While the number of these remaining attacks may seem statistically significant, if you look at the total number of animal attacks over the rest of the month and take an average, you discover that there are actually fewer incidents around the full moon." Ezra had worked that one out. Callum had been surprised, to say the least.

"I don't understand," Malcolm Shaw interrupted from the first row. "Are you saying there isn't a problem?"

Callum gritted his teeth. "Not at all. We suspect that anomaly may be due to normal lycan presence. Animals are less likely to be aggressive when there are a large number of predators around."

Another murmur went around the room, but it seemed like no one else was going to interrupt, so Callum continued. "Since the incidence of attacks was not informative, we turned our search in another direction."

Ezra flipped to the next screen.

"This is a map of reported wolf deaths that could have occurred around the full moon based on decomposition."

That earned Callum a respectful, eerie silence. He caught Ezra's eye, and Ezra clicked over again.

"This is that same map with positively identified wolf deaths ruled out. Those remaining on the map are possible lycan remains."

A sharp collective intake of breath. Callum understood their shock. There were three incidences remaining: two up near Coeur d'Alene in Idaho and one in central Montana, halfway between Billings and Great Falls. There was no way to pass that off as a mere coincidence.

Now came the hard part. Callum paused and took a sip out of his water bottle in a futile attempt to calm his stomach. "The Montana remains are a confirmed lycan." To press home the seriousness of his claim, he continued, "The farmer who found the body three months ago said it was the biggest wolf he'd ever seen, so he...." He closed his eyes. "He took him to a taxidermist, who told him the strangest thing—that the wolf's stomach was full of pizza and smelled like beer."

One of the female Alphas gave a sharp cry and covered her mouth. Good. Callum was getting through to them. Maybe now they would stop trying to save face and come forward when they suspected something had happened to one of their pack members.

"What of the other two?" Darius Maulsby wanted to know when the commotion had died down.

The other two—that was worse. "They were found together two months ago at the full moon. The park ranger in Coeur d'Alene spotted this." Callum gave the signal, and Ezra flipped to a picture of one of the wolves' hind legs, which was tattooed with a rosary.

More murmurs, and another anguished cry, this one from another part of the room. Grimly, Callum said, "If you can identify this woman, come speak with Ezra or myself after we're done or contact the National Fish and Wildlife Service up in Coeur d'Alene. She deserves better than anonymity."

Knowing the worst, most shocking part was yet to come, Callum steeled himself. "It is possible that the third body is that of a wolf and not a lycan, but test results were inconclusive." She'd had a stomach full of meat. It just hadn't been attached to much. "There wasn't enough left of her to identify. She and the previous victim tore each other to pieces."

That generated the biggest reaction yet. Some Alphas were stunned into silence. A few covered their mouths; still more glanced around the small conference room, as if wondering which of the other Alphas could identify the dead lycans or possibly afraid someone was going to finger them as the victim's Alpha.

Callum thinned his lips into a line and looked at Ezra, who was pale but determined. He touched Callum's wrist for a moment and leaned over so he could speak into the lapel mic. "Please," he said, "if you have any information about our victims, we could use all the help we can get. We're trying to determine if the cause is environmental, but it's difficult to track where they've been since we know very little about them. Even if you just want a copy of the program I wrote.... I've been working with the National Fish and Wildlife Service and state police and FBI, but there are some smaller municipalities with local sheriff's departments I haven't been able to reach. If you think you can facilitate cooperation, I'd be glad to get you a copy of the software."

Ingenious. Callum didn't know whether Ezra had planned that or whether it was spontaneous, but he wished he'd thought of it. Inter-pack Alpha politics could be tricky. Callum couldn't ask for too much help without losing the respect of the other Alphas, as ridiculous as that was. Likewise, the other Alphas couldn't simply offer too much information without losing face.

Not unless the person they were helping was a beta lycan. Having Ezra around was like having an ace up his sleeve. He just hoped they'd get some information they could use.

Chapter Eight
Wag the Dog

THERE were seven of them, and they were all standing in front of Ezra and staring up at him with wide shining eyes and disconcertingly expectant faces. It was a decided contrast to the conference of a few days previously, when Ezra and Callum had been staring out at a much larger sea of adult lycans.

"Um," said Ezra uncertainly. All seven children looked even more eager, though for what, Ezra wasn't sure. Nor was he sure why Wyn had thought that it was a good idea to make him the sole entertainer for an audience of minors. She had told him about ten minutes before the doorbell rang this morning that there would be children coming over.

"Who's coming here for what now?"

"Some of the pack parents are going out for the day and leaving their kids with us."

Ezra had stared at her in horror for long minutes. "*Us?* As in you and *me?* Me, in charge of children?" Yep, he definitely should've gone to work today, Saturday or not.

Wyn had turned away from the stove to arch a brow at Ezra. "What's the big deal? They'll be here for a few hours, and then they'll go home."

"Sure, but in one piece? You can't leave me in charge of children!"

"I won't be leaving you in charge of anything. I'll be in charge. All you have to do is bask in the attention they will certainly give you."

Now that Ezra was staring down into their curious faces, he was pretty sure that this wasn't going to be as easy as Wyn had attempted to make him believe.

One of the children, a girl with two blond plaits, stepped up close. She was particularly familiar, as Ezra recalled her being opinionated and bossy. She did not disappoint. "Uncle Ezra? Do you know how to play hide-and-seek?"

"Um, yes?"

"Will you play with us?"

"Uh…." Ezra regarded her with uncertainty.

"I'm sure that Uncle Ezra would love to play hide-and-seek with all of you." Wyn was smiling, and there was a devious twinkle in her eye. "Maybe you should run off to hide while Uncle Ezra counts to one hundred." Before anything else was said, all seven children turned and ran from the room.

"Oh my God," breathed out Ezra to an empty room. "Now what?"

Wyn blinked in surprise. "Um, you count to one hundred and then go find them?" She patted his arm consolingly before turning and escaping to the kitchen.

After reaching one hundred, and then adding on an extra fifty, Ezra finally conceded that it was time to go and search out the children.

Children were exhausting, Ezra decided an hour later as he collapsed into a living room chair. He closed his eyes, but was jerked from his rest when one of the boys, Konnar, yelled, "Aunt Wyn!"

"Did you all have fun playing hide-and-seek?"

"Yes!"

"But Uncle Ezra is bad at it," bossy Allison told her. Ezra considered pointing out that his size precluded him from using the best hiding spots, but he'd probably lose that argument.

Wyn gave a delighted laugh. "Well, maybe we should give him a break. I made up a picnic lunch that we can take to the park."

"Yay!" The children were delighted.

Ezra was not. "What?" Ezra turned panicked eyes on Wyn after the children had all run to put on their shoes. "We're taking them out in public? Where we could lose one?" he whispered harshly.

Wyn only laughed at his reasonable concerns and ushered him to the door.

It turned out that taking the kids out was a fairly smooth operation. The children were all used to having surrogate aunts and uncles watching over them, and they all seemed happy to obey any orders. It also helped that Allison bossed all her playmates to hurry up and to get to the park sooner. Soon, werecubs were rushing down the slide, sitting on swings, and crossing the monkey bars.

"Keep an eye on them while I pull the food out, will you?"

Ezra headed closer to the playground. He watched them from a distance for only a moment; soon Dallas was calling out, asking Ezra to come push him on the swing.

By the time Wyn called them to eat, Ezra had been asked to push both Allison and Beau on the swings, to help three-year-old Kenzie down the slide, and then to assist Olivia, Konnar, and Nick across the monkey bars. They all wanted to play with him, but all seven quickly turned away from their new friend to run for the food when Wyn called. Ezra, equally hungry, ignored the surprise feeling of mild rejection.

After the food was gone, Allison stood up and announced, "We're playing tag." She then smacked Ezra's arm and declared, "You're it!" before running away.

Stunned, Ezra took a moment to look at Wyn, and this moment of hesitation cost him, as the rest of the children (save Kenzie, who was curled up in Wyn's lap) took flight.

Ezra rose to his feet and gave chase. He caught Beau first. Beau caught Konnar, and Konnar caught Olivia, who took off after Ezra. Laughing, Ezra let himself be caught, then turned back to give chase. He couldn't stop laughing as he feinted for Dallas, then held his hands up mockingly toward Olivia before finally catching Allison. The girl giggled as Ezra picked her up and held her in triumph.

"I've got you!"

Allison squealed and wiggled.

"You're it!" Then Ezra let the girl go and took a few loping steps away from her. He turned back to see which way she'd move only to be distracted by the sight of Nick, Beau, and Konnar standing together in the field looking at something on the ground.

Now watching their impromptu serious council, Ezra did not notice Allison take after Dallas or see Dallas turn toward him. His quick gait away from the boy was purely coincidental as he moved toward the trio, his speed increasing as the boys crouched down, apparently to get a better view of whatever was on the ground.

Ezra arrived just in time to see Beau reaching forward.

"Hey, boys!" They jumped and looked up at him, each sporting a guilty expression. "What have you found?" Ezra crouched next to them, barely aware of the other three children playing behind him.

"Dunno," said Beau.

"Found it," said Konnar, perhaps to reinforce their innocence.

Nick simply shrugged, his eyes wide.

Ezra leaned forward to get a better look. On the ground were what appeared to be two stickers used to monitor a hospital patient's heart and, more alarmingly, the needle from an IV.

"Right. Definitely shouldn't touch that. How about you go back to the game?" The boys all looked relieved not to be in trouble and scampered off. "And no touching any other strange things," he yelled after them. Then he turned back to the items and picked them all up.

What the hell was IV needle doing in a park? Silently, so as not to be overheard by young ears, Ezra began to curse the mysterious lowlife who had left such a hazard in a public park where children could find it and hurt themselves. He was quite annoyed by the time he brought the items to Wyn, who was now cuddling a sleeping Kenzie.

"After-lunch nap," Wyn said with a smile that faded as Ezra got closer. "What is it?"

"Look at this." He told her how the boys had discovered the items.

"How odd," said Wyn. "What a strange—I mean, I've heard of drug needles being found in parks, but an IV?"

Ezra nodded. "And with heart monitors?"

"Strange." Their musing was quickly cut short when six children came stumbling back to the picnic blanket, panting. Dallas and Allison both threw themselves on the ground dramatically, seemingly tired beyond endurance. There was an argument going on over who had won the game.

"It's getting late," Wyn cut into the argument. Fortunately she knew how to distract kids. "Your parents will come for you in an hour; we have to get back to my house to meet them." When everything was packed up, and Wyn turned to Ezra to ask, "Could you carry Kenzie? I don't think she'll be able to stay awake to walk." Her smile held hints of a smirk.

Ezra eyed the child, who, though awake, stood rubbing her eyes sleepily. He wasn't sure how to scoop her up. Fortunately, Kenzie helped to solve this in part by walking up to Ezra and holding her hands up to him, waiting. Hesitantly, Ezra leaned forward and gripped the child beneath her arms and lifted. Kenzie wrapped both arms around his neck and then rested her head on his shoulder. Ezra stared at her at very close range before shifting his grip on her so as to get a better hold.

"Rest her weight on your hip," Wyn said with a laugh, and Ezra did so somewhat clumsily. Finally, once she was settled and Wyn had the basket, the group made their way from the park. The other children had energy once again. They seemed to drift, shift, and float around Wyn and Ezra, only falling in line when Wyn called them to attention at street crossings. When they reached the end of their street, Allison shouted, "Last one to Wyn's is a toadface!" and they all burst into a run.

"Toadface?" Wyn was smiling.

"I don't want to be a toadface." Ezra kept his expression deadpan. "I hope I get to the house before you."

"Ha! You're carrying a child; I just have the basket! Fat chance, Toadface!" Then Wyn took several skipping strides forward, leaving an encumbered Ezra behind.

"That's cheating!"

"No! It's life!" Wyn didn't stop.

Ezra lost several key seconds trying to regain a comfortable hold on a slipping Kenzie. A car drove past him, and he jumped. Finally, he paused to shift the child; carefully, he repositioned the sleeping girl up his hip, not wanting to drop her.

Satisfied that she was once more secure, Ezra looked up and found that he was now standing only one driveway away from Callum's and that the car that had passed him was pulling into it. While Ezra watched, three men got out of the car.

Over the past few days he'd gotten used to seeing visitors come and go—Callum was much in demand whenever he wasn't working—but Ezra was surprised to realize that he recognized the third visitor, and *not* because he was pack. Alpha Darius Maulsby had just unfolded himself from the passenger seat. He was just as tall and foreboding as Ezra remembered.

Ezra watched as the man took a cursory look around before heading directly to Callum's front door. Surely he couldn't be unaware of Wyn, the children, and Ezra—he had just driven past some of them—but he did nothing to acknowledge their presence.

The men with him did. The kept looking around like they thought they were in the Secret Service, shifting their attention between the children, Wyn, then Ezra, and back again.

What are they doing here? Ezra wondered. *Why did they come all this way to see Callum?* Relatively speaking, Great Falls wasn't that far from Missoula, but it wasn't exactly just around the corner. *What can he possibly need to say that can't be said by telephone?*

When the front door finally opened, there was a brief pause before Darius and his companions walked inside. Even after the door latched shut, Ezra stayed watching it.

"Ezra!"

Snapping to attention, Ezra looked to see Wyn standing on her driveway. The kids were playing Ezra-didn't-know-what on the lawn. "Come watch the kids while I get this inside."

Right. Ezra stepped inside for a moment to deposit the sleeping Kenzie on the couch, then went back out and settled himself on the front step.

A sharp cry startled Ezra from his reverie. Olivia was on the ground screaming, her knee covered in blood. Allison stood over her and was yelling at the top of her voice at Beau and Dallas. After taking in the scene and realizing that Olivia was in need of first aid and comfort, Ezra jumped to his feet, turned around, and dashed to the front door.

"Wyn!"

"What?"

"I—help!" His desperation was probably clear in his voice, as Wyn was suddenly there, her face white and panicked.

"What?" she asked again, this time sounding less irritated and more anxious.

"There's—outside—injury!"

Wyn rushed out the door, passed him on the porch, and—

"Oh really! It's just a skinned knee!" She shot Ezra a look before rushing away. Clearly she thought he had overreacted.

Ezra eyed the screaming child and the way that Allison was yelling at the boys for hurting her friend, and couldn't help but respectfully disagree. Blood and screaming children weren't "just" anything.

DESPITE having two days' warning the second time around, Ezra was not prepared to see all of the pack again as they gathered for Dallas's birthday party. Most of a lycan's closest friends were also lycan, and parties often became community events. So Ezra found himself at another pack event surround by dozens of people, all of whom were still curious about him.

Unlike the last time, this gathering was taking place at someone's home. The ground floor of the house had been opened for mingling, though the backyard was reported to be the focus of the event.

Ezra had arrived with Callum, which he was sure was fueling the gossip that had only become more persistent since he had taken up residence at Callum's. It had taken less than twenty-four hours for everyone to find out that he was no longer staying at Wyn's. At least Wyn's budding relationship with Blaise provided everyone with something else to gossip about.

Despite Callum's initial resolve to find Ezra somewhere else to live, neither of them had broached the subject. Ezra had thought about it, especially while he was jacking off in the shower while fantasizing about Callum, but he didn't bring it up because he didn't want to leave. As frustrating as it was to live with the object of his desire, the benefits outweighed the disadvantages. He couldn't deny the pleasure in seeing Callum first thing in the morning or relaxing together at the end of their stressful days.

Dallas's mother greeted them warmly at the door and then directed them to the backyard, where children were playing.

Callum nodded and gave her one last smile before turning to leave. He arched a brow at Ezra. "You coming?"

Ezra could feel eyes on him. Various mothers, all stationed in the kitchen with the food, were closely following the casual interaction between them, he was certain. "Sure," he said. Anything to avoid further scrutiny.

The backyard was busy and crowded full of people taking advantage of what was likely the last of the year's good weather. Adults were gathered around the barbeque talking about the art of the grill or perusing the large table of snacks and side dishes. Among them children played, running between bodies and dashing beyond onto a large stretch of grass.

Dallas found them by running headlong into Callum. The man gave a grunt at the impact but didn't hesitate to lift the birthday boy and offer him congratulations.

The boy held up two hands showing a total of six fingers. "Uncle Ezra, I'm six now!" His expression was expectant, though for what, Ezra didn't know.

"Wow," Ezra finally settled on saying, unsure if he should add anything else. It seemed to satisfy the kid, who said nothing in response but turned back to tell Callum about his day.

In no time, Callum was dragged away to partake of something that, from Dallas's tone, must be incredibly exciting. They disappeared behind a body, and Ezra suddenly found himself quite alone in the crowd until a small hand rested on his arm and a voice said, "Birthdays are often like this." Emma LaPorte wore a warm smile as she stared after Callum and Dallas.

"Sorry?"

"Callum and Jax try to give special attention to anyone celebrating anything. With the kids, that means playtime."

Ezra turned from her and looked back to see that Callum and Dallas had joined the other children to play tag and noticed that Jax, too, was running around. "Huh."

"What's that noise for?" She turned warm eyes to him.

"Nothing." Ezra tried to pass it off but got only an arched brow for the trouble. "It's just… I keep thinking of Alphas as being the responsible ones, being the ones with the extra worries and the extra stress. I hadn't thought of it like this before. Like… being a minor celebrity and a role model. But those kids are basking in the attention. Especially Dallas."

"There are *good* things about being an Alpha. It's not all bossing people around and worrying about newly bitten members." Emma gave him a saucy smile.

"So I see." His tone was rueful.

"Come on, let's get some food. Maybe find a seat in the sun."

Thirty minutes later, Ezra was extremely grateful to Emma. The other lycans had continued staring at him without shame, which was enough to put Ezra on edge even with her company. He wasn't sure he'd still be composed, or still at the party, if she hadn't mounted a campaign to distract him.

She was regaling him with tales of her children when Jax appeared beside them.

"Ezra! You made it." She gave him a saucy smile.

"Yes…." He wasn't quite sure what he had done to earn that smile *this* time. "Was there any doubt?"

"Well, if I was going to go to a party where everyone would be staring at me and talking about me behind *my* back"—her voice rose steadily as she spoke—"I'd be reluctant to attend."

"Jacqueline!" Emma admonished, but Ezra was too relieved by the noticeable change in the lycans around them to be upset with her.

THERE had been a time when Ezra's life wasn't so difficult. A time when things were easier. A time when it didn't feel like so many people were out to make him miserable.

Lucien, the beta of the all-consuming hatred for him, had found Ezra during one of the few minutes that he was alone. Callum had been called away to pay further attention to the children, and Jax was busy defending Wyn from questions about her relationship with Blaise. Ezra hadn't minded being left alone until Lucien had stepped up from behind him to stand at his left side.

"Hello."

Reminding himself that he didn't want to be a prick to anyone in his new family, Ezra gave a grudging hello in return.

It didn't take Lucien a full five minutes to get Ezra wishing that he had just been a prick instead.

"The whole pack is talking. No one can figure out why he hasn't just fucked you yet."

Ezra gritted his teeth.

"I mean, it's obvious that you want him to, and what's the point in denying himself a little fun? Unless he doesn't want to deal with you the morning after."

For a brief moment, Ezra considered responding, but he knew it would do little good. He could only hope that ignoring Lucien would eventually get rid of him.

Neither did walking away. Ezra tried, but Lucien just followed him.

"Callum's not ready to settle down yet, and he probably knows how clingy you'll get if he actually gives you what you're gagging for."

Ezra couldn't take any more. "Lucien, I strongly encourage you to shut the fuck up and back off. It's painfully obvious that I'm not the one who's bitter about not bending over for the Alpha, and unless you want to get into a very loud conversation about how much *you* are gagging for it, then I suggest you leave me alone." Ezra was very careful to keep his voice low, and he didn't regret it in the slightest when he saw the indignant flush spread high across Lucien's cheeks. His eyes flashed with some unnamed emotion when he finally tried to speak.

"Why you—I've never—insulting little—"

"I'm going to walk away now, and you're not going to follow me," Ezra said. Then, ignoring the furious look the other man was giving him, he did exactly that.

Deciding that it was best to get as far away as possible, Ezra headed for the house. He'd noticed how many of the adults had been floating from the house to the backyard and back again. Several of the older lycans had opted to stay in the house, no doubt to enjoy the quiet.

Pulling the door shut with a sigh, Ezra turned and found himself face to face with Jax. Seriously, how did she do that? He could have sworn she was in the kitchen with Wyn.

"Sorry." Jax made a face. "I was just about to intervene. You want to stay away from that one."

Ezra snorted. "Easier said than done."

Jax gave him a sympathetic pat on the arm. "He's ambitious. Wants to move on up in the pack, wants respect. And he figures he can get it the old-fashioned way." Ezra's look must have indicated his confusion, because Jax clarified, in typical Jax fashion, "Naked and on his back."

It was a good thing that Ezra wasn't trying to drink anything at that moment, as he was pretty sure that he'd just choked on nothing. "Seriously?"

"He's wanted to be Callum's kept boy ever since Callum got elected."

Really? Lucien wanted to trade his body just so that he'd get more respect? Didn't he see the fallacy in that logic? Also... ew. Ezra's face seemed to say enough, because Jax nodded.

"Exactly. Thankfully for the rest of us, Callum's actually got a brain, and it isn't in his dick. He shot Lucien down pronto, though judging by the to-do they had a few years later, Lucien didn't take him too seriously."

"What?"

"I figure Lucien thought he was just too young the first time. He was only seventeen, so he tried again a couple years later. Callum's not much of a gossip, so only he and Lucien know how that conversation went, but judging by the stick that's been up Lucien's ass ever since, that second rejection didn't go as well as the first." Jax sighed wistfully. "Oh to have been a fly on that wall."

"So... why doesn't he like me?"

The look Jax gave him suggested that she thought he was pretty stupid, which Ezra supposed wasn't unfair. On further reflection, it was kind of obvious. "Okay, so maybe I get why he thinks he should be jealous of me." He gave her a wan smile.

Jax clapped him on the shoulder. "Okay, enough of the history lesson. Did you see what Wyn made for dessert?"

Chapter Nine
Every Dog Has Its Day

THE truck pulled to a stop in front of the ramshackle cabin Callum had been visiting with the younger lycans on their first change every year since he'd become Alpha. In the passenger seat next to him, Ezra fidgeted restlessly, staring out the window at the darkening sky.

Twenty minutes till moonrise.

Callum put the truck in park, then threw open the door and hopped out, grabbing their duffel bags from the back of the truck as he went. Ezra got out more cautiously, taking in the scenery, breathing deeply. "What is this place?"

"Pack land," Callum told him. The pack had several holdings—some land, a nursery, a Christmas tree farm, all more or less adjacent. "That cabin's been part of it for 200 years, in some form or another."

Ezra turned to take in the small A-frame building. "It doesn't look that old."

"Pocketknife problem," Callum explained. "Sometimes it needs a new roof or new siding or an electrical generator, but it's still the same cabin, essentially." He gestured to the path. "Well. Shall we?"

Ezra nodded, and they headed up the path. "Is this feeling normal?"

Callum glanced at him. "What feeling?"

"Like pins and needles. Everywhere. Including in my head." Ezra made a face.

"Must be the last of your DNA resequencing." It was certainly not something Callum remembered from his own first change. He located the lockbox, then punched in his code to reveal the key. "It doesn't sound like something any of the first-timers I've helped through the change has mentioned." He put the key in the lock, giving the door handle a bit of a jiggle before turning it; it *was* old. Finally it unstuck, and he pushed the door open, motioning Ezra in ahead of him. "After you."

Callum put the key back in the lockbox, then pulled the door closed behind them and knelt down to unlatch the—

"Is that a doggy door?"

Callum looked up at Ezra and raised his eyebrows. "What, you didn't think we were going to stay in the cabin all night, did you? And doors are kind of tricky to open when you don't have any thumbs."

"But... don't we have to work tomorrow?"

Rolling his eyes, Callum got back to his feet. "I hear your boss is pretty understanding about needing time off around the full moon." He shrugged. "It's not a regular thing, but you shouldn't have to spend your first full moon inside."

Besides, Callum told himself, he took all the cubs out at least once their first year. Oh, if there were more than two of them, he needed an extra chaperone—wolf or not, subject to the rule of the pack Alpha or not, they were still kids—but... well. He would have been kidding himself if he hadn't admitted that he didn't want to share Ezra tonight.

Or any other time.

"Right," Ezra said. "Thanks for that."

Callum nodded, stripping off his coat and hanging it on one of the pegs by the door. "Sure." Would Ezra still be thanking him if he knew what Callum was planning for later?

He would, actually, which was a bigger problem. Ezra was genetically predisposed to be attracted to him. He couldn't help it. It was one of the many reasons that Callum had kept all lycanthrope betas—not just those who belonged to the pack—out of his bed to date. At least with human partners, he could be sure that their attraction was their own and not due to some accident of biology.

Ezra, on the other hand, presented something of a moral conundrum. While his physical and sexual attraction weren't in question, his free will was. Sure, Callum had ensured that he would be able to disobey should he want to, if Callum ever slipped up and put a pheromone compunction behind the orders he was inclined to give in bed, but the idea of removing even the slightest bit of Ezra's agency was just as repugnant as the thought of having him in the first place was intoxicating. Something told him that breaking the cardinal rule for Ezra would be well worth it—unless and until it blew up in his face, and then it would all go very bad very quickly.

With a sigh, Callum turned up the dials on the gas fireplace and began stripping out of his clothes. Maybe the full moon would shed some light on his thoughts.

"Um," Ezra said from behind him. Callum could feel his gaze boring into his back, warmer than the flames from the stove beside him. "What are you doing?"

Callum's ennui evaporated, and he allowed himself a small smile as he reached for his belt buckle. Ezra wouldn't be able to see it anyway. "What does it look like?" he asked, toeing off his shoes and socks before letting his jeans drop to the floor and sniffing the air discreetly.

There was the reaction he was looking for. He peeled off his boxers too before scooping up his clothes and tossing them over the back of an old armchair by the fire.

Ezra said, "Um." He was staring, and not at Callum's face, either.

Callum let him. "If you ever want to wear those clothes again, you should get changed too," he pointed out.

Ezra swallowed. "Right," he said, turning away as he unzipped his jacket.

Callum had already seen him more or less naked when he'd examined him post-bite, but maybe it was the stripping itself that was making him nervous. "I'm just going to do a quick check and make sure everything's still in working order," he said. "I'll be back."

In actual fact, the cabin itself didn't have a whole lot of stuff to work. It did have plumbing, but it was too early yet to worry about the pipes freezing. Callum's keen ears told him the refrigerator in the kitchen area of the great room was functioning just fine. Aside from the common living area/dining room/kitchen combination, there was just the one large bedroom and the en suite bath, but Ezra didn't have to know that. Callum slipped into the bedroom, pulling the door mostly shut behind him.

As promised, the sheets had been changed that afternoon. Callum could tell that much without so much as inhaling deeply. He should have known he could trust Wyn—though she had taken some liberties with the specifics, he noted ruefully, taking in the economy-sized bottle of lube and decorative bowl of condoms on the nightstand. Asking for her help had been, well, mortifying. Especially considering he still wasn't sure he wanted to go through with his plan.

He was going to have to face Wyn's speculative gaze either way.

Quietly, he moved to the bedside and, after a second's hesitation, stashed Wyn's helpfully provided supplies in the table rather than on top of it. He just hoped, as he turned down the covers, that she hadn't put rose petals in the bathroom or something. That was crossing the line, in his opinion, and he'd edged far closer to it than he ever had before tonight already.

A quick check of the bathroom proved it to be largely intact, though cleaner and with a better quality of towel than it was accustomed to. There *was* a bottle of bubble bath—did Wyn think he'd lost his mind?—but it looked decorative enough that he decided to leave it. Besides, the moon would be up at any minute. He didn't have time for much else.

Ezra hadn't exactly hurried to undress in his absence. Callum returned to the main room of the cabin just in time to see his jeans and boxers hit the floor—and to hear the heavy thud as they hit the wood. Callum made a note of the shape of the pocket as he closed the bedroom door behind him. It seemed he wasn't the only one who had plans for that evening.

Strangely, that didn't put him at ease. Maybe it was the moonlight.

More likely it had something to do with the way the firelight played on Ezra's skin. Callum forced himself not to stare. *Business now, pleasure later.*

Ezra cleared his throat. "So now what?"

"Now we wait for moonrise," Callum said, peering out the window. "It won't be long."

NOT surprisingly, Callum was right. Perhaps half a second later, Ezra got a chill as every hair on his body decided to stand on end simultaneously. His skin began to itch, first the small of his back, then the backs of his hands, and then everywhere else as thick hair began to grow out of it. The nail beds on his fingers and toes throbbed as his fingernails lengthened and thickened, curling into wicked points. Then everything went hazy as pain tore through his body. His knees broke and his jaw lengthened and narrowed. He screwed his eyes shut against the onslaught, and when he opened them again, everything was in black and white, and he was on the floor.

No, that wasn't quite right. He was *closer* to the floor, but he was standing—on four legs.

Across the room, a hulking black form was watching him silently. There was a crest of lighter fur across his chest and a splash of white on the end of his muzzle. Ezra's nose left him with no doubt that this was Callum.

Callum stood, then crossed the distance between them quickly, his tail parallel to the floor, and stopped a few inches in front of Ezra's nose. It was a little disconcerting at first. Ezra wasn't used to having to look up at him. Until now, they had always been the same height, but Callum the wolf was at least thirty percent larger than Ezra, taller and broader and—though Ezra would take care about when he mentioned it when they were human—*fluffier*. Acting on an unfamiliar instinct, Ezra lowered his body, inching forward until he could reach Callum's muzzle. Before he really knew what he was doing, he reached out with his tongue, licking it twice before biting him gently.

The reaction was immediate. Callum growled, a pleasant rather than threatening timbre, and captured Ezra's muzzle between his jaws.

For a minute, Ezra panicked, but he quickly realized Callum wasn't exerting any real pressure. It was just his way of telling Ezra who was in charge. Ezra went with his instincts, sinking the rest of the way to the floor and turning over on his back.

Callum released his hold and stepped over Ezra's prone body, sniffing him thoroughly before backing off. He seemed to be waiting for Ezra to get up again. Once he was on his feet, Callum barked once, sharply, and then squeezed out the doggy door and into the night. The message was pretty clear, both in the body language and in the scent trail he left behind him: *Follow me.*

With a concerted effort to coordinate four legs when he was used to just two, Ezra loped after him.

Outside in the moonlight the world was somehow sharper and fresher than Ezra had ever seen it. He heaved deep lungfuls of fresh air, tasting the rich brown of the earth and the pungent aroma of the pines; a hundred different species of animal, each more intriguing than the last; the cold rush of a nearby stream; and above it all the dark scent of pure, uncontested power.

Callum.

Ezra raced to keep up with Callum's longer strides, having no difficulty following his scent or the flash of black tail in the underbrush. Callum led him steadily up the slope, across the stream he'd smelled, the water fresh and cold in his nostrils, though his thick fur kept most of the chill from his skin.

He lost track of Callum as they came to the top of a small hill, and when he turned around to look, following his nose, Callum bowled into him from the side, growling playfully and nipping at his ears and muzzle. Ezra yelped as the air went out of his lungs—Callum was *heavy*, pinning his spine to the ground with one massive paw to his chest—and bit back the best he could reach, careful not to put any real pressure behind the bites. Eventually Callum let him up and coaxed him back to his feet with a prod of his nose to Ezra's side and trotted over to the clearing at the very top of the hill, where he proceeded to wait for Ezra to catch up, bushy tail held aloft.

Then he backed up a half a step, widened his stance, lifted his nose, and howled at the moon. For a long, still moment, it echoed into the night, and then Ezra's keen ears picked up three answering howls ringing out: *here we are.*

Callum looked at him expectantly, and Ezra hesitated only half a second before raising his own voice, feeling more alive than he had in weeks.

EZRA squeezed through the door with only a little difficulty, the fur on his belly snagging on the unsanded wood trim, and hurled himself down on the small carpet in front of the pot-bellied stove just in time for the strange tingling itch to set in. He was aware of Callum throwing himself through the opening only a few seconds later, his keen ears picking up the sound of huffed, panting breath and claws scrabbling on untreated floors. Then he felt it as the moon started to slip below the horizon, a tug behind his ribcage and pressure everywhere. The tail was first, shrinking slowly and painfully back into his spine, making him arch his neck, and then he felt it in his teeth and gums as his jaw broke and shrank. Spasms wracked his paws as fingers and toes uncurled and nails receded into their nail beds. Ezra howled as his knees broke and re-formed, his body elongating, stretching out until he was human again, hairless and naked.

He'd anticipated the pain, though it was dissipating rapidly, but not the electric buzz of leftover moonlight zipping across his naked skin, setting the hairs on his arms and legs standing straight up. He felt alive, energized, his body on fire with sensation. The scent of fur and fire and bare skin crawled into his nose and burrowed deep into his brain, spreading down into his nervous system and out to his extremities.

A deep, satisfied hum from somewhere to his right filled his ears, and suddenly the only thing he could smell was Callum, dark and intoxicating and powerful. He blinked his eyes open, having been unaware that they'd closed, and sat up, inhaling sharply as color returned to his vision, overbright and too vivid.

Then he turned his head.

He'd seen Callum naked not eight hours before, of course, but that didn't stop him from looking now, didn't stop the rush of blood southward. But now Callum was looking back, gaze so intense that Ezra could feel it on his skin. His eyes were dark, molten.

Close, he was so close, and Ezra couldn't look away, couldn't even move—could only wait, paralyzed, while Callum took the first hesitant step, and hope that the stupid pheromones were still saying "come and get me," because, yeah. He wanted.

The next thing he knew, Callum was kneeling over him, arms bracketing his head, knees warm against the outside of his thighs. Ezra inhaled sharply and got a nose full of really horny lycan.

After licking his lips, Ezra tried his voice. "Are we—" He cleared his throat. *Are we really doing this?* he wanted to ask, but then Callum lowered his mouth, and Ezra bent his head back without a thought, baring his neck in a textbook submissive pose.

He felt the shudder that went through Callum's body as warm breath and a cold nose ghosted across his skin. Then the slick, teasing tickle of a tongue on his jugular.

Pulse pounding, Ezra struggled to draw a breath. "Please tell me you're about to fuck me."

Callum lifted his head just enough that Ezra could make out his eyes, half-lidded with the pupils blown huge. "What do you think?" he said rhetorically, and he shifted a fraction of an inch, just enough so that his erection brushed Ezra's thigh.

Ezra didn't have a lot of spare brain activity for thoughts after that. He managed a sound that was suspiciously reminiscent of a whimper when Callum dropped his face back to his neck and inhaled deeply, but the sudden sharp scrape of teeth across his throat shocked him into silence. The skin there had never been so sensitive; Callum might as well have been doing it to his dick.

"I think—" Ezra's breath hitched. Callum shifted again, insinuating himself between Ezra's legs instead, and slid one hand up the side of Ezra's thigh. The thumb of his opposite hand caressed Ezra's left collar bone. "What—what was the question?"

All he got in answer was a deep, throaty chuckle. Then Callum's left hand slithered down into Ezra's hair and fisted it, tugging sharply until his head was all the way back. "Never mind," Ezra said hoarsely as one finger trailed down over his Adam's apple. It was a pretty clear statement of intent.

Then Callum was savaging his mouth, lips crashing down over Ezra's and tongue plunging in to tangle with his. It was like being kissed by a hurricane, sheer power of intent pushing in every direction at once. Between Callum's mouth and his hands and the way he'd just shifted forward so that their naked cocks rubbed up against each other, Ezra had to raise his own arms to take in as much of Callum as possible just in self-defense. For several long, hot, breathless moments Ezra did nothing but revel in the touches being burned into his flesh and build desperate sense memories of the planes of Callum's back. But before they could get to the good part, Ezra's brain decided to switch back on again, and he jerked his head back, hissing at the pull on his hair. "Wait, wait," he gasped, already mentally kicking himself for not taking what he could get. Was this what Callum had meant when he'd said that pheromone manipulation could go both ways? "I thought you didn't play with pack members."

All at once, everything stopped. Callum pulled back, relaxing but never quite releasing his grip, and regarded him steadily. His lips were shiny-wet and swollen. "I'm not playing," he said seriously, and before Ezra could catch his breath they were kissing again.

Then, just as suddenly, he was being dumped onto his stomach, the air whooshing out of him in a rush as one of Callum's warm, broad palms settled onto the middle of his back. Half a second later he felt Callum stretching out over him, the hot, damp tip of his erection leaving a scorching trail across the backs of Ezra's thighs and the curve of his ass as Callum reached for the leg of the jeans Ezra had been wearing earlier. It didn't take him long to find the lube Ezra had stashed there just in case.

"How"—Ezra hissed as Callum sat up and the head of his cock slipped between Ezra's cheeks—"how'd you know?"

There was an overloud *snick*, and the sudden distinctive scent of lubricant filled the air. "Educated guess," Callum told him, nudging his legs further apart with his knees. "Breathe out."

That was all the warning Ezra got before Callum breached him with two fingers, firm and steady, all the way in without slowing. He felt the burn everywhere in his body, a current of heat shooting up his spine to his brain and then spreading out until it pooled again in his dick. The hand on his back held him flat to the floor as Callum twisted and scissored his fingers inside of him, stretching the ring of muscle before angling just right. Ezra saw stars as Callum rubbed against his prostate. He dug his nails into the wood floor beside the rug as Callum withdrew his fingers only to press forward again, harder, a second later.

"That's—" Ezra lost his train of thought as Callum added another finger and a lot more lube, and he dropped his head to the rug and arched his back in supplication, a keening whimper slipping out without his permission. He moved with the thrusts as much as he could, the rough weave of the rug beneath him chafing against his leaking dick.

Callum pressed him back to the floor with what sounded like a growl, and a bolt of want rushed right to Ezra's cock. He barely recognized the sound that came out of his own mouth, something between a groan and a wordless plea.

Callum rumbled something low against the skin of his shoulder, but Ezra was in no place to answer or even decode what he'd said, too busy *wanting* to be able to use the language center in his brain.

Then: "Ezra."

Ezra shuddered as the word cut through the fog surrounding his mind and breathed deeply, the heavy scent of arousal filling his nose.

"Is there a condom in your pocket?"

Fuck. Ezra hadn't had any on hand, but he'd bought a package the day before—only they were all the way across the room, in the pocket of his coat, which was lying on the kitchen counter. "In my coat," he groaned, hissing in protest as Callum's fingers left his body.

Then suddenly there was a shoulder in his oblique and the room tipped on its axis and—"What are you doing?"

"Saving myself a trip." Callum gently dumped him onto the kitchen table and reached for his coat pocket.

And Ezra suddenly had an unobstructed view of Callum in all his glory. *Holy shit.* Okay, so he'd seen Callum naked before, but that was a totally different context. Now….

Ezra didn't realize he'd been licking his lips until Callum ran his thumb across them and promised, "Later." Then he closed his hand around Ezra's shoulder and tugged until he was sitting at the edge of the table.

Ezra didn't waste time thinking about it. He tilted his head back until Callum kissed him again, biting down on his lip when Callum crushed him against his chest and grabbing Callum's side for balance. Then he thought, *Fuck it,* and slid his palm inward across Callum's flat abs, then down until he could wrap his fingers around the heavy cock. Callum was hard and leaking, and he growled into Ezra's mouth when Ezra flicked his thumb over the slit.

Breaking away with a hiss, Callum thrust the foil packet into Ezra's free hand. "Deal with this," he demanded roughly. Then he pulled Ezra's head back and covered the pulse point in his neck with his mouth, his right hand skating down Ezra's side to his thigh, lifting it up, coaxing Ezra to wrap it around him.

It took a considerable amount of concentration on Ezra's part and a small miracle from the powers that be to get the condom on. He was shaking with want, and every time Callum ran his teeth over his neck, which was often, he lost track of what his fingers were doing and had to start over. Callum must have been paying attention, because the second Ezra had it on him, he released his hold on Ezra's hair, got a grip under Ezra's other leg, and pressed forward. Ezra held him steady until the head breached him and then got the hell out of the way.

Fuck. This was the itch he'd been trying to scratch when he'd gone to the bar, what he'd wanted ever since Callum had shown up on his father's doorstep in that suit. Ezra let out a satisfied groan as

Callum pulled back and then slammed forward again, his fingers digging into the skin of Ezra's ass. The table juddered as the legs slipped on the floor, but it was sturdy and held his weight.

Ezra scrabbled for purchase on Callum's sweat-slick back, breathing heavily through his mouth and nose. Around them the air was thick with cloyingly persistent pheromones. They were so much clearer now, despite his lack of focus, so much easier to identify now that he had finally transformed. The messages they conveyed were primitive but effective—Ezra's a desperately sexual invitation, *I'm ready, I need it, please*, and Callum's a deeper, heady echo, a claim of ownership. *I want you. You're mine. Let me.*

Too breathless to beg with words, Ezra was balanced on a razor wire between arousal and oblivion. His erection was caught between their bodies, smearing fluid over Callum's stomach every time he thrust forward. Succumbing to Callum's silent demands was easy, inevitable. He opened his mouth to a bruising kiss, let Callum taste him, snag his lips with his teeth, lick wetly across his tongue. Then the pheromones again, *Let me*, and Ezra dropped back and supported himself on his arms as Callum pounded into him; shuddered at the hot touch of Callum's tongue over the mark Jax had put on him; and came, keening, in hot, throbbing pulses at the rough touch of Callum's human teeth on his skin.

There was a hot puff of air in his ear, and then Callum was coming, too, fingers leaving bruises on the skin of Ezra's ass and thighs even as he lowered Ezra down to the surface of the table. Ezra spent a few long, sweaty moments with Callum's heavy head on his chest, just breathing.

Then Callum pressed a kiss to the side of Ezra's neck. "Are you going to fall over when you stand up?"

"Probably," Ezra admitted with a wobbly laugh, still buzzed. "You got a bed in this place?"

Callum drew back with a smile. "Come and see for yourself."

CALLUM awoke from the sudden chill. When Ezra sat bolt upright in bed next to him, he pulled the covers away from their bodies, and the cabin didn't have central heat. *Definitely time to install a gas fireplace in the bedroom*, Callum decided. Without looking, he flung out an arm to drag Ezra back down to the mattress and then tugged the covers back into place.

"Ow," Ezra complained.

Callum squinted at him, uncomprehending. "That hurt?" he rasped.

Ezra flushed. "Not *that*, no."

"Oh." Callum wasn't always the quickest in the mornings. "*Oh.* Sorry?" He wasn't usually around to deal with the aches and pains of the day after. Was there a protocol for this? Should he offer a massage?

Actually, maybe he'd better keep his hands to himself if Ezra was sore already.

Ezra didn't bother responding to his apology other than to roll his eyes and tuck himself back in against Callum's side. "Thinking of calling in sick," he offered, "but I don't know what my boss will say."

"He'll never know as long as you make it in by noon." Callum stretched, reveling in the slide of Ezra's bare skin on his own. Lycanthropes were tactile creatures by nature, craving the touch of the members of their extended family. He'd never had sex with a pack lycan before, though, and he'd never stuck around long enough to cuddle. It was something he could definitely get used to. Apart from the chill upon waking up, of course. "Did you have a bad dream or something?"

"Ugh." Ezra made a face. "I dreamt Beau picked up that IV needle he found in the park and caught a zombie virus."

At first, Callum wasn't even sure where to *start* addressing that comment. "Wait, you found a needle in the park with the kids and didn't tell me?"

"Didn't I?" Ezra frowned. "I meant to, sorry. I'm getting used to telling you everything, really. There were some heart monitor leads too. Weird, huh?"

A little shiver ran through Callum at that, and the hair on the back of his neck stood on end. It was a long shot, but.... "What happened to the needle?"

If Ezra thought it an odd question, he didn't comment. "I think... I put it in the picnic basket."

"And...?"

"Um... well, Wyn carried it home and into the house, but then there was an injury. Olivia scraped her knee. I... have no idea what Wyn did with it," he concluded sheepishly. "Sorry."

"Never mind," Callum said, reluctantly throwing off the covers. "Wyn knows better than to toss a needle in the trash."

Ezra propped himself up on his elbows. "Where are you going?"

"Playing a hunch." Callum sighed inwardly. He really would have rather gone back to bed for a few hours, but for some reason, his instincts were telling him this was important, and he was an Alpha—his instincts were not to be ignored lightly. "Come on. It looks like you've got to work today after all." For once, leaving off the signal pheromones felt natural. Callum allowed himself a small smile as he went back out to the main room in search of his bag. It looked like he wouldn't be giving Ezra any more accidental boners.

It was more fun to do it on purpose, anyway.

A little over an hour later, they pulled up in Wyn's driveway, and Ezra got out and went to ask Wyn about their find. Callum couldn't hear everything that was happening, but judging from the relieved look on Ezra's face, it was good news. He disappeared inside and came out of the house a few minutes later clutching a brown paper bag. He was also bright red, and Wyn was grinning manically. She tossed Callum a jaunty wave before turning back into the house. Ezra said nothing, so Callum obliged and didn't ask what Wyn had said. Then they were back on the road again, headed toward the lab.

"Where should I put it?" Ezra asked as they entered the lab adjacent to Callum's office.

"Leave it on the table over there," Callum answered, motioning with a jerk of his head. "Here, give me your coat and get suited up."

Ezra handed over his jacket, and Callum went to the coat rack to hang it up before joining Ezra in donning a lab coat, gloves, and goggles.

"Are you going to tell me what you're thinking now?" Ezra asked. "I mean, I'm assuming you think this might have something to do with the whole Teller thing, but I'm not sure how."

"Like I said, it's just a theory." Callum carefully opened the bag and then reached in with a pair of tongs and removed the needle as well as the heart monitor pads. "But we tracked Teller's scent back through that park when we caught him the first time. It was dark, and we weren't looking for evidence, just the man himself—we could easily have overlooked this."

"The first time?" Ezra echoed, holding out the tray so Callum could set the items down. "You think he had a heart monitor and IV drip before you caught him?"

Callum caught a faint whiff of dread and couldn't blame him. Hearing his hypothesis spoken aloud made it that much more real, that much more terrifying. The idea that someone could do this on purpose, could experiment on lycans like that…. "It's just a theory."

"Yeah, well, let's test it so we can disprove it. I'd like to be able to sleep tonight. What do we do?"

Callum tweezed up the heart monitor pads and examined them closely. There were a few hairs still stuck in the adhesive, maybe enough to get a DNA profile. He put the pads in a sample jar and screwed on the cap. "Bring these to Crystal in the DNA sequencing lab. Tell her it's her new top priority."

"Okay. What are you going to do with that?" Ezra motioned toward the needle.

"I'm going to try to find out what they were feeding him," Callum said grimly. There was a tiny fragment of tubing still attached—it was possible he'd be able to collect some sort of residue. He slid the IV needle into a test tube.

Rather than take his leave immediately, Ezra watched him for a few more moments. "What are you thinking?"

"That it might not be an epidemic," Callum said grimly, eyeing the tube. Would there be a large enough sample to test? He couldn't tell. The microscope was probably his best bet. "I need that DNA test, Ezra."

Ezra nodded, pale-faced. "Right."

Callum put the sample in the pocket of his lab coat. The lab across from the DNA sequencing room had a dark field microscope and a library of samples for comparison. In a few minutes, he could test his hypothesis.

He really, really hoped he was wrong.

EZRA bolted upright in his desk chair when the door to the otherwise empty computer lab opened behind him, and rubbed frantically at his eyes, trying—most likely in vain—to wipe away evidence of his impromptu nap before he turned around.

"There you are," Callum said, his quick brown eyes taking in Ezra's state immediately. But there was no hint of reproach in his gaze or his voice. "Burning the midnight oil? We have to go soon, you know."

Ezra looked up at the clock that hung over the door. God, was it that late already? They'd be stuck in the lab if they didn't leave shortly. "I was checking up on my web crawl," he said, voice cracking a little with disuse. "Must have fallen asleep."

"It happens," Callum said wryly. "Sometimes regardless of the caffeine drip." He indicated the three unwashed mugs Ezra had accumulated in a vain attempt to keep himself conscious. "Did you learn anything new?"

Ezra shook his head tiredly. "Too much to go through tonight. I'll have to work on it tomorrow." His eyes took in the coat Callum had draped over his left arm. "Time to go home, I guess."

It wasn't exactly that Ezra didn't have any experience sleeping with someone he worked with. But he sort of also lived with Callum, though maybe that would change in a few days when his first full moon was past and, with it, most of the inherent dangers in turning into a lycanthrope. The point was that Callum was his boss, and his host, and the leader of the damn pack, and Ezra wasn't sure where he stood, other than apparently Callum had all the damn power, which was hot in the bedroom but frankly a little disconcerting anywhere else.

Callum passed him his coat. "Come on. If we leave now, we'll make it home before moonrise."

Home. Funny, but that was how Ezra thought of it too—even if he'd only been squatting in Callum's guest room for a short time. Yep, this was going to be awkward.

Ezra donned the coat automatically, flashing back to a month previously, when Callum had ordered him in and out of his clothes casually and he'd been unable to resist. That in turn brought with it an unexpected pang of grief. He hadn't even had time to mourn his father properly.

"You're quiet tonight," Callum commented as he turned the SUV into the drive, and Ezra finally snapped out of his daze.

"I'm just tired," he excused himself, reaching for the door handle. Callum had said lycans normally just curled up and went to sleep anyway, right? That sounded pretty fantastic, actually.

Ezra waited for Callum to unlock the door, then toed off his shoes in the entryway and hung his coat on the peg behind the door. "You've got about twenty minutes if you want a shower first," Callum said.

No need to be on tenterhooks, then; that was as clear a dismissal as Ezra could have hoped for. Nodding absently, he headed toward the stairs. Apparently he wasn't so tired that he couldn't feel disappointed—crushed, even. Fuck it, this was ridiculous. He was a grown man. If he wanted something, he could damn well say so—

"Ezra."

Ezra turned on the bottom stair, doing his best to keep his expression neutral. "Yes?"

A slight pause. "Are you coming to bed after?" His expression was pensive, borderline hopeful.

When Ezra didn't speak—too torn between being embarrassed and stunned to react—Callum took a step closer, but not close enough to crowd him, and gentled his tone. "Ezra, I'll be the first to admit that I don't have a lot of experience with this relationship thing, so I'm just going to be straightforward with you. You are not my dirty little secret. You are not my bit on the side. I don't know what you are yet, but you are sleeping in my bed until you decide you don't want to."

Oh. Well. That didn't sound so bad, actually. And—"Are you using pheromones on me right now?" Ezra said a little incredulously.

Callum blushed, a reaction that was so incongruous with what they'd done to each other in the past twenty-four hours that Ezra almost laughed. "Not on purpose," he said with an embarrassed groan. "I'm really bad at this, huh?"

Would it be bad form to agree with him? Ezra wondered. Because, okay, yes, he was appallingly bad at "this"—whatever "this" was—and they were supposed to have a handle on this now that Ezra had been blooded, but Ezra didn't want to discourage him too much. "Maybe you just need some practice," he suggested hopefully.

Callum herded him up the stairs with a wry half smile. "Maybe I'll just follow your lead for a bit."

Now there was an interesting prospect. Ezra glanced up at the clock. "What time did you say moonrise was?"

Callum followed his gaze. "About fifteen minutes, now. Why?"

Hmm. Well, it'd be tight, but Ezra had faith in them. He flashed an uncertain grin. "Race you to the shower?"

Chapter Ten

Hungry Like the Wolf

"IT'S going to snow," Blaise observed with narrowed eyes as he climbed out of the truck, shaggy head tipped back to take in the slate-gray sky.

Ezra had been afraid of that. He shivered, wrapping the long end of his scarf around his neck one more time before slamming the passenger side door. He'd forgotten how much he didn't miss Montana winters. After the relatively pleasant week they'd just had, this one seemed to be coming on strong. "That could make this a little more challenging," he pointed out. Not to mention unpleasant. "Is there a trick to this?"

Blaise gave him a bemused look. "Just take me to where the kids found the stuff. This isn't the sort of field work I usually do, you know."

Ezra had no earthly idea what sort of field work Blaise usually did, other than act as Callum's bodyguard. But it wasn't like that was a full-time job or anything. "What *do* you usually do?" he asked, leading the way into the park. "Callum spends a lot of time locked down in the lab."

"Yeah, well, he's not the only one," Blaise grunted, and Ezra flushed. Then Blaise sighed. "I'm a CPA."

Ezra tripped over the wooden box around the swing sets and would have eaten dirt, but Blaise caught him by the shoulder just in time. "Thanks," Ezra managed. "I thought—did you say you were a CPA?"

"You didn't think Jax got all the brains, did you?"

Maybe not, but Blaise had certainly got the lion's share of the brawn, Ezra thought with a critical eye.

"I do the books for the pack holdings. Rental properties, community center, the nursery."

Ezra was starting to feel like he could use some letters after his name. Damn. But back to the task at hand. The picnic had been in the more wooded area of the park, far enough in that you couldn't really see the parking lot or the road. "They were playing tag," he explained, trying to get his bearings. A sudden thought occurred to him. "Hey, speaking of the kids. Lycans don't change until they're teenagers, right?"

Blaise grunted an affirmative, his eyes not on Ezra but on the brush surrounding them.

"Well… who watches the kids?" Realistically, Ezra knew the older ones didn't have to be watched while they were sleeping, but what about nights when the moon rose early, or infants? Infants woke up during the night all the time, didn't they?

Blaise actually turned his attention away from the trees at that. "Their moms, usually," he said, as if he didn't quite understand why Ezra was asking the question.

Was Ezra missing something? "But aren't they kind of, you know… hairy and thumbless? It would be kind of hard to warm a bottle, wouldn't it?"

"A female lycan stops changing when she gets pregnant," Blaise told him. "This the place?"

Ezra looked around and nodded. "Yeah." They were about as close as he could pinpoint it. Then he pressed on, "Permanently?" He'd had a blast the night of the full moon. He couldn't imagine voluntarily giving that up for good.

"From the pregnancy through to about eighteen months or so. That's why it's important to have pack Alphas around all the time. Alphas lead to stability. Stability leads to a higher birth rate. That means there's usually at least one person around who can watch the kids at the community center for a few nights. The older kids help out too."

Huh. "I think that's the most I've ever heard you say at one time," Ezra commented. He kept circling around, looking for whatever it was they were supposed to be looking for, which was easier said than done.

Blaise grunted in response.

"So, you and Wyn?" Ezra gambled.

A snort. Blaise half-raised from his crouch by a bush and lifted an eyebrow. "You and Callum?" he countered.

Stalemate. Or maybe checkmate. Ezra was definitely more uncomfortable than Blaise was.

Blaise jerked his head. "Come look at this and tell me what you see."

Ezra headed over to him, watching the ground carefully to make sure he didn't disturb any other evidence they might have missed. At first, he didn't see anything but trees and bracken, underbrush, and dead leaves. Then, after a moment of staring, he saw it: a thin cloth, maybe blue once, now stained with something that was either dirt or blood. Ezra stayed back so his nose didn't identify it for him. "Is that a hospital gown?"

Blaise cocked his head and glanced at him sideways. "That's what I thought." He started to make his way toward the gown, each step deliberate as he made his way down the incline and into the bracken. Ezra followed after him.

"So... we've got an IV, heart monitor leads, and a hospital gown." He paused a moment to let that sink in. "What does that mean?"

"No idea." While Ezra enjoyed Blaise's company, it really wasn't for his scintillating conversation. "It's like, someone escaped from a hospital. But if they're running from a hospital, then what's with the stuff Callum found in the IV? I mean, they wouldn't be giving people that shit in a hospital, would they?" The most annoying thing about Blaise's continued silence was that Ezra felt a need to fill it.

"Unlikely. Most humans don't even know about it. Not even the doctors."

True. Ezra contemplated in silence.

Blaise reached the gown and bent over to retrieve it. Ezra, still positioned behind the large man, took the opportunity to appreciate the view. He might have started... something... with Callum, but that didn't mean he couldn't ogle.

Then Blaise stood back up and turned to face him. He was holding the cloth out at arm's length so that both of them could see it clearly.

"Definitely a hospital gown," Ezra said. He knew what they looked like.

"And that's definitely blood."

Well, that confirmed Ezra's worst suspicions. The bottom of his stomach dropped out and then rose back to its rightful place; he was caught up in memories of his mother, lying in a hospital bed and coughing—

"Yeah. Not a lot, though. Probably spilled when they pulled out the IV."

"Oh." The silence hung in the air for a moment before Ezra managed to say, "Is there anything else with it?"

After taking a long look around, Blaise shook his head in the negative. They continued their search, Blaise beginning by circling out from where he had found the gown. Ezra turned and walked up the incline back toward the spot where he thought they had found the IV, careful to keep his eyes on the ground the whole way there.

Thirty minutes later Blaise called out, "Find anything yet?"

"No!"

"Me either." His shout wasn't nearly as loud this time around, and Ezra turned to see Blaise headed in his direction. "I don't think we're going to find anything else."

"Oh, thank God," Ezra said with a sigh of relief. "I'm getting tired of looking at grass."

Blaise's lips gave a definite twitch at that. "Well, if the gown was there and the IV here… then he probably came running from that direction." Blaise pointed back toward where they'd found the gown. The trees were thicker on the far side.

"You think?" Ezra stared off in the distance.

"The stickers for the heart monitor would have been on his chest, right? Under the gown, so…."

"Stands to reason that he'd take them off after he got the gown off," Ezra finished. "Good thinking."

"You say that like you're surprised."

"It's the muscles." Ezra gave a lazy shrug, surprised when Blaise only smirked in response.

To break the tension, Ezra gave a flourishing gesture forward. "Shall we?" The only response was a snort as Blaise started walking. "I guess we shall."

As they walked, both men kept their eyes on the ground, but neither of them found anything by the time they reached the stand of trees. A brief look at each other, and then both of them were making their way into the copse. They didn't find anything else among the trees either, though Ezra was willing to concede that they might have missed something small. A heart monitor lead would be much more difficult to spot in the brush than on the grass.

On the other side of the trees, they stumbled onto a road. It was narrow and unpaved and had two indents carved into the dirt by several years' worth of cars. The road met up with the paved drag a hundred or so feet to their right and headed off to their left for a short way before curving sharply away from them. The road beyond the turn was hidden from view by the trees that lined the other side of the road. It seemed that the small copse was only part of a much larger woods.

"I had no idea that we were so close to the woods," Ezra said inanely.

Blaise gave him a funny look and then stepped out onto the dirt road. "This road doesn't get a lot of traffic."

"There are wheel ruts carved into it," Ezra pointed out, because worn-in tire impressions denoted use, even Ezra knew that.

"Ezra, I've lived here my whole life, and I've never seen anyone use it. I had forgotten that it was here." Blaise was walking away from him, eyes on the dirt beneath his feet.

Taking that in, Ezra joined Blaise on the road. "So where does it lead?"

"What?"

"The road."

"Oh. Nowhere."

There was a long pause while Ezra waited for Blaise to explain that, but apparently he wasn't going to. "Then why is it here?"

"I'm not sure."

"Want to find out?"

A few feet down the road, Blaise stopped, bent over, and picked something up off the dirt.

"What is it?"

"The third heart monitor sticker." And it was. It matched the two that the boys had found in the park.

"Well at least now we know we're on the right trail," Ezra pointed out as they resumed walking.

It turned out that Blaise was mostly right. The road really didn't lead to much of anyplace. Well, no place public. They did pass what appeared to be a private driveway, but given that the entrance was blocked off with a gate and a sign that read NO TRESPASSERS, they figured that it hardly counted. Eventually the road simply ended in a large dirt circle. Judging by the tire tracks, its only purpose was to help lost cars turn around.

"Well...," Ezra said as they both stood in the middle of the dirt road, staring around.

"I'm thinking that this guy, wherever he came from, he started from this road."

"What?" Ezra spun around to stare at Blaise. He had been so caught up in finding out about where the road led that he had almost forgotten about their mystery person.

"We found that sticker on the side of the road, and there were tire imprints in the dirt. Last time it was raining hard enough to leave prints like that was—"

"A little over a week ago," Ezra finished for him. He took a moment to think over this idea. If the guy hadn't run away from the hospital, if he had been brought here by someone, then... well, this would be a likely spot for them to have dropped him off. "Let's go back. Maybe we can find something to support your theory."

Back where they discovered the last lead, they spread out and began searching for something else.

"Hey, Blaise, come take a look at this!"

"Are those—"

"Footprints?" Ezra finished. Pressed into the dirt was a confused and chaotic pattern. There were several impressions from what appeared to be large boots. They were not all the same size, and they crisscrossed over one another. Ezra was no expert, but he was pretty sure that more than one person had run over the same patch of road. "Look how they just start out of nowhere." Ezra pointed to the ground where the prints began, less than a foot away from the tire groove.

Blaise made a grunt of agreement and then, "There's another print—this one looks barefoot."

It did indeed, though it was partially covered by a larger boot print. "So. We have our barefoot patient who jumps out of a vehicle and men in shoes who follow him?"

"Looks like."

Ezra huffed out a breath. "Well, that jibes with what Callum found in the IV drip, I guess. Someone's pumping people full of alpha hormones. Against their will, if this is any indication." You didn't run away from doctors who were trying to help you. Besides, what medical purpose could those hormones possibly serve?

Blaise grunted agreement, then cocked his head to one side. "Rock paper scissors for who has to tell Callum?"

CALLUM was surprised when he opened his front door and found two women on his front doorstep. Since he had assumed that the chiming bells were heralding the FBI agents, Callum had been expecting to find men, and aging men at that—he knew the likelihood of working with not only one but two female field agents.

"Hello, are you Callum Dawson?" The petite blonde was the first to speak. She was barely five foot four and seemed to be compensating for it with her long hair, which reached her butt despite being braided. She had bright blue eyes and lips that were naturally curved with a smirking lilt.

"I am. And you must be the agents from the FBI."

"You bet, sweetheart," said the blonde.

It was her partner who elaborated, in a voice as smooth as honey. "I'm Siobhan Veyron, and this is my partner, Dannika Louis. We were told that you had some information for us about a series of kidnappings and attacks." Agent Veyron was a striking contrast to her partner. She was tall, at least six feet, with curves in excess and short dark hair. Even Callum wanted to call her a bombshell.

She was also lycan. She was undeniably emitting the familiar musky scent of an alpha.

"I'm surprised. I didn't think the FBI would be sending a lycan." His voice was steady and not overtly aggressive, but he didn't open the door or step back.

Agent Veyron looked unsurprised by his hostility. Callum thought that Agent Louis might be shocked, but it was difficult to tell, as he and Agent Veyron were locked in a staring contest. "I was bitten five years ago. An accident. But it comes in handy when dealing with certain people and cases," she said.

Callum waited another moment until Agent Veyron finally broke their staring contest. Nodding his acceptance of her submission, he abandoned his aggression. "Come in." Callum waved them into his home, explaining, "There's a lot for us to tell you, so we may as well be comfortable while we talk."

Since Callum led the way, he was afforded a good view of Blaise's face when Agent Veyron followed her partner into the room. Blaise's mouth didn't actually drop open, but it was a close thing.

"Agents Veyron and Louis, I'd like you to meet my second in command, Blaise LaPorte, and my research assistant, Ezra Jones. They've both been invaluable in researching this…." Callum pursed his lips for a moment, thinking; he finally settled on: "Crime."

"Please, Mr. Dawson, it's Siobhan and Dannika," Siobhan said in that smooth voice. "Neither of us is that formal."

As handshakes were exchanged, all three men made the same assertion.

"So, Cal." Dannika flopped onto the couch, stretching out her feet. "Why don't you tell us what's been going on?"

Siobhan settled next to her partner with much more grace. "Please, Callum, tell us about why you called."

It took only twenty minutes for Callum and then Ezra to get both women caught up. Siobhan in particular was interested in all the details. When she learned about the computer program that had searched out other victims, she had wanted to know all about the search parameters that Ezra had used. Ezra was in the middle of explaining how he had worked to distinguish lycan from genuine animal attacks when Jax arrived.

"Dawson! I thought you told me that the FBI wouldn't be here for a while yet." She gave him a smirk and then turned to introduce herself to the women.

The look that Dannika gave Jax while they shook hands was long and appreciative. Though Jax gave her scrutiny in return, she saved her more favoring looks for Siobhan's shape. Sheesh, even Jax was admiring the woman. Given the way that Dannika rolled her eyes as she threw herself back into her a seat, this was par for the course everywhere they went.

"So Callum has been telling you all about our problems, then?"

"Yup." Dannika made a popping noise with her lips. "All the details. Something fishy is definitely going on. Don't worry, though. Siobhan and I are excellent detectives."

Siobhan rolled her eyes. "Dan and I are here to help, and we'll work hard to get answers." She paused then before adding, "And we're hoping that you'll be willing to keep working with us."

It seemed obvious to Callum that Dannika was biting the inside of her cheek, hard, but Siobhan seemed not to notice.

Jax was the one to ask, "Work with you?"

Man, even Siobhan's nods were graceful. "Given our lack of manpower and resources in the area—"

"It's not like we can bring forensics to the local PD, not without there being questions," Dannika cut in.

"We were hoping that you would oblige us by helping our investigative efforts."

It would have made sense—if Callum and Jax weren't who and what they were. "Siobhan, I called the FBI because I don't know how to conduct a murder investigation, not because I don't have the desire to *look for clues*. These people who are dying, who are hurting—that could be *my* pack. No way in hell are you stopping Jax and I from finding answers." He locked his gaze with Siobhan's, waiting. She had to understand that she was here to help him, not the other way around. When she finally broke the staring contest, Callum turned to find Jax and Dannika locked in a similar battle, though Dannika seemed far less inclined to concede.

"Dan," Siobhan murmured, "Boise?"

Callum had no idea what that city meant to either of them, but it obviously meant something. Dannika cut her gaze to the side toward her partner before letting out a sigh.

Deciding to give a little ground, Callum asked, "Where should we start?"

Both women agreed that it would be best to start by going over all the evidence already accumulated before attempting to speak with Teller. In order to see any evidence collected, they would have to head to Callum's labs.

"How about someone rides with us to show us the way?" Dannika said as they headed down the drive. "Jax? You want to ride with the ladies?" The smile she gave was positively flirtatious.

"Why not?" Jax smiled back, but hers was more warm than sexy.

"Nice car," grunted Blaise when a sizable black sedan came into view.

"It's a rental," Siobhan said with a shrug.

"Still. Nice."

"Isn't it just?" Dannika patted the hood of the Lexus. "They tried to give us this tiny little Toyota—how am I supposed to fit Siobhan in an Echo?"

"Like you weren't just looking out for your own fetish."

"It's not a fetish! I just appreciate a nice car. Besides, you're the one who flashed her tits to get the free upgrade."

Color rose on Siobhan's cheeks, and she spared a glance in their audience's direction. "I didn't flash anything!"

"Sure you didn't. Your rack just got so heavy that you had to rest it on the counter, and the clerk just happened to look down your top. I understand." Her voice was sweet and sympathetic, but the effect was ruined when she tossed a cheeky wink at Ezra.

THERE was no way to fit all six of them in Ezra's matchbox office, so the lunchroom was the most logical choice. When Callum and Ezra arrived with their accumulated information, they found Jax, Blaise, and the agents sitting around the table in the middle of the room.

"Let's see what you've got," said Dannika, stretching out her hands and making "gimme" motions.

Callum hesitated. Sure, he could just hand everything over, but the papers weren't in the most logical order—Callum's fault. He'd been going through them furiously, looking for the one little detail that would tie it all together, and he'd screwed up Ezra's obsessive organization.

It was Siobhan who said, "Let them tell us how they want," and Callum was grateful when Dannika stopped trying to take his folders.

Callum and Ezra settled in, Ezra taking the folders, scoffing under his breath as he put them to rights. Dannika and Siobhan both pulled out paper and pens.

"Ready to get started?" Dannika asked, seemingly to the room at large.

It took several minutes for Ezra to lay out all the charts and show all their documentation for everything that had happened. By the time he had finished, Siobhan was nodding her head and Dannika was holding her bottom lip hostage between her teeth.

"This is pretty complete. Usually when we're brought in like this, Dannika and I need to spend a couple of days running around and getting caught up. The only thing that we'll need to do to finish off our research is to talk to"—she glanced down at her notes—"Mr. Teller?"

The air suddenly felt heavy and strained to Callum. "You won't get much out of him," he said, wishing that she hadn't brought him up. The subject never failed to make Ezra tense.

"I know that you said he's unbalanced," Dannika said. "But we really do need to give talking to him a try."

"We'd be remiss if we didn't at least give it a shot."

"Well," Jax cut in, "you lot can arrange that later. Now that the FBI is all caught up, what do we do next?"

With a sigh, Dannika blew a few wispy bangs out of her face. "Now? Now we start talking strategy. Where we go from here, etcetera, etcetera."

Jax sat up straighter, flattening her hands on the table. "Where do we go from here?"

"Well, first order of business is to figure out who could do this. I mean, we've got an obvious roadblock in coming up with suspects: not everyone knows about lycans. We need to start narrowing down that list," Dannika explained.

"So... how do we do that?"

Siobhan gave a small smile. "Actually, I'm pretty sure that Ezra could give us a hand with it, since we need to compare data."

On cue, Ezra reached under his chair and pulled out an ancient laptop he'd found somewhere in storage and then updated with cannibalized parts: a butt-ugly piece of Frankensteined technology, but it worked. "Figured I might be needing this. It's only got about an hour of battery life, but it's this or take notes and come back to you, so...." He shrugged. "Just give me a minute to log in to the servers."

When he was set to go, he looked up over the laptop screen and gave a short nod. "I'm ready. You guys can do your thing," he said to Siobhan.

It was Dannika who spoke. "We're looking for somebody who knows werewolves. Either a government official, someone in the FBI, maybe even someone who is himself a lycanthrope. Better include immediate family, too, in case someone found out who shouldn't."

"That's a long list," Ezra murmured as he started tapping at the keys. "Countrywide?"

It was fortunate, Callum supposed, that the lycan community had its own census. In order to better keep track of each other, and to better protect themselves from hunters, Alphas all across the United States had started providing a list of their pack members to a central source. That database was the perfect tool for Ezra.

In response to his question, Siobhan shook her head. "Better narrow it down. Start with Montana and the bordering states. We can widen the search later if we come up empty."

"Whoever's doing this has a strong scientific background. They've got some research experience and access to lab equipment," Callum put in thoughtfully.

Ezra shot him a look. "I'm not the IRS, you know. I don't have access to that kind of information."

"I'm sure the FBI can get it and forward it to us," Jax put in smoothly, turning her head toward Dannika and giving the woman a hard look. "Right?"

And that was why Jax was Alpha.

Dannika reached into her pocket and took out her cell phone. "Sure thing, dollface." She tipped her head at Ezra. "You got e-mail on that thing?"

Ezra rattled off his CDC e-mail address, and Dannika nodded and waved her cell phone at them as she stepped out of the room.

Blaise, Siobhan, and Callum all turned to look at Jax. "What?" she said flatly.

"Back to the task at hand," Siobhan put in smoothly. "We need to cross-reference that list with those who know about werewolves. That's going to put you at the top of the list," she told Callum baldly.

"I'm pretty sure I'm innocent," Callum said a little more sharply than necessary. "But feel free to check my basement."

"My point is that you should consider whether anyone who works in this department could have done it," Siobhan said. "There may not be many lycans on staff, but the whole department is more or less qualified to do the sort of experiments we suspect are taking place."

Shit. Callum hadn't thought of that. This was why he hadn't become a detective: he just wasn't a suspicious bastard at heart. He took a moment to chew on the possibility. He'd have liked to be able to say that he trusted everyone he worked with, that he knew them well, but it just wasn't true. While the CDC had presumably done thorough background checks on everyone from the janitor through the DNA and infectious disease specialists, Callum didn't know all of them. Some of them were new, others were shy, and Callum had spent the last four months holed up in his lab trying to figure out what the hell was going on with the lycan population.

Callum turned to Ezra. God, he'd brought Ezra in here without a second thought. Any one of his people could be a sadistic—

"Callum."

Callum forced himself to take a deep breath and look at Jax instead. She held his gaze until he settled, and he nodded, blowing out a long breath.

Dannika came back in from the hallway. "Yeah, I know, I'll owe you one. Another one. Thanks, Mark." She ended the call. "So?"

"So, everyone in this department is now a prime suspect," Ezra said morosely. Then he perked up. "Well, except for me. Seeing as I'm a victim."

If he really felt that way, he was doing a decent job of hiding it, Callum thought wryly.

"What if it's more than one person?" Blaise said. "We saw at least two sets of tracks. Could be that someone who knows about lycans hired somebody with the scientific knowledge."

"I'm not the bloody CIA either," Ezra grouched. "I can give you that cross-referenced list, but…." He trailed off with a shrug. "It'll take a while for the program to run and for the computer to find anything."

Siobhan suggested that Callum take them to see Teller while they waited. By silent agreement, Jax and Blaise stayed with Ezra while Callum guided the agents out of the room to see Teller.

THE meeting with Teller had gone just as well as Callum had expected.

Instead of acknowledging the agents that had arrived to see him, Teller had given Callum a long, despairing look before turning away and mumbling to himself. The only true reaction they got out of him came after both women had pressed him for an answer, and he had turned fierce, furious eyes on them and began to shout, "Sing a song of sixpence and a pocket full of rye. Four and twenty blackbirds were baked in a pie." Teller's voice gave out after the second line of the nursery rhyme. His eyes turned puzzled, his expression introspective. His voice was much quieter and troubled when he spoke again. "But when the pie was opened, they all began to sing. Wasn't that a dainty dish to serve to a king? The king was—the king—the queen was in the garden hanging out the clothes, when along came a blackbird and snipped off her nose!" He finished with an anguished wail, trembling in a huddle, and wouldn't be roused again.

Dannika was the first to speak when they left the room. "Well."

"I told you you weren't going to get much out of him."

"I was expecting PTSD, that's not—"

"No. It's not. Or not only. I think… we theorize that whatever causes the hormonal imbalance does permanent damage to the synapses. To the pathways in the brain. Teller has been obsessed with children's entertainment since the… event."

"Why didn't you mention this before?" Siobhan looked displeased and a little sulky.

Callum just sighed. He wasn't going to get defensive about it. "There's nothing we can prove about Teller. Not yet. Who's to say it's not just severe trauma?" When Dannika opened her mouth, he opted to add, "Our psychologists certainly haven't. Yet."

YAWNING, Callum poured himself a cup of coffee. He was several sips into his mug before he thought to wonder where the coffee had come from. Ezra was just now getting out of the shower. So who…?

"Morning, sunshine!"

Callum spun to find that Jax, Blaise, and Wyn were sitting around the table, which was piled high with breakfast items that, now he was aware of them, smelled heavenly.

"Did you break into my house and make coffee?" Callum wondered aloud and made for the food.

"Yup! You didn't answer when I knocked. I waited a whole fifteen seconds. So we decided to come in. The FBI agents are on their way."

Callum simply grunted in return. He might have formed actual words in response if he had actually managed to get more than a few hours' sleep. Or if he hadn't had half a croissant stuffed into his mouth.

Ezra joined them, smelling fresh and clean and looking amazing, and sat down at the table to moan long and loud over the breakfast set before him. Damn. For a brief moment, Callum thought about taking Ezra back upstairs, and fuck the rest of them. Then Jax smacked the back of his head and he was reminded that there were many other important things in life.

Blaise, Callum, and Ezra were still working away at the mountain of food when Dannika and Siobhan arrived, both of whom took in the table with ravenous gazes.

"We only had a few slices of toast at the hotel before coming here," Dannika explained between bites. "God, this is amazing."

"Wyn's an amazing cook," Jax explained with pride.

"You *made* all this?" Dannika turned to Wyn. "Marry me?"

The impromptu proposal was short-lived as Blaise started growling, and Callum had to raise his mug again to hide his grin at watching the hulking man posturing for a tiny lesbian. Dannika didn't look so much frightened as she did resigned when she told Wyn to never mind and stole another cinnamon bun, several strawberries, and three more pieces of bacon.

When everyone but Blaise and Dannika had eaten their fill, Siobhan turned to Ezra and asked how the program was running. Ezra gave a small jerk of surprise but got up and hurried out of the room.

When he returned, he plunked the open laptop down on the table.

"I completely forgot about this," he said in between clicks of the track pad. "I was going to check it this morning but then—" Abruptly, he stopped and stared at his computer screen. "Huh."

"Yahtzee?" Dannika asked.

Callum tossed her a confused look, then leaned over so he could peer at the screen over Ezra's shoulder. Siobhan had been right— several of the names that he could see on the list were familiar, though he didn't see his own at the moment. Finally he saw what Ezra was looking at. "Malcolm Shaw?"

"Well, he's a big enough douche bag," Ezra muttered.

Jax snorted. "That's for sure. He's on our shiny new suspect list?"

"I created a matrix, last night, to cross-reference names of not just the scientists but of employers and company CEOs." Ezra did some more clicking and started pulling up information about Shaw. "Shaw, like many Alphas, heads up several companies. One of which has been putting a lot of money into the research of one Dr. D. Maxwell. He does lab research at Black Hills State University. He's a professor there, and guess what he specializes in?" Ezra turned triumphant eyes on their group.

"What?"

"Biochemistry with a focus in endocrinology," Ezra read aloud from the screen.

"Endo-what?" Jax was the first to break the silence.

"It's the study of endocrine glands—hormones. Which would certainly be a great background to have if you were experimenting with artificial hormone injection."

"And you think this Malcolm Shaw would be willing, capable, of that." Siobhan's face, when Callum turned to look at it, was inscrutable.

"Ezra wasn't wrong. He's a douche bag," Callum said. God, no wonder he thought Malcolm was such a creep, if this was what he got up to in his off hours.

Jax gave an inelegant snort. "He's an arrogant, sexist pig. He's the kind of man that will look down your shirt and ask for a poke while telling you not to worry your pretty head about men's work."

"So I don't suppose that this connection is enough for an arrest warrant?" Callum asked into the silence.

Siobhan huffed elegantly. "Not even close. We could bring him in for questioning, but if he *is* our guy, that would only tip him off. Who knows how many of us he's got locked up that he might decide to dispose of?"

"It'd be better if we discreetly had a look around," Dannika agreed. "Where's this guy live?"

"It's a couple hours' drive from here," Callum told her. "You'll get there by lunch."

Siobhan gave a satisfied nod. "Give me some directions?" she asked of Callum, who nodded. "Great. And in the meantime, we should keep looking for suspects, so, Dannika's going to call her friend the data analyst."

The diminutive blonde looked at her partner. "I am?"

Siobhan nodded. "In the spirit of taking full advantage of our geek connection."

"You know, you could call her." Dannika gave her partner the stink-eye until both ladies held out fists and began a round of Rock, Paper, Scissors.

Dannika lost two rounds in a row.

She seemed to deflate with a sigh. "Right, I'm going to go call my analyst." She looked despondently at Ezra. "I'm going to need to borrow your laptop."

Shrugging, Ezra handed it over, and Dannika left the room, muttering under her breath this time. Callum looked at Siobhan askance.

"One of the FBI data analysts has a crush on her," Siobhan explained. "Misguided, but adorable, not to mention useful. It might take a day or two, but we'll get the information we're after."

"What are we supposed to do in the meantime?" Blaise wanted to know. Callum had to admit that he was a little curious himself.

"I know this isn't what you want to hear, but act as naturally as possible," Siobhan instructed. "It's possible the culprit already knows you called in backup, but if he or she doesn't, it's best to keep it that way. Go home. Do whatever you normally do on a Saturday."

"And pretend like we know nothing?" Callum frowned at her.

"I know you want to help, but right now you need to let Dan and I do our job. We're not cutting you out, but we need to be careful with how we move forward. I know what I'm doing. And if anything comes up or something weird happens, you have our numbers."

THE young beta took a running leap at the door, his body colliding with the metal. Davis watched him through the one-way mirror. Tonight they would set the beta out. Subject B-H30-5 was the most promising so far: his aggression was up and his arousal, though elevated, wasn't all-consuming like some of the other subjects'. Some of them got so desperate for a fuck they would roll over and beg any alpha, regardless of gender and sexual preference. This one seemed to prefer fighting the other lycans and the humans he came into contact with.

Davis had high hopes for B-H30-5. He was obviously itching for a fight, and he had proved himself time and again amenable to fighting whomever the Boss wanted him to fight. When given the option, he'd only take out the one he was told to. The only other subject this promising had been B-K24-1, who had escaped en route to a target. The Boss had been livid when he had learned of the escape; Davis hadn't envied the men who had allowed it to happen. Still, it was best not to dwell on his high hopes for B-K24-1. B-H30-5 would prove satisfactory, he was sure.

Tonight, they would dose him with more adrenal alphatropin 7H and then unleash him on the public.

Though Davis wasn't able to move B-H30-5 until the Boss had arrived and told him to cooperate, he had fitted him with handcuffs and promised that a fight would be had soon. B-H30-5 hadn't listened, of course, but when the Boss arrived, he had submitted to being moved easily enough.

Two hours later, they had the van parked on a side street in Butte's downtown area.

They settled in and only had to wait fifteen minutes before a well-dressed man walked past the street's entrance.

The man—Assistant District Attorney Doug Weiman—had been the Boss's target choice. He spent every Saturday evening at his private club, but he was too cheap to pay for their parking service, preferring to leave his car a few blocks away.

That was going to be the last mistake he ever made.

Davis had obtained a picture of Weiman and had also managed to procure a scarf that the man had recently worn. The Boss had made sure to let B-H30-5 know that he wanted the man dead, and the subject had been receptive.

"He's coming," growled the Boss. "So how about I let you out of this car and you sic 'em?"

"Yeah." B-H30-5 got out a breathy, eager gasp—the first word spoken in hours.

When the door opened, B-H30-5 was out like a flash, nose in the air and sniffing.

"Should we wait?" the driver asked.

"You *do* know the prey's name, don't you?" The Boss was looking out the windscreen, but Davis wasn't in doubt as to who he was talking to.

"Yes. One Doug—"

"We'll find out if he was successful in tomorrow's paper. Let's leave the scene, yes?"

Davis nodded. It was a good idea. They would lose B-H30-5, but there were others.

Chapter Eleven
A Dog's Breakfast

THE phone rang at 3:00 a.m. Still mostly asleep, Callum ignored it. He didn't want to get out of bed, and he didn't want to hear what someone thought needed to be said at 3:00 a.m.

The phone rang again, and this time Ezra shifted and let out a loud unhappy moan. Damn, Callum would have to answer it or risk Ezra waking.

"Wha—?"

"Alpha Dawson? I'm sorry to call so late—er, early, rather, but I thought I should call you ASAP."

Callum grunted. Was that Siobhan? She hadn't addressed him so formally in days. "What's going on?"

"I just got a call from the sheriff's office in Butte. Dannika and I put out the word that we wanted to know about any suspicious violent activity—"

Alarm filled him, and he didn't try to stop the Alpha voice. "What happened?"

Siobhan obeyed. "They found a body. Torn to pieces in the east end of downtown. Probable cause of death is blood loss from multiple injuries."

"Lycan?"

"Human."

Something about her tone made him uneasy. "And?"

"They've found a suspect—a young man, covered in blood. He was half-mad—they had to take him out with tranquilizer darts."

Relief replaced the building tension. He was still alive. Though how sane he was remained to be seen. "Where is he now?"

"On his way here. I was able to convince the local police that he was part of an ongoing investigation and to let Dan and I take over. He's being transported to the NFWS now. The ETA is 5:00 a.m."

"Right. Okay." Callum took a minute to think. He needed to dress and shower. "I'll meet you there."

"Okay. See you then."

Callum turned off the phone and let it clatter onto the nightstand.

"C'll'm?" Ezra's face was mashed into his pillow.

"Go back to sleep, Ez." He ran a hand over the other man's messy hair.

"M'kay. You too." He reached out a sleep-heavy hand that flopped around a bit before finding Callum's arm.

Callum knew he wouldn't be able to sleep—he had neither the time nor the desire—but there was no harm in lying down. He didn't have to leave for at least an hour, and showers were overrated anyway. Sliding down, he settled himself so that Ezra could cuddle up close. He placed one hand on the small of Ezra's back, rubbing small circles and trying to ignore the persistent thought that Ezra could have been like the unnamed body in Butte.

"Who was on the phone?"

He really didn't want to bring Ezra into this, but he needed to say something if he was going to be leaving thei—*his* bed in an hour. "Siobhan. I need to go meet her in an hour."

"An hour? 'S the middle of the night."

"Early morning." His hand wandered up Ezra's back in a long caress.

"Oh." The silence lasted so long Callum figured Ezra had gone back to sleep. "How come?" Or not.

"What?" Perhaps if he stalled long enough, Ezra would fall back to sleep and forget about it?

"Why do you need to meet Siobhan in the middle of the night?"

"Early morning."

"Why?" Ezra opened on sleepy eye and tilted his head to look at Callum.

"Because we might have a lead." Damn Ezra's persistence. That was more than Callum had intended to give up.

"It couldn't wait?"

"Not this one."

"Why not?"

"Go to sleep, Ez. We'll talk in the morning." Not that Callum truly expected that to work, but it was worth a shot.

Ezra grumbled and half sat up in bed, looking at Callum

accusingly. "You smell worried," he said. "Would you be sleeping if there were a worried alpha in the room with you? No. So just tell me what's going on, and then I'll go back to sleep. Promise."

Callum had his doubts about that, too, but he figured he could always leverage Ezra into keeping the promise afterward. Besides, Ezra had a point—there was no way he'd be able to sleep until Callum reassured him. "Siobhan called about an attack up in Butte."

Frowning, Ezra wiped at his eyes. "But it's not the full moon."

"The attacker was in human form," Callum admitted. At Ezra's obvious distress, Callum put a hand on his cheek. "They caught him, but he's very sick, Ezra. I have to go in and interview him as soon as possible in case"—*he dies*—"his condition deteriorates."

Ezra calmed a little, soothed by the touch. Callum was, too, which wasn't surprising, just… different. He wasn't used to being so affected by the presence and emotions of another. "What happened to the person he attacked? Are they okay?"

Fuck. Callum wouldn't lie to him. "He's dead," he said softly. Then he thought about what Siobhan had told him and added with a slight wince, "Which is probably for the best."

When Ezra swallowed, Callum felt it against the heel of his hand. "Oh." He took a deep breath. "So you have to go, huh?" It wasn't really a question.

"Sorry," Callum told him. When all of this was over, he and Ezra were going to take some time away, find a cozy little spot where no one would bother them for a week. It sounded distressingly like a honeymoon, though of course gay marriage wasn't legal in Montana. Hell, if Senator Feyen had had his way three years ago when the vote had come up, Callum could have been arrested for the things he got up to in the privacy of his bedroom.

If Ezra had the slightest notion how Callum's thoughts had wandered, he didn't show it. "'S'okay," he murmured. "You have an hour before you have to leave?"

Callum nodded.

Ezra flopped back down to the mattress. "Good," he said, the full measure of sleepiness back in his voice. "You can make yourself useful as my personal hot water bottle until then."

Despite the gravity of the situation, Callum felt a smile tug at his lips as he settled down to comply, spooning with his lover, sliding his arm around Ezra's waist. He rubbed his nose over Ezra's nape, inhaling his scent. Ezra's fingers interlaced with his own. Half a minute later, Ezra was asleep.

WHEN his hour was up, Callum somehow talked himself into leaving his bed. The internal struggle was only outweighed by the physical one required to untangle himself from Ezra's sleep-heavy body. Ezra's cuddling was… persistent. Still, Callum had escaped and left his hot-water-bottle status to be here, standing with Siobhan and Dannika in a quiet building, waiting for a prison transfer to arrive.

God, another one. He wondered if this one would be in better or worse shape than Teller. He wondered if he would be sane at all, if he would have descended completely into madness, or worse, if he was completely rational.

"Do we know who this lycan is?"

Siobhan shook her head. "Not yet, no. He hasn't been terribly coherent. Though he hasn't been sober since the police got him—tranquilizers make any sort of interrogation fruitless." Right, he had forgotten about that. Siobhan gave a sigh. "Hopefully we'll be able to get his name out of him, or at least enough information to figure out who he is. Should be fairly easy if someone is missing him."

And if they're not? Callum didn't have the heart to ask it aloud. Because if no one was missing the lycan, then it meant he was a loner, or worse, that his pack had failed him. That his *pack* had let him be taken and then done nothing about it. The idea was enough to turn Callum's stomach, and he didn't want to have to share it with anyone else.

Dannika, who was silently huddled around a steaming cup of coffee, made a small noise. "No point in wondering and guessing—we'll get our answers when he gets here." Figured that the one who was so clearly not a morning person would be the most pragmatic about things.

"Will Jax not be joining us?" Siobhan asked.

"No." Callum eyed the woman. Jax had been the one to suggest that Callum act as primary contact for the FBI. She would focus on pack issues, trusting that Callum would inform her of any major changes and bring her into important discussions. *You're the one they need to talk to about the science, anyway,* she had pointed out, and Callum hadn't really wanted to argue. He didn't think he could be gracious or wise enough to wait for news secondhand. "I decided to let her sleep. She'll know everything I know in the morning. It's not like having us both here will make a difference."

Siobhan nodded. "I guess."

"The only purpose her being here would serve would be that we'd both be tired in the morning. That doesn't seem very productive to me."

Dannika shrugged. "Just so long as she doesn't get mad at us in the morning."

Callum had been ready to argue the point further—it had been Jax's idea!—when Siobhan's phone gave a loud trilling ring. Callum and Dannika both jumped and then glared at Siobhan, who simply reached into her pocket to fish it out. How she had remained unperturbed by the loud noise, Callum didn't know.

"They're five minutes away," she said when she hung up. She slipped the phone back into her pocket.

Dannika tossed her empty cup into a nearby trash bin. "Goody." Her voice was dry as desert sand. "Well, let's go meet the cavalry and their newest outlaw."

Callum noted the unhappy curl to Siobhan's lips and was grateful when she didn't say anything. He really didn't want to have to deal with two women bickering over tactful behavior at five in the morning when his stomach was tied in knots at the prospect of meeting this lycan.

It turned out, though, that the first meeting—or first sighting, rather—wasn't nearly as dramatic as Callum had feared. It helped rather a lot that the other lycan was unconscious. For the time being, Callum wouldn't have to find out how unbalanced the young man was. It was disturbing enough to see his emaciated frame, his dirty body and unwashed hair, his bloody hands and his split knuckles. The kid—and he was a kid, probably younger than Ezra by a few years—was one of the most pitiful sights that Callum had ever seen. The desire to cry and the desire to scream warred within him so violently that Callum was almost grateful; neither impulse could win, and so he managed to hold off both reactions. Instead, he went through the motions of checking the newest inmate in and focused all of his available attention on that.

Then Callum got a good sniff of the man and felt like throwing up.

BY MIDMORNING, Callum was walking back into his house. And straight for the liquor cabinet.

He wasn't unaware of Ezra when he passed him, but he didn't stop to chat. He couldn't. First, before anything else, he needed a drink.

After pulling out a tumbler and a bottle of Jameson, Callum poured himself a finger's worth and tossed it back. He grimaced at the burn but didn't hesitate to pour himself another glass.

"Want to explain what's up with the alcoholic routine?" Ezra asked. Though Callum didn't turn around, he knew the other man was standing in the doorway. In his mind's eye, he could see him, looking as tentative as his voice sounded.

"Bad morning," was all Callum said before he downed the whiskey.

"*Ri-i-ight…*," Ezra said, his disbelief obvious.

More whiskey. "Really bad morning."

"Are you going to tell me—?"

The sound of the front door opening brought Ezra up short. Then Jax was yelling, "Callum, where are you?"

"In here!" he called back. His eyes were trained on the bottle of Jameson. To have another glass or not, that was the question.

"With the whiskey," added Ezra in a dry tone. Callum ignored him.

"Whiskey? You're drinking at 10:24 in the morning now?" When Callum finally turned, it was to see Jax standing in the doorway half a pace behind Ezra, looking baffled.

"Bad—"

"—morning," Ezra finished with him.

"What could possibly—?"

"There was another attack. Siobhan called this morning. This time the victim was killed."

Jax swore. "Is that why…?"

"She called at 3:00 a.m., and he didn't drink then."

Callum felt vaguely embarrassed at Ezra's casual mention of being in bed together. He was grateful that Jax was too preoccupied to say anything.

"So what changed?"

"They found the lycan that did it. He's like Teller, infected with… whatever." ARD, or whatever was causing it. Callum turned and pulled out a second tumbler.

In his peripheral vision, he could see Jax nod. This wasn't entirely unexpected news, all things considered. "So why—?"

"He's a beta," Callum said bluntly.

A sharp inhalation greeted this piece of news. "What—are you sure?"

Callum glanced her way briefly to give her a look and then turned back to the task at hand: filling the second tumbler with a finger—two fingers—of whiskey.

"Fuck, fuck, fuckity-fuck!" Jax crossed the room and snatched the glass from Callum's hand before he could turn all the way around to offer it to her.

When the whiskey was gone, she held it out for more. Callum obliged.

"I don't understand," Ezra said. "Why the whiskey?"

Callum was pretty sure that Jax was giving Ezra the same blank stare that he was.

"It was bad enough thinking, knowing, that one of our own was taking out alphas in such an… inhumane way. But betas? Drugging betas so badly that they go wild? That's beyond sick, it's—it's—"

"What?" Ezra's voice had cooled slightly, but Callum was too upset, and a little bit dizzy from downing so much whiskey so quickly on an empty stomach, to truly take note.

"It's barbaric," he finished.

"Twisted," Jax added, her voice filled with anger.

"Disgusting," Callum finished.

"I see. So, hurting an alpha is bad, but going after poor helpless betas is worse. How silly of me not to realize that one is a greater crime than the other!" Ezra threw his hands in air, clearly annoyed.

"Are you angry at me?" He turned to Jax. "Is he angry? Are you seriously angry at me?"

The crossed arms and jutting chin both said yes.

"Why are you angry at me?"

"For—for—acting like a stupid caveman! Like it makes any difference that this one was a beta!"

"Of course it makes a difference!"

"I don't see why it should! Lycans are lycans! They're blood and they're being tortured. Who the fuck cares if it's alphas or betas?"

"We care!"

"I can see that! I don't see why—"

"Because we're supposed to protect you! You're ours to take care of!" Callum glared at Ezra. "And that anyone could just... just ignore that—that instinct.... God, it's unimaginable."

Ezra's lips were still pursed tight, but he unclenched them to say, "Explain."

"You don't know what it's like," Jax said, speaking once again now that Ezra and Callum were no longer shouting. "It's pure instinct, the desire to protect."

"It's like, every beta you meet has this...." Callum searched for the right word. "Scent—aura?—that speaks to your gut, to your bones, and demands one thing: protect me, keep me safe."

"But we don't know for sure that whoever's doing this is an alpha," Ezra pointed out. "Or even a lycan."

It was a valid point, but it didn't make Callum feel any better.

"Alphas don't just protect because we're taught to," Jax pointed out. "We do it because we need to."

Harming a beta that way was nearly unfathomable to Callum. He didn't understand how anyone could do it, even a human. "We do it because we don't know any other way to be," Callum whispered to his empty whiskey glass.

Then a hand was taking the glass from his and placing it on the cabinet. Then it and another wrapped around his face. Ezra tilted Callum's head up so that they were looking at each other. Then they were hugging, and Callum was holding on tight. He buried his face in Ezra's neck and breathed in deep, capturing his scent. He gave in to the urge to hug his lover tight, like he'd wanted to do ever since they'd brought that beta into the NFWS hospital.

He was young. Young, pretty, and submissive. And made crazy by the hormone imbalance. God, it had been like Teller all over again. Not in his behavior—the beta had been acting like he was high on designer drugs and filled with too much testosterone, while Teller was clearly suffering from PTSD—but everything else had felt so much the same. The sick lycan covered in blood, the madness in his eyes, the knowledge of what this young man had done because of something that someone had pumped through his veins. And the feelings of dread and the weariness that came along with all that knowledge. It had put Callum's teeth on edge, kept sending him back to that morning they had found Teller and to the morning Ezra had seen him. He had wanted nothing more than to come home and hold Ezra tight.

But then he had seen him and had been filled with such rage at the bastard who had done this, had done this to men who were barely more than boys, men who were as vulnerable as Ezra, that he had known he couldn't touch Ezra just yet. Not until he had dulled some of the emotion with whiskey.

Strong fingers stroked the back of his head and neck, and Callum let out a grateful sigh. Fuck, that felt good.

"We'll find him, and we'll stop him," Ezra was whispering softly in his ear, and Callum wonder how long Ezra had been talking to him. How long he had been promising that they would put a stop to this nightmare.

"We're going to win this one, Callum. We'll keep him from hurting anyone else."

Fuck it, it didn't matter how long Ezra had believed in him. What mattered was that he did.

ALL things considered, Ezra couldn't say that he was overly thrilled to see Dannika and Siobhan again. Knowing where they had been, and given the news they had recently delivered, he wasn't exactly eager to hear what they had to say. Especially once he got a good look at their drawn faces.

Still, not wanting to hear whatever bad news they had wasn't a good enough reason to slam the door in their faces, so he let both women in.

He turned and led both women into the dining room, where they had been settling down to lunch.

"Just in time for lunch." If Ezra was a more cynical person, he might have suspected that Dannika had timed their visit on purpose.

They ate in a companionable silence—the agents seemed unwilling to broach the subject of their visit, and for a while, their hosts said nothing on the matter.

The inevitable couldn't be put off for long, though, and after everyone had had a chance to get some food in them, Callum cleared his throat. "How'd the conversation with our John Doe go?" Despite their efforts, the young beta who had been found in Butte had remained unidentified.

"I think you were right about the hormone making them unbalanced." Dannika rubbed at her forehead.

Siobhan looked similarly strained. "It was as bad as talking to Teller. We couldn't get any sense out of him."

"It's like trying to question a parrot. They'll say a lot, but none of it's very helpful."

Siobhan's mouth twisted sourly. "He kept begging for orders, wanted me to tell him what to do next." She was clearly uncomfortable with the memory. "But when I told him to tell me his name, he couldn't remember and started rambling about needing to be punished for his behavior."

"It would have been kinky if it weren't so pitiful." Dannika grimaced at the sharp disapproving look Siobhan gave her. "Sorry, it just… left a bad taste in my mouth."

"Now that's true. Talking to him was… distressing. Especially knowing why he's so damaged." This was greeted with understanding silence.

"So, you got nothing?" Callum looked so disappointed at the thought that Ezra reached out under the cover of the table and put his hand on the other man's knee.

"Mostly nothing."

Siobhan nodded in agreement with her partner. "Mostly he rambled, but we were able to glean a few things from the rambles." Callum perked up at that. "One, we know that someone's been giving him orders. He kept asking for 'more' even though I hadn't really given him any. Two, his attack on that poor man? It wasn't an accident."

"What?"

Ezra noticed that he wasn't the only one to sit up straighter at that.

"Yeah, we know." Dannika leaned forward to grab an orange and, peeling it, she explained, "Among all the babble, he kept telling us over and over again that he had been good, that he had hurt the man, and why wasn't *he* pleased with him."

"He? He who?" Callum looked eager.

"That's just it. He wouldn't tell us anything about it, and he never gave a name. We tried to get him to implicate Shaw—or anyone else for that matter. Nothing doing. Only ever called him 'he' or 'Master', but sounds like whoever this was told John directly to go after that man. To kill him."

"Like an attack dog." Dannika scowled.

Something curdled unpleasantly in Ezra's stomach. God, how could anyone do this?

"Or an assassin," said Siobhan with a pinched look.

The curdling might just lead to vomiting.

"Assassin?" Callum, as usual, was the one brave enough to break the silence.

"Think about it. The victim was an assistant DA—easy enough to make enemies. And if you were an alpha and wanted to kill people, it would be a handy way of doing it. Betas too high to refuse your orders and the ready excuse of the ARD to cover your tracks."

Dannika gave a nod. "Exactly. If it hadn't been for those kids finding that needle—and it's reasonable to assume that losing that needle was a complete accident—you'd still be thinking it was a natural infection and breakout. So long as people thought as much, you could propagate a series of 'random' attacks, some or all of which were calculated and deliberate to take out enemies."

Callum looked ill. "Damn it all to hell. That's just sick."

Ezra bumped the toe of his shoe against Callum's and offered a half smile when their eyes met. "We'll get him," he whispered, knowing he'd hear. "We will find him and stop him."

Callum tried to smile.

"Still, having a better idea of motive doesn't get us any closer to pointing the finger at Shaw or finding out if someone else is doing this." Dannika looked fairly annoyed by this fact.

Siobhan was wearing a similar frown. "Indeed. We have a better idea for motive, but we still don't know much about who's doing this, only that there is an alpha involved somehow and they probably have something against this Weiman guy. It's anyone's guess if that alpha is actually in charge. It could just be a human who's getting an alpha to issue the orders on their behalf."

Someone had to say it, and Ezra might as well be the one to bite the bullet. "So to sum up, we're really not any further ahead."

In a move that was altogether discouraging, the FBI agents only nodded.

"Well, coffee, anyone? We should take another look at that list." Ezra stood and gathered his plate.

"He's got a point," Dannika admitted. "Siobhan, why don't you go with Ezra and Callum to take another look at that list? Maybe cross-reference it with a list of cases Weiman was prosecuting and see if that turns up any new leads. I'm going to give Mark and Coz a call, see if they've got any new intel for us." Then she, too, marched out of the room—but the only thing in her hand was her cell phone.

"THAT cocksucker!"

The telephone flew across the room. It hit the wall with a *thuck* and left the drywall dented, before falling to the floor with a resounding clang.

The man didn't wait to watch it. He was already pacing away, his body vibrating with anger.

"Vile, inbred whoreson!" He screamed and launched a paperweight. It barely missed the girl cowering in the corner. He wasn't sorry; her incessant whimpering was getting on his nerves.

He turned his back to her and stomped to his desk. Fucking Dawson. The whoreson continued to plague him—and this time was the worst. The fag had called the FBI. The fucking FBI!

"Cocksucking, fudge-packing faggot!"

The lamp was next.

Fifteen minutes later, the man stood panting and disheveled at the center of chaos that had once been his office. The girl was finally quiet. He could finally stop to think.

Smoothing down his suit jacket, he began to consider what he knew. His maid had told him about the phone call that had brought such disappointing news: Dawson had contacted the FBI about some of Davis's subjects. Highly annoying and potentially inconvenient, but now that he had relaxed, he began to consider the other important fact his informant had supplied him with. The FBI agents were *girls*. A tomboy and a dwarf. Thankfully, the FBI couldn't be taking Dawson too seriously if they had sent children to him. No, likely they had sent the girls down to placate Dawson and nothing more.

Still… if the FBI were now aware, if only peripherally, of his plans, it was probably best to step things up. He wanted the he-bitch and he wanted him now.

"You!" He snapped his fingers at the bitch still curled in the corner. "Get up and find me a phone that works!" She stared at him wide-eyed. "Now! I need to make a phone call!" She didn't waste another second.

The he-bitch was an aberration, genetically weak. If he could figure out why he was broken, then he could fix what inbreeding had destroyed: the natural order. Then he could fix all of the unnatural women.

Taking another deep cleansing breath, the man turned to his chair and sat down. Yes, it was definitely time to take Dawson's bitch. He flicked some lint off his pant leg and waited for a phone. He had calls to make.

Chapter Twelve
Let Sleeping Dogs Lie

SO IT turned out that detective work was actually really boring. For one thing, everything took a long time. It wasn't like on *CSI* where they would tap a few keys and get all the answers they needed. Dannika and Siobhan spent a lot of time researching on the computer, as well as calling contacts and doing footwork.

While both women had continued their investigations into Shaw, they had asked Ezra to continue compiling a list of lycans with known science backgrounds and connections. Unfortunately, doing so took a lot of time.

Worse still, there was very little that the rest of them could do other than to provide the occasional insight into various people of interest. Dannika and Siobhan kept telling them to keep going on with their day-to-day lives and let them take care of everything.

Not that Callum or Jax listened to that advice. With the help of Ezra, Wyn, and Blaise, they kept up their own investigations, working in tandem in hopes of breaking the case as soon as possible.

Still, as the days ticked by, it seemed to Ezra that nothing was getting done, that no answers were found, and whoever was doing this was still out there. Still hurting… and killing.

It was frustrating to be stuck in what felt like slow motion just waiting for something to happen. As with most things in life, of course, when things sped up, Ezra wished they hadn't.

EZRA had barely made it to the door when it flung open, smacking into the pile of shoes stacked up behind it and rebounding. Dannika Louis stormed into the house, dropping a pint-sized travel bag by the coat rack and heading straight for the couch. Siobhan followed at a slower pace, though her mood was obviously on a par with Dan's. At least she took her shoes off before she got to the couch.

"Uh," Ezra said to the now-empty doorway. "Won't you come in?"

"Where's Callum?" Dannika asked, ignoring his question.

"It's Sunday. He's at the community center." He'd tried to weasel out of it, saying he was busy, but Wyn wasn't having any of that and had dragged him along anyway. Ezra had only been allowed back to the house to get a sweater. "Did something happen?"

Which was a stupid question—something had *obviously* happened.

Dannika just grunted, but Siobhan sighed and answered him. "Depending on your definition of 'something'." She shook her head. "Malcolm Shaw's not our man."

What? But Ezra had been so sure. "Come on, that dick had to be guilty of something."

"Yeah," Dannika muttered. "Being a greedy sonofabitch."

"Are you actually going to tell me what's going on?" Ezra finally said impatiently.

"You were right that Shaw's doing lycan-related research," Siobhan said.

Ezra sighed. "Okay, I'm dying of curiosity, but if I don't go back to the community center Callum will have my ass."

Dannika smirked. Loudly.

"So I'm going to go get him, and maybe Jax, too, and then you can explain what happened to all of us together," Ezra continued without acknowledging the blush staining his cheeks. "Make yourselves at home," he muttered to himself as he grabbed his coat from the rack and closed the front door behind him.

It didn't take much to get Callum's attention; he looked up from his plate the second Ezra opened the door, and he must have read in Ezra's face that something was up, because he finished listening to Anya's story and then nodded and excused himself. Jax followed.

"What's up?"

"Siobhan and Dannika are back," Ezra said quietly, making sure they wouldn't be overheard. The last thing he needed was to further disrupt the family dinner. That would get him on the shit list with the chefs, and they'd promised to make his favorite next week. "I said I'd come and get you."

His arrival hadn't gone unnoticed—a few pack members had glanced up with Callum, and more still when Callum and Jax had excused themselves from the table. One of the grandmotherly types was smirking knowingly and nudging her neighbor with her elbow. Lucien was, of course, glaring.

"What do you think will cause a bigger commotion?" Jax asked thoughtfully. "Both Alphas leaving the table in the middle of family dinner, or Berta spreading the rumor that you two skipped out for a quickie?"

Ezra blushed. "We could take Blaise instead," he suggested.

Jax tilted her lips up in a teasing smile. "Making sure everyone knows you have a chaperone? That's sweet." Then she sobered. "You want me to get him?"

Sighing, Callum shook his head. "No, that's all right. It's not like the rumor mill isn't already rife with speculation."

"Oh, there's a betting pool," Jax said cheerfully. "All right, you go do your thing. I'll try to smooth things over here without freaking anyone out too much."

Callum gave her a tight smile. "Thanks."

As they put the community center behind them, Ezra glanced to his left. "A betting pool?" he said with some slight trepidation. After all, it was pretty obvious they were already sleeping together.

"I'm supposed to pretend I don't know about it," Callum said as Ezra fell into step beside him. "Let them have their game at my expense. It's traditional."

Right, because that made it okay. "What are the stakes, do you think?"

"Babysitting hours, probably."

"But what are they betting on? We're already, you know." Ezra waved his hands around a bit to illustrate what they were already.

Callum looked uncomfortable.

"What? It can't be that bad."

They stopped on Callum's doorstep, and Callum reached out a hand to hold the door closed when Ezra went for the handle. He lowered his voice, looking anywhere but at Ezra. "They want me to make an honest woman out of you," he finally said.

For a minute Ezra just stared at him. This was going to be another one of those awkward moments unless he magically came up with the right thing to say. "Well," he said at length, "I'm not getting a sex change, so that's off the table."

He didn't get a chance to see Callum's reaction, because Dannika pulled open the door and rushed halfway through it before noticing their presence. "Good, you're here." She grabbed them by the sleeves of their jackets and dragged them into the house. "You need to hear this so we can get dinner. I'm dying for a burger."

Ezra let Dannika shove him down onto the couch. Callum followed at his own pace. "I take it there's been a development," he said drily.

Dannika snorted. "You could say that."

"Why don't we start at the beginning," Siobhan suggested tiredly.

"The beginning is boring."

"The stakeout was a bust," Siobhan began. "Maxwell works out of the university labs, so obviously he's not keeping any test subjects there. And he is there *all the time*."

Dannika put in, "Serious workaholic. If he weren't such a twatwaffle I'd say he needed to get out more, but I see no reason to inflict him on the rest of unsuspecting humanity."

Callum cleared his throat. "Okay, so the stakeout was a bust?"

"Plus this guy hasn't got the mindset to be a criminal mastermind. We watched him for three days and he never made us."

"Maybe that means he actually *is* a criminal mastermind," Ezra pointed out.

Siobhan grimaced. "Trust me, evil masterminds don't normally let you witness their fumbling sexual encounters through their open bedroom windows. It's bad for their image."

Ugh. "Ew." Not a mental image Ezra ever needed. "But I thought you said he was doing lycan-related research?"

"He is." Dannika again. She made a face. "After his disgusting little display we were pretty sure he was just a regular creeper, but we had to make sure in case he knew we bugged the house."

"You bugged the *house*?"

Dannika grinned. "The Patriot Act is a beautiful thing. Anyway, so while he was taking a break from his office, by which I mean he was nailing some bimbo with his pathetic little—"

"Nice, Dan," Siobhan interrupted.

"I broke into his lab," she finished, rolling her eyes. "*Fine*, if I have to leave out the juicy part. Anyway, he's got a freezer full of lycanthrope placenta, which is gross but not really illegal. From his notes, it looks like he's trying to share the natural restorative powers of the moon with those of us who don't howl at it a few days a month. Preferably in an oil-free moisturizer."

"He's making *wrinkle cream*?" Callum said incredulously.

"With *placenta*?" Ezra added, because, double ew. Who wanted to put that on their face?

"On the plus side, he's not turning innocent lycans into homicidal maniacs." Siobhan blew out a breath. "Of course, that means we have no idea who is."

WHAT followed was another exhausting and fruitless few days of reading through the piles of information they had on dozens of lycans. And thanks to Dannika's ever-so-helpful FBI analyst girlfriend, they had a bit more information to work with. Even more background information on several of the suspects that had yet to be cleared.

Yawning around his toothbrush, Ezra tried to unknot the muscles of his back with a few tired rolls of his shoulders. Damn, he hadn't spent so much time hunched over a computer and reams of printouts since college.

Ezra leaned over to spit out the mint foam and just managed it before he was overtaken by another yawn. He had forgotten how tiring *thinking* could be. In his post-MIT days, he had had little occasion to pull such marathon sessions and so had forgotten that living on computer radiation and coffee for several hours was an unpleasant experience.

With a final rinse and spit, Ezra left the bathroom and headed for the bedroom.

"Tell her thanks again, and that I'm sorry. I know her job is easier when both of us are around to listen to her lawyer talk." Callum walked into the bedroom, phone against his ear while he talked. With no shirt.

Very slow elevator-eyes were the only correct response to the situation at hand. Callum had apparently changed into his pajama pants to head downstairs to lock the front door. And to make a phone call.

"I know she understands why... just. Look, I really appreciate that both of you took up the slack today. I haven't been around to do my job much lately and.... Yeah. Yeah, I know. Just... tell her anyway," Callum insisted before saying his goodbyes. His gaze was searching out Ezra's even before he turned off the phone. "Jax says hi." Then he was tossing the phone aside and walking toward Ezra.

"How is she?" Ezra took a step forward.

"Fine."

The embrace that followed was welcome. Two arms twined around his body, and Ezra responded in kind. He placed his head on Callum's shoulder and shivered when the other man let out a long sigh that brushed across his neck.

"*Her* day went well, at least."

"Hm, hey. Our day was productive." His voice was somewhat muffled, pressed as he was into Callum's neck, but Ezra didn't worry about it. Callum would understand.

"No it wasn't. All we did was read."

"We researched, which needs to be done to get answers. Just... not everything you read is going to be helpful in the end, but that's the nature of research, Mr. Scientist."

There was another deep sigh that tickled and left goose bumps in its wake. This one sounded more relaxed than the previous. "That's Dr. Scientist to you."

"Right, sorry. Forgot." The skin that stretched from Callum's ear to his shoulder was smooth and bare—and temptingly within reach. So Ezra kissed it.

His lover didn't object. Instead, he lifted one hand and placed it over the nape of Ezra's neck. Strong fingers began to massage the muscle.

Ezra rested his forehead against Callum's shoulder. "Mmm, that feels heavenly—ouch!"

"What?" Callum sounded alarmed.

"Nothing urgent, just a knot in the muscle." Ezra ended with a moan as Callum began to knead the muscles of his neck with strong fingers. Knotted-up neck muscles were something he'd learned to deal with after years in front of a computer screen.

"Jesus, you're tight."

Ezra didn't *say* anything, but Callum seemed to know what he was thinking anyway.

"Not like that."

"You disparaging my sex appeal?"

"I'd never dream of it. Seriously, your neck is all knot. Want a massage?"

"Mmm, yes please." Wait. What? Callum gave out massages? Since when? And why hadn't Ezra gotten one before? "Why haven't I had one before?" Ezra pulled back to look Callum in the eye.

Callum just shrugged. "I haven't offered before?"

"Right." Ezra pulled out of Callum's arms and backed away, stripping off his shirt. He crawled onto the bed and flopped down onto his front. "Get your hands over here, loverboy, and start rubbing."

A snort came from the left, Ezra turned his head to see that Callum had moved and was now rummaging in his bedside table. "How romantic."

"Hey, you lost out on romance when you failed to mention, for *over* a month, that you give massages. That is cruelty, my friend. I'm pretty sure there's a clause in the Geneva Convention."

Callum found what he was looking for and shut the drawer with a snick. Then he climbed onto the bed, straddling Ezra's hips and opening up a jar of... massage oil, apparently.

"*Fuuuuuck,*" Ezra groaned as Callum began by attacking the large knots in his back.

It turned out that Callum was really fucking good at this.

Several minutes later, Ezra was a puddle of goo, purring at the back rub that was now on offer. Now that his muscles were loose, Callum was simply stroking the skin.

Ezra wasn't sure when it happened, but at some point after Callum had started those soothing touches, Ezra's limp body began to stiffen again, this time because Callum was straddling his body and sitting on his ass. The strokes didn't change, but they were suddenly leaving tingles and making Ezra shiver. The moans that came out then were deeper and tinged with lust.

Surely Callum, with his strong nose and sharp ears, couldn't miss Ezra's building arousal—though Ezra figured anyone, lycan or human, would know. Certainly if Callum had been ignorant before, he wasn't after Ezra responded to a brush of fingers across the small of his back by arching upward and grinding his ass into Callum's crotch.

"Ezra, was there something you wanted?" Callum's voice was deep but amused.

"What, you don't give out happy endings?" Ezra managed to joke even if it was a little breathy.

That got laughter from the other man. "Well, depends on the customer. Jax usually doesn't merit more than a shoulder rub."

"Callum," Ezra huffed, "don't mention Jax in bed."

"Noted. So, happy ending, huh? Like… this?" The statement was punctuated with Callum slipping fingers below the waist of Ezra's pants and shifting the elastic downward.

"Hmm." Ezra just parted his legs in response.

Callum moved to settle between Ezra's legs and pulled the pants all the way down and off. *He's still dressed,* Ezra thought muzzily as Callum settled himself between his knees. The thought was quickly chased away by the wet lips that began kissing their way across Ezra's back. Which felt amazing. The oil was warm and slick between them…. Wait, the oil?

"Oil?" Ezra managed to get out.

"It's edible," Callum murmured into the small of his back.

"Edible? Schemer."

"Maybe. But how could I not with this ass?" Callum ended the sentence with a playful bite to the flesh.

"Hey." The grumble was halfhearted and muted by the pillow.

"It's a compliment. This is the finest ass I've had the pleasure of fondling"—he gave both cheeks a firm grope—"fucking"—here his fingers moved down to brush over Ezra's hole—"and tasting." And Callum shifted down and, parting the cheeks with his well-placed fingers, put his mouth right on Ezra. His tongue gave a long lick up, and Ezra let out a loud groan in response.

Fuck, not a lot of guys would do this, and it had been ages since someone had last offered to eat him out.

And Callum was really fucking good at it too.

He started with teasing licks that quickly gained force, and soon he was alternating between those light touches and firmer strokes and, eventually, pushing inside. At the feel of the warm muscle first entering, Ezra let out a loud desperate moan.

God damn. His fingers spasmed and curled in the sheets, and he lifted his hips to push back. Dimly, he wondered what Callum thought of him—one massage and then the application of a tongue, and Ezra was moaning like a whore—but he was much too occupied with thoughts of *guh* and *more* and *yes* to truly worry.

Just when Ezra was contemplating the idea of rubbing off on the sheets—he just needed to come—that wonderful maddening tongue pulled away. Ezra whimpered.

"Shh," Callum crooned, crawling up the bed. And then flipping Ezra over onto his back.

Ezra swallowed the yelp of surprise at the manhandling—fuck, that was hot—but let out the moan that followed when Callum leaned in for a kiss. There was a unique taste to Callum's mouth, and Ezra let out another moan. God, that was filthy in the best possible way.

Ezra curled both hands around Callum's head and kissed back hungrily, sliding his tongue into Callum's mouth and sucking on his tongue when it chased Ezra's back. The moments seemed to bleed together, one sliding into the next, as both men tried to take their fill of kisses and touches. Though Ezra was sure that there could never be *enough*. Desperate, he pushed at the waistband of Callum's pajama pants.

"Fuck!" The feel of their naked bodies pressed together was enough to make Ezra's full body shudder. "C-Callum. Fuck me. Please!" To drive home the point, Ezra wrapped his legs around Callum's hips and arched upward. A hard cock slipped down between his cheeks, the wet head slipping over the slack muscle of Ezra's opening. He was still licked open and loose. Ezra whimpered. "Callum, now?"

"Damn, fuck. Soon, Ez, soon."

Ezra started to groan in frustration, but the groan changed direction when wet fingers pushed into him.

One, two…. The fingers were scissoring, stretching the muscles and pushing in more and more lube, and Callum was whispering in his ear about how hot Ezra was, how tight and perfect, and how Callum was going to fuck him.

The fingers pulled out and Ezra let out a noise of pure frustration. It turned into a happy moan, though, when Callum slid his tongue back into Ezra's mouth for another wet and dirty kiss.

Then the world was tilting and rolling and Ezra was on top of Callum, staring down. "Wha—?"

"I want you to ride me."

There was only one response to that demand in that voice: Ezra whimpered again.

Callum's hands found Ezra's waist, and he pulled up and guided Ezra into straddling his hips. Callum's cock was somehow already wrapped and slick, waiting for Ezra.

With Callum's help—Ezra's muscles were so loose from the massage and the lust it was honestly a wonder he didn't fall on his face—Ezra managed to get himself hovering over Callum's body. He wrapped a shaking hand around the hard flesh and began guiding them together.

After that utterly fantastic rim job, Ezra's hole didn't even try to deny Callum. It fluttered open around the tip, and Ezra slid down Callum's cock, moaning like a whore again, while Callum gave a groan and his fingers clenched around Ezra's hips.

When all of Callum was sheathed inside him, Ezra paused to pant and marvel again at how good it felt. Stuffed so full and aching, Ezra clenched around the hot flesh just because he could, wanting to really feel it.

"Fuck! Ezra!" Callum's hands clenched hard again, and he bucked his hips upward. Ezra followed the movement up and then began to ride.

Callum was a genius! Ezra needed to do this more often. Hands braced on Callum's chest, he rose again and watched Callum's face as he slammed back down. Being able to control the pace and angle, being able to see the pleasure move across Callum's face, was amazing.

But as amazing as it was, it couldn't last forever. All too soon, Ezra's rhythm was faltering, his thighs were trembling, the muscles unpracticed (all the more reason to do this again!), and despite the fact that Callum had hardly touched him, Ezra's climax was approaching.

When Ezra slipped and fell forward onto Callum's chest, slamming his hips back down on Callum's cock, Callum grunted and shifted his grip to Ezra's arms before rolling them back again.

Ezra was on his back once more, his legs wrapped around Callum's hips. There was a brief pause as Callum got himself balanced, and then he started fucking.

His tempo and force were brutal. Callum thrust hard and fast now as both men raced to the finish.

Ezra found new energy and soon was writhing around, gripping at the sheets, Callum, and himself; his climax was so close. "Callum, Callum, please. Oh please, I'm gonna—I need—more!"

When Callum whispered, "That's it, touch yourself" and then, "Come," that was it.

Sound faded out, fireworks exploded, and Ezra touched a live wire.

When he came down, Callum was still hard, shifting his hips slightly, waiting. "There you are," he said when their eyes met, and then he was thrusting again, short, hard strokes.

Still buzzing, Ezra wrapped his arms around Callum's shoulders and moaned. "Yeah, yeah, fuck me. Come in me," he encouraged. Callum did just that, shaking and moaning Ezra's name.

Then Callum was shifting out and off of him, and Ezra sighed a little at the loss.

As Callum left the bed to discard the condom, Ezra lay sweating, chest heaving. *Wow.* He was going to need a few more minutes to recover from that, and not only because of all the pheromones and hormones and sex smells lighting up his amygdala. The visual—Callum's naked backside retreating down the hallway into his bathroom for a clean damp washcloth—wasn't anything to sneeze at either. The effort of holding his head at a funny angle just to watch, however... well, it *would* have been worth it if Ezra hadn't known Callum was going to come back to bed and be naked beside him, where he could experience it with his skin and not just his eyes. So Ezra let his head flop down, too, arching his neck back into the pillows and stretching as the earthy night air from the open window cooled his overheated body.

Half a second later, his eyes drifted shut. It was bad form to fall asleep after sex, but probably it wasn't so bad if you were already living together. Besides, he knew from experience that Callum would probably wake him up in the middle of the night so they could have sex *again*—

Ezra's train of thought screeched to a halt.

It was November. They hadn't left the window open.

Ezra sat bolt upright in bed, his mouth already opening to call for Callum, but by the time he caught the hint of menace and disgust over the heavy scents of sweat and come, it was too late. Someone clamped a hand over his mouth and jerked his head backward.

Ezra had seen enough thrillers to know not to breathe in, that if he inhaled, the chloroform in the cloth covering his nostrils would knock him out. Panicked, Ezra held his breath. Shit. Shit! What should he do? Running on instinct and adrenaline, he lashed out. One of his hands knocked against something sharp, but his foot caught the softness of a belly, and he was rewarded by a *whoof* of air from one of his assailants.

Not loud enough. Callum would never hear that, not two rooms down with the water running. Ezra had maybe twenty seconds to make a lot of noise without opening his mouth, without needing to breathe. Otherwise… otherwise he was in big trouble. The kind he might not live to tell about.

With renewed determination, Ezra lashed out again. If he could unbalance one of the men holding him, maybe knock over the lamp on the bedside table, Callum would come running, and then, if these goons had any sense, they'd scram. But instead he felt the pinch of a needle piercing the skin of his bare upper arm. The pain made him gasp, and the sickly sweet stench of the chloroform invaded his nostrils again. Black spots swam in front of his eyes, and his body grew heavy. His last thought before he lost consciousness was to hope they weren't going after Callum next.

IT WAS the feel of Ezra's cum pressed between their two stomachs that prompted Callum into separating their bodies and heading for the bathroom. He pressed one last kiss to the underside of Ezra's jaw and then untangled their limbs.

On the way to the bathroom, he stretched languorously. Damn, he felt good. He always felt good after sex with Ezra, relaxed and reenergized, no matter how bad the day had been before that.

In the bathroom, he turned on the tap and waited for the water to warm before he ran a cloth in the water. Then the sound of the rushing water reminded him of his bladder, which was suddenly uncomfortably full.

After shutting off the water, he relieved himself and then washed his hands before finally wetting the cloth.

He was on his way back to the bedroom when the first smells hit him. He could smell strangers in his home, the scent of the evening air, but mostly the sharp, vile stench of Ezra's terror. Callum ran, the cloth forgotten on the ground.

Adrenaline filled his body. His strides were long as he thundered down the hall and into his bedroom. It was empty of people—no Ezra or the strangers he could still smell. The only sign of anyone having been there was the open balcony windows. The doors were open, the drapes fluttering in the frigid evening breeze. They had taken Ezra right out of bed and pulled him naked out the window and into the night.

All this registered with Callum in the few seconds it took for him to cross the room in a galloping stride, heading for the balcony. He didn't stop to think, just rushed outside. With one leap, he vaulted up to the balcony rail and then pushed off. He fell down the two stories and landed hard but steady on all fours in the grass. After pushing himself up, he ran after the lingering scent of Ezra's fear.

His nose took him around the house to the street. There was a van just pulling away.

"Augh!" Callum gave a shout and put on an extra burst of speed to get to the van. But it was already accelerating too fast—soon it would round the corner and be gone from view. Desperate, he took in the license plate, repeating the numbers to himself as the car disappeared from sight.

The car that had a naked, frightened Ezra in it.

Tremendous rage filled him, and Callum let out a yell of frustration.

The human part of Callum's brain tried to calm the wolf instincts enough so he could think. Taking several harsh breaths, Callum considered. He could not simply run after the van like the wolf wanted. The wolf demanded that Callum chase down the strangers that had taken his mate, but it would do little good, even if he went for his car.

By the time he got around the corner, the van would be gone. No, he needed to think about this like a human.

"*Callum?*" That was Jax. He looked to find her clad in pajamas, rushing down her front lawn and toward him. "What's going on?"

"They took Ezra!"

"What?" She was close enough now that he could see the shock painted across her face.

"They came into our bedroom and took him!" Callum was still panting.

"Who?"

"I don't know!" he shouted, loudly and in her face.

"Don't yell at me, I didn't take him!" They stood, toe to toe, breathing harshly in each other's face. "And this doesn't do us any good."

Fuck. She was right. He wasn't really mad at her anyway; it just felt good to yell.

"Look, let's go inside. I'll call Dannika and Siobhan, and you can put some clothes on."

It was then that Callum realized that he was naked. "Oh. Right." There was a tittering, awkward laugh, and Callum looked up to realize that they had an audience. One that was growing.

He felt a vague sense of embarrassment at having been seen naked and fuming by so many people, but he was too worried about Ezra to truly feel it.

With a sharp nod, he turned and headed into his house. He could hear Jax telling the others that they should go back to bed, that they'd get an update in the morning when she knew more.

Callum headed straight up to his room to pull on a pair of pants and a T-shirt. Then he was bounding back down the stairs, relieved to find Jax already on the phone.

"He doesn't know who it was, just that someone took him. Well, they had to have been fast about it. Callum wasn't wearing any clothes, so he probably hadn't left Ezra alone for long." There was a pause. "I found him naked in the street, yelling out his frustrations."

Rolling his eyes and biting back his frustration at the time Jax was losing, Callum held a hand out for the phone.

"Wait, he wants to tell you something." *Dannika,* Jax mouthed at him as she handed over the phone.

"Dannika? I got a license plate." He rattled it off before adding, "It was a large van, black."

"Right, just a sec...." He could hear her passing the information on to Siobhan. "So I'm going to hang up now so Siobhan and I can get clothes on and head over. In the meantime, that search on the plate will run. We should have some answers by the time we get there."

EZRA awoke to darkness and pain and the gag-inducing stench of fear. He was bound hand and foot, and when he struggled, he found that his wrists and ankles had been tied together. He was lying naked on his side on an industrial-style concrete floor. Someone had stuffed a gag in his mouth, and he'd been out for long enough that his lips were cracking from dehydration.

Making a promise to himself not to panic, Ezra squinted into the dark and squirmed around a little, trying to discover more about his environment. By shifting his weight to his chest and inching his legs up, he could sort of worm around a little—not that there was much to see. When his eyes adjusted, he could make out more concrete (the wall to one side), some industrial-looking fencing fashioning a sort of cage on three sides, and best of all, a recessed drain in the floor. Ezra's nose told him that was where the stench was coming from.

He was doing remarkably well on the no-panicking front until someone screamed—a long, terrified, blood-curdling scream that made Ezra want to inch his way into a corner where he could have something against his back, so that at least he knew nothing would come for him from that direction. But before he could do anything of the sort, the lights came on, blinding him with their sudden intensity. The door to his cage screeched open, and a rough hand reached down and clamped around his upper arm.

It fucking hurt, but Ezra tried to squirm away anyway. If they thought he was going to go easy, they had another thought coming. Then a sinister sort of feeling came over him, and he jerked his head back. Fuck, those were alpha signal pheromones, no two ways about it—strong ones too. And they came with a compulsion: "Be still."

Ezra had a split second to decide: resist, or keep his cards close to

194 | Ashlyn Kane & Morgan James

the chest and maybe have the element of surprise later. Gritting his teeth, he froze, trying to convey with his facial expression what utter pieces of cat excrement he thought these assholes were.

He recognized the scent before a hand fisted in his hair and twisted his head around. "I should've known," he spat.

Darius Maulsby sneered down at him over the shoulder of the meathead who was giving Ezra whiplash.

Chapter Thirteen
Hair of the Dog...

BY 8:00 a.m., they had to admit that they had nothing.

The van had been reported stolen over a month ago. The license plate that Callum had read had indeed been registered to a large black van. The van had been owned by a small catering company based out of Greybull, Wyoming, of all places. The company, which provided food and dinner service for small gatherings, had used the van to move food and utensils from one kitchen to another for the first three years of its life until it had been lifted from a church parking lot during a wedding. A police report had been filed and the insurance company had paid for a new van. No one knew who had been in possession of the van for the last forty-three days.

"Damn it!" Callum turned away from Blaise and the four women who were settled around Jax's kitchen table. Callum's house had been declared off-limits by Siobhan and Dannika as soon as they realized that Callum and Jax were traipsing all over a crime scene, so they had relocated to Jax's home and had been joined by Wyn and Blaise.

Callum scrubbed his hands over his face and gave a frustrated sigh. He wished that he could go home, be surrounded by familiar calming things, at least. But even if he broke the embargo to go across the street, it would only be to join the local police who were now going through his home looking for forensic evidence. Siobhan had called them in, not wanting to wait for the FBI to fly out from Salt Lake.

"We'll find him," said a soft, trembling voice. Callum didn't turn to look at Wyn. "We'll find him. We have to." There was a certainty to her voice, despite its shaking, that made Callum's chest ache.

They had nothing. Their only suspect and true line of investigation had gone bust only a day before Ezra was taken, and their only new lead had been a dead end. They had nothing to tell them who had taken Ezra or why, and yet Wyn believed that they would find Ezra, if only because she could not conceive of them failing. And that quiet, if desperate, hope was almost enough to break Callum's heart.

"We have nothing."

"So we keep looking. We keep looking until we find something. Because you are going to find him, Callum. You are going to find my best friend, and you are going to bring him back to us!" Wyn's voice had been rising in pitch and volume until it finally cracked and gave out on her. The broken sound of the "us" seemed to echo and linger in the kitchen.

Even with his back turned, Callum could hear the sound of Wyn sobbing and of Blaise taking her in his arms.

Callum planted his hands on his hips and bit his lip, willing the tears not to fall. He was not going to cry. He couldn't cry right now. Because Wyn was right: right now, he needed to find answers, needed to find a lead, so that he could find Ezra.

Swallowing hard, Callum blinked several times to chase away the tears. Then he turned back to his companions. Releasing a long breath, he said, "Right. If what we have doesn't tell us enough, then let's find more. The only person who has reason to come after Ezra or me is whoever it is behind these attacks. So let's go back to that—our first suspect didn't do it, so let's find another suspect."

Wyn was right: he could do this. He *would* do this. Because the alternative was unthinkable.

EZRA gritted his teeth as the meathead shoved him down into the cold metal chair. The whole room reeked of a cornucopia of chemicals: bleach, maybe formaldehyde, and something sweet-sour that crawled up his nose and down his throat. Underneath it all the stink of fear and sweat and blood and piss and hatred made Ezra want to gag.

The hired muscle bound him to the chair, first with a leather strap around his neck, then canvas ones across his waist, wrists, ankles. Over his shoulder, Ezra could see Darius and a man—not a lycan; Ezra was inexperienced, but even he could tell that much—stood supervising, well out of Ezra's spitting range should he attempt the only method of resistance still available to him.

By this time Ezra was well beyond terrified and comfortably detached. It allowed him significantly more freedom than the cowering in blind terror that was the alternative option. "Callum Dawson's going to kill you, you know."

"Callum Dawson is a pathetic weakling without the sense to lead a flock of brainless geese, never mind a pack," Darius said with a sneer.

Well. Now they were getting somewhere. Right? It wasn't like Ezra could get into any more trouble. He might as well pump the guy for information. "Right," he said. "Because obviously the Missoula pack has been falling apart under his guidance, whereas the Great Falls pack is strong and flourishing despite lacking a female Alpha—"

Darius snarled. "Davis, I want that sample. The sooner we discover the source of this perversion, the sooner we can be rid of him."

The human lackey—Davis, the man in the lab coat—stepped forward and tied a length of rubber tube around Ezra's right bicep. The swab he gave Ezra's forearm was, Ezra felt, hardly even cursory. Then the needle pinched into the flesh of his inner elbow. Ezra tried to focus on the conversation instead. "Perversion?" he echoed, taking a guess. "We call it 'gay' these days. Little more PC."

"Political correctness is a disease of soft-minded liberals force-fed to the rest of us to distract from the blight of moral corruption and the decline of family values."

Something about the words, or the way he said them, rang a warning bell somewhere in the back of Ezra's mind. Davis slid the first vial of blood away and replaced it with a second, though, and Ezra was distracted. "Not the first time you've heard the PC line, I'm guessing," Ezra murmured, transfixed by the sight of his blood filling the sample vial. But neither man seemed to be paying him any attention.

"I want a report on that workup on my desk first thing," Darius snapped.

Davis never looked up from taking Ezra's blood. "Yes, sir."

"CALLUM!"

When Siobhan shouted his name, he was in the kitchen making coffee and something to eat. He had been trying to put some normalcy, some calm routine behavior into the obsessive mess that his day had become. It had been almost a full twenty-four hours since Ezra had been taken, and their small group had spent the entire day searching through the information, trying to find some sort of connection that made sense. Unfortunately, very little did.

So Callum had decided to take a break from staring at spreadsheets and lists, at computer screens and printouts, and to find himself something to eat and drink. Some caffeine. Callum wasn't sure how long it had been since he'd last slept—not since the night before Ezra had been taken—but he did know that he wouldn't get any now even if he tried. His brain just wouldn't shut up long enough for him to actually sleep. He was sure of it.

When Siobhan called, Callum was standing in front of the coffeemaker, trying to remember if the machine needed anything more than coffee grounds and water. It was just possible that he had zoned out. He jumped to attention at his name, though, and was halfway to her before he registered the desire to move. "What?"

"The van!" Siobhan was grinning with a ferocious, satisfied gleam in her eye. For a moment, Callum could picture her as a wolf.

"The van?" Callum knew he was a little overtired, but he was pretty sure that they had stopped looking into the van hours ago.

But Siobhan was nodding. "Yes. I started tracking the owners. It took me forever! See, the catering company, Motor Mouth, was a subsidiary, and the company that owns it is owned by another. Anyway, I had to go through several different companies before I finally got to the head."

Callum was ready to pounce on it, to demand, "And? Who is it!" when he was interrupted by Dannika.

"Who the hell buries their ownership of a catering company?"

Callum really didn't care about why the company was being hidden; he just wanted to know who was doing the hiding. The angry clench of his jaw and the hard curl of his fingers were uncontrollable.

"I know! It's so weird." Siobhan nodded enthusiastically. "At least until you create a full web of the companies and their links. Motor Mouth is just one of many companies he owns in Greybull and the rest of Wyoming, Montana, and Idaho."

Jax let out a long whistle. "Sounds like this guy's got his fingers everywhere."

"Oh, his claws are dug in deep. Whoever does his accounting is a genius. So are his lawyers. I wouldn't have been able to make the links between most of these companies if it wasn't for Coz's help. Seriously, this guy brings new meaning to the phrase 'silent partner'. Take this bookstore in Idaho—the only reason we're suspicious of it is because he owns the building, and the rent that he charges rises and falls with the store's profits. Oh, the growth is all masked as additional fees for, like, repairs and stuff, but it's totally bonuses being paid on up the chain."

"Well, fuck. Why on earth...?"

Siobhan shrugged. "Who knows? Building an empire, making money...."

It was then that Callum finally managed to get over his rage—seriously, why the hell were they dawdling?—enough to say, "Who. Is. It?"

Siobhan turned to him with a fire in her eyes and finally told him.

"Maulsby. Darius Maulsby."

BETWEEN the darkness, the cages, and the smell, the warehouse was more like death row at an animal shelter than anything else. From the sounds of things, he thought there were maybe six or seven people stuck in there with him. Everyone he could see was naked, and two or three of them were covered in blood and bruises and other things Ezra didn't want to think about but that he couldn't quite put out of his mind. He'd been a little dizzy when they'd finally finished with him in the lab room, but he thought he remembered passing guards holding what he hoped were tranquilizer guns.

That must have been several hours ago now, maybe even a day or so, judging by the feeding schedule. At some point a gaunt young woman in a filthy lab coat had come along with a pair of joined stainless steel bowls that she'd pushed jerkily under the bars in the door of Ezra's cage, slopping the water from one into the other beside it. Ezra had been starving already, but he knew dog food when he saw it, and he wasn't *that* hungry. Yet. Though he noticed she didn't stop in front of all of the cages and imagined that he could very well be soon.

Then the room filled with the sound of heavy footfalls from one end of the warehouse, echoing off the bare walls and ceiling. Hearing them, the girl skittered away from the cages and disappeared behind a door at the end of the room.

Ezra scooted back against the wall as the footsteps came closer, and he watched as three men approached the cages across from him.

One raised his arm and pointed one of those maybe-tranquilizer-guns at the door.

It opened, and the other two men went in, dragging out the poor bastard who'd been inside, a lycan with wide, wild eyes and filthy hair and skin. Then the four of them marched out, the guard with the gun bringing up the rear.

Over the next few hours they came for everyone, returning dragging limp bodies that reeked of sweat and blood. Sometimes they took the lycans one at a time, sometimes in pairs. Always Ezra could hear them snarling, raving, the thunder of heavy objects crashing into walls.

Ezra closed his eyes and hummed nursery rhymes at the top of his lungs until his throat was too sore to continue.

The girl in the lab coat came back again, shoving more dog food and water under the bars. The water tasted coppery and abraded his sore throat, but Ezra forced himself to swallow it before crawling back against the wall again, keeping as far from the door as possible.

Maybe if he were very quiet, they would just forget he was there.

THE information on Darius Maulsby was a game-changer. Now that he had somewhere to focus his efforts, Callum was finally able to switch his emotions off and get down to the details. Maybe it was cold, but it was a skill that made him a good Alpha and a good scientist, and it was going to bring Ezra home to him. That was all that mattered.

Darius's pack was based out of Great Falls. Callum spread a battered AAA map out on Jax's kitchen table. With a black Sharpie, he made an X over Great Falls, then another over Missoula, and several more from memory, anywhere they had evidence that Darius had been.

Callum stared at the map for forty-eight seconds. It wasn't helpful. He shoved it off to the side and grabbed a pad of paper Jax had swiped from some hotel chain or another and started making a list instead.

Darius Maulsby. Callum hadn't seen him since the last time Darius had been in town and had paid him the customary courtesy visit. What did Callum really know about him, other than that he was a dick? He had money and liked power. He was misogynistic to the core—God, with the experiments on female alphas and Di lying in a hospital in a coma, Callum couldn't believe he hadn't made the connection earlier. He'd bet dollars to donuts Darius had put her there.

Darius hated Callum, presumably because he'd wanted control of the Missoula pack and Callum had edged him out in the election without contest. Callum tried not to think too hard about that, because that right there was more than enough reason for Darius to go after Ezra, even without his ignorant sneering at male betas.

He was a turned lycan, not born, so there had to be a file on him somewhere; applications and character references. Dannika's analyst friend Coz seemed fairly proficient with computers; maybe she could dig something worthwhile out of it.

There had to be something.

"Hey."

Callum acknowledged Dannika with a nod and a grunt, letting his brain free-associate. There was no telling how many shell companies Darius owned, and any one of them could hold the title to whatever hole they were keeping Ezra in.

"Brought you some coffee."

Okay, that deserved a little eye contact in thanks. Callum had no idea how long he'd been at it, but his eyes suddenly felt like sandpaper. "Thanks."

She set the mug down in front of him. "Anything I can help with?"

He shook his head and wrapped stiff fingers around the mug. "I don't know. Maybe. I might need to borrow your pet geek."

Dannika shifted in obvious discomfort. "She's not a geek."

The sulky defensiveness was kind of adorable. "Has she got us anything else?"

"Actually, that's what I came in here to tell you. Siobhan's printing the reports off now."

Callum drained his mug and grabbed his notes. "Let's go."

Jax had run out of computer paper sometime during the third copy, and the sheets Siobhan handed him had the landscaping layout of someone's house on the back. The font had been condensed to something barely legible in order to squeeze onto the available paper, but Callum wasn't exactly worried about eyestrain at the moment.

"So," Siobhan began, "Darius Maulsby. Like we said before, quite the entrepreneur."

Dannika sat on Jax's coffee table, nodding. From the way she barely bothered glancing at the printout, Callum figured she'd been the one on the horn to Coz—again. "He has at least a dozen major shell companies—we're talking millions of dollars of holdings—and Coz says there's no evidence that he's siphoning pack resources to do it. Their coffers are healthy."

"So where is the money coming from?"

"According to the paper trail Coz tracked down, two years ago Maulsby opened a spending account at a Bank of America branch with a $10,000 cash deposit. Then, over the next several months, he kept making those deposits. He's got over $5,000,000 put away in that account now, and there's another one with $15,000,000 tied up in bonds, also purchased with cash."

"Who carries around that kind of money?" Jax wondered aloud.

"People who don't want it to be traced." Callum clenched his printout tighter in his fist. "What else?"

"One of the companies is called BioGen Inc. On paper, they're a research group looking into the development of drought-resistant crops. But if you dig a little deeper, you discover that the seed company signing their paychecks is just another one of Maulsby's shell companies. This guy's money just goes around and around." Siobhan shrugged and passed the explanation on to Dannika.

"Coz is looking into BioGen's employment records, and so far there's nothing—ghosts. They don't exist. No driver's licenses, no criminal records, no record of employment or income tax filed before 2010, no school transcripts. So she went back a little further and managed to find some newspaper articles. All of the supposed employees died during infancy."

"Maulsby's not his real name," Callum said, thinking aloud. "That's why he came out of nowhere. That's why he opened those accounts with cash."

Dannika nodded in agreement. "Coz ran him too. He's got a thicker background story, but she agrees with you. He isn't who you think he is."

"But why change his identity?" Jax wondered. "What was wrong with whoever he was that he had to start over?"

"And does it matter?" Callum wasn't sure if they were looking for Darius Maulsby or whoever he used to be, but there had to be a way to track down his whereabouts without finding his previous identity.

"What if we go back to the beginning?" Siobhan suggested. "We have Darius Maulsby—"

"And we have a scientific research company," Callum finished, running both hands through his hair in frustration. "So where's the third piece—the scientist. He has to have one, right?"

Jax stood, shoving her hands into her back pockets. "Unless he doesn't. We don't know his real background. Maybe he was a scientist before he became Darius Maulsby."

The table creaked sharply as Dannika sprang to her feet, already digging in her pocket for her cell phone. Two toneless beeps later, it was pressed to her ear as she paced the room. "Hey, Coz. Yeah, I know you're busy. I need another favor." Pause. "Please."

She took a deep, shuddering breath. "Okay. We're looking for a male scientist from the Midwest. Someone specializing in genetics. Maybe somebody with a record or someone who was fired under suspicious circumstances or has been out of work for a while. Okay. Okay. Thanks, Coz. I owe you."

The phone clicked shut. Dannika seemed suddenly self-conscious and small, and Callum noted the exhaustion around her eyes. "She's looking into it."

"Thanks," Callum said quietly. Sometimes it was hard to see past his own grief.

Dannika nodded tiredly, and Callum could actually smell her frustration. Before she could say anything, though, her cell phone started declaring its wish for a—something. Dannika picked up hurriedly and left the room.

Siobhan watched her go with a vaguely bemused expression. "That was fast."

Callum curled his hands into fists helplessly, trying to avoid gritting his teeth, trying not to count the seconds that passed with Ezra in Darius's hands.

Apparently he wasn't as good at turning off his emotions as he thought. If they didn't find him soon—

Dannika popped her head back into the room. "I have a name." Some of the fatigue had seeped away from her face, replaced by a spark

204 | Ashlyn Kane & Morgan James

of some kind, maybe optimism. Callum hardly dared hope. "This guy Davis Gamber lost his job as a research geneticist in Spokane two and a half years ago, just before Darius Maulsby surfaced. He hasn't worked since, according to the IRS, but his bank account's healthy. He just might be our guy."

The relief flooding through him almost knocked him out at the knees. "Do we have an address?"

"We have a cell phone number." Callum's gut clenched as Dannika held up her phone. "The second he picks up, we need to be ready to go."

IT WAS only a matter of time before they came for him again. Ezra knew that. So as disturbing as it was, he made himself watch the guards, watch the girl who came with the food, trying to judge timing, trying to figure out where the electronic controls for the cages were. Clearly the cage setup was impromptu, or at least not designed to hold anyone of any intelligence—it didn't take Ezra long to work out that the wiring for the cage controls ran right across the back of his cell. Unfortunately, it was such a poorly executed mess that he couldn't tell which of the eight twisted strands was for his door. Somewhere, an electrician needed to be fired.

Or maybe hugged, Ezra thought, considering. Definitely hugged, if he ever got the hell out of here.

The guards walked through every half an hour or so, not really looking at anything so much as intimidating their charges with their mere presence, Ezra figured. Every third or fourth time through, they swapped out used-up prisoners, and they were gone for a little longer than usual after that.

Ezra waited until the guards had walked through the warehouse for the third time without exchanging prisoners. The two women they had taken to the lab an hour and a half ago were still audible through the walls, but Ezra couldn't afford to pay attention. The second the footfalls were out of earshot, he scrambled to the front of his cell, craning his neck up to try to trace the wires. He was only going to get one shot, maybe two, before the guards came running. He needed to be out of sight before they got there.

Ezra counted out thirty-five seconds after the last footfall before picking up the stainless steel bowl. A piece of rounded rubber had been wrapped around the bottom edges, and he scraped it against the concrete floor until it peeled off. The metal underneath was sharp, unfinished, just as he'd hoped. Looking around quickly to ensure that he wasn't being observed, Ezra used the sharp metal to slice into the insulation of the wiring he hoped controlled the door to his cell.

After peeling away the outer layer of insulation, Ezra let out a sigh of relief and thanked God for his second-year circuits class. There were four wires, and if the idiot who'd wired the place had followed standard conventions, the black was hot, the white completed the circuit, and the green was the ground. That meant the yellow one controlled the signal to the door.

Of course, if the yellow one *didn't* control the signal to the door, Ezra was in for a big shock. Literally.

Carefully, he picked up the rubber he'd peeled off from around the edges of the dish and wrapped it around his fingers before picking up the bowl again and cutting through the yellow wire.

So far, so good. Bracing himself, Ezra put the dish down and quickly licked the tip of his finger before pressing it briefly to the copper strands inside the yellow insulation.

Nothing.

Letting out a shaky breath, Ezra picked the bowl up again. He was extra careful this time, scraping the insulation away from the black wire without cutting through it. A spark at the touch of metal proved it was live, so he backed up a bit, licking his lips as he peeled the insulation away from the ends of the yellow wire. Then, crossing his fingers, he leaned forward and touched twisted copper to the exposed hot wires.

A loud buzz reverberated through the room as the door opened, and Ezra cursed. Apparently the door alarm was hardwired into the controls. It was too late to do anything about it now, though. This was his only chance. He scampered through the door before the circuit could overload and slam it shut again, and made a beeline for the room at the end of the warehouse.

He skidded through the door like he was being chased by the hounds of hell and threw himself flat against the wall, his heartbeat thundering in his ears. By the time he'd calmed down enough to look around, to notice that the door was still open a crack, there were hurried footsteps and shouts coming from the warehouse, and there was nothing he could do but wait and pray he wasn't discovered.

The room he found himself in now was tiny, little more than a storage closet, but it was furnished with a cot, a secondhand shop dresser, and an incongruously cheerful string of colorful patio lights hanging from the ceiling.

The girl who'd been serving him his dog food breakfast was curled up on the cot, her eyes wide and her mouth open.

If she screamed, he was toast.

Ezra raised a shaking hand and pressed a finger to his lips. The girl was filthy, and if this was where she was staying, she was practically a prisoner herself, but there was no telling. She could have Stockholm syndrome by now. In fact, Ezra would be surprised if she didn't.

Finally, after an endless moment, she nodded her acquiescence, her face still a picture of terror, and Ezra turned his concentration back to the commotion outside.

All of the guards were human. Ezra knew that by scent alone, and it wasn't even close to the full moon. Manipulating that many alphas into causing this much pain would have been practically impossible unless Darius had been recruiting from an asylum—or maybe a prison. Anyway, *they* wouldn't be able to smell *him*, not the way someone with lycan senses would, but there were plenty of people they could go to. Ezra had to get out of that room before they came back with someone who could sniff him out. He had a sudden vision of being hunted down by one of the lycans that had been locked up in the cells opposite him, and a chill shot down his spine. There wouldn't even be enough pieces of him left to identify.

Heavy footfalls, coming closer. Ezra swallowed. God, he wasn't even going to get far enough to be hunted down like some kind of animal. He should've just bolted when he could—

"Under here," the girl hissed, pointing beneath her cot as she mussed the covers so they would fall over the edge.

Ezra didn't think he'd fit, but he didn't have a choice. He squeezed underneath, scraping his shoulder and bumping his head, and the girl dropped the covers into place. He could feel her settling on the bed, probably trying to make it look as if she'd been sleeping, and then he heard the door open.

For several long, heart-pounding seconds, Ezra didn't dare

breathe.

Then the door slammed shut again, loud enough that he felt the rattle in his bones, and he stayed on the floor for a few more breathless seconds, shuddering with relief.

The girl pulled the covers up and stuck her head down to look at him, her filthy hair falling in her face. "What's your name?" she whispered.

"Ezra," he whispered back, darting his eyes to the door and then up again. "What's yours?"

"Isabelle." She bit her lip. "Are you running away?"

Gambling on what he understood about beta wolf psychology, Ezra said, "I have to get back to my Alpha." The girl leaned forward a bit like she was trying to smell him. Callum probably would have said such an overt move was yet another taboo, but Ezra got the feeling this girl hadn't been very well socialized for the past few years. "He'll be worried."

Isabelle nodded. "If you don't go back, he might get angry."

Oh, he was definitely going to get angry, but Ezra was pretty sure Isabelle meant *at him*, and that was just... yeah, it was time to go. He carefully dragged himself out from under the cot. "Do you know how I can get out of here without being seen?"

Quietly and with a lot of prompting from Ezra, Isabelle walked him through the layout of the warehouse. To get outside, he'd have to go all the way back across the room with the cells, then out into a storage area that acted as a front for the illegal detention going on behind it.

So of course the storage area was where the guards liked to hang out when they weren't schlepping someone to or from the lab room. Awesome.

They froze again as more heavy footfalls sounded outside the room, then faded away in the direction of the lab. It wouldn't be long before Darius started screaming. Definitely time to go.

Ezra stood. Somehow in the past twenty-four hours, the whole naked thing had stopped being a big deal. Or he was deeper in shock than he wanted to think about. "Listen, thanks." Isabelle was still huddled on the filthy bedclothes. He didn't want to think about what the stains might be. "Are you... do you want to come? I mean, you could join our pack? If you want."

He watched as the openness in her expression closed off, as her mouth thinned into a line. Maybe Stockholm syndrome, maybe just defeat, he couldn't tell. "I'd better not." She shook her head. "Come on, you should get going. They'll be back before long, and I don't want to get caught with you here."

Yeah, Ezra hadn't really held out a lot of hope for that, but it was worth asking. He nodded once, put his ear to the door, and slipped out as quietly as he could.

Back in the cell room, Ezra's adrenaline started pumping again. He felt lightheaded, and every sound of his bare feet on the dirty floor was too loud.

And then it got worse.

One of the still-caged lycans was conscious, and she'd dragged herself to the front of the cell and curled her hands into claws around the bars. Her teeth had shifted, slicing into her lower lip, and her blown pupils never left Ezra as he skulked by.

"Help me."

The hair on the back of Ezra's neck stood up, and he took a deep, shaky breath. Bad idea. The compulsion was there, beneath a thick layer of blood and sweat and grime.

"Please."

She was getting louder, and God, Ezra wanted to help, but there was just no way. She wouldn't be able to walk, not with the shape her legs were in. He could see that one of them was definitely broken. The best way to help would be to get the hell out of there and come back with reinforcements. "I can't," he whispered back, stopping in spite of himself. His legs seemed to be rooted to the floor. "Please, you have to let me go. I promise I'll come back, but I can't help you."

"Help me," she rasped again.

He took a deep breath. *I will*, he promised silently, and he determinedly put one foot in front of the other.

Behind him, the female alpha started screaming. It was all the impetus Ezra needed to break into a run.

There was a guard in the front room, but he was facing the wall as he spoke quietly on his cell phone, and beyond him—in another situation, Ezra would have laughed—there was a gleaming exit sign not thirty feet away. He wasn't going to get a better chance than this.

Forcing himself to move slowly, Ezra crept toward the door.

Twenty-five feet.

Twenty.

The guy with the cell phone made an exasperated noise. "No, you're not *listening*—" and turned toward the spot Ezra had entered from.

Ezra stood stock-still, adrenaline coursing through his system. When it became clear the man didn't see him, he shuffled forward again.

Ten feet.

Five feet.

His fingers touched the cool metal of the door. Just a few more steps and he'd be free—

A hand clamped down around his elbow, right where the blood had been drawn the day before, and he was slammed up against the wall hard enough to rattle his teeth. The spark of hope faded to desperation as an enormous fist connected with his jaw and everything went black.

EZRA woke up sputtering with a throbbing sensation below his left eye and a killer headache that wasn't helped by the ringing of the kennel buzzers in the background. There was water dripping from his hair down his face and chest. He coughed. "You know, if you want me conscious, I'm partial to coffee."

The hands holding him up gave him a rough shove forward, and he stumbled, catching himself just before he fell. Ah, the lab. Ezra hadn't missed it. He looked around, taking everything in. "Where's your pet scientist?" he asked—too loudly, it turned out, as the kennel buzzers cut out.

"Davis is experiencing a promotion as a reward for all of his hard work," Darius said smoothly, baring his teeth.

Whatever the fuck that meant, Ezra was sure he didn't want to know.

"Unfortunately," Darius continued, "you seem particularly disinclined to cooperate. Dawson's influence, no doubt. A shame—I had hoped we might be able to cure you of this disease."

That sounded ominous in more ways than one. Ezra swallowed

against the rising dread and tried to put on a brave front. "I'm sorry, could you clarify something for me? How did a pompous windbag like you get elected pack Alpha?"

That was the last straw, apparently. Snarling, Darius grasped Ezra's forearm in a clawlike grip, fingernails cutting into the flesh, and dragged him back over to the hated metal chair. He threw him down into it roughly, securing the tie around Ezra's free hand and the leather strap around his neck before rising again and pulling Ezra's arm out straight. The guard at the far door made to help him, but the alarm for the kennel went off again. "Go see to that," Darius bit out. "I can take care of this weakling."

With a nod, the guard hefted his tranquilizer gun and left the room.

"Now," Darius said, his fingernails so tight on Ezra's arm that droplets of blood were beading down and gathering at his elbow, "we find out what kind of wolf you really are."

The syringe on the tray table was huge, much bigger than any of the ones Ezra had seen him use on the other subjects, and he picked it up, appearing to consider the dosage for a moment. Ezra struggled in his grip, but it was no use. He was tied down. He wasn't going anywhere.

The needle was only centimeters from his skin when Ezra scented something on a sudden breeze that shouldn't have been there: something strong, and righteous, and angry—livid. Something proprietary. *Callum.*

But Ezra barely had time to be relieved. His wasn't the only sensitive nose in the room.

"Well, well. Callum Dawson. Two for the price of one, I see." Darius's cruel smile revealed hints of his pointed canines, and Ezra realized that at some point, the man's lycan teeth had descended. He didn't lower the needle, though, turning away from Ezra to face Callum, who was standing in the doorway, looking like every pissed-off action movie hero ever—only better, because he was all Ezra's.

Quelling the urge to squirm, Ezra kept his eyes locked on Darius.

"It's over, Darius," Callum told him, his voice and gaze steady though Ezra could smell the tension. "We know what you've been up to. Did you think we wouldn't find out?"

Ezra worked his left hand gently against the canvas restraint. It was scraping some of the skin off the back of his hand, but Darius hadn't strapped him in tightly enough. If he was careful, if he was quiet and Callum held Darius's attention, Ezra might be able to get away.

Then Callum took a step forward, and Ezra winced when Darius jerked his arm harshly. "Not another step, Dawson, or your pretty little toy is going to have a close encounter with his more violent side."

Shit. Now the needle was closer than ever. Ezra pulled his left arm harder in terror. Just a little farther and the meatiest part of his hand would squeeze through the loop....

"On second thought." Darius let go of him, and for a moment Ezra was so relieved he didn't even move to free himself.

The relief was short-lived. Darius reached out for something on the counter behind him. It looked like a giant dart gun, with a canister of compressed air for propulsion. Darius cradled the weapon almost lovingly, then turned a narrowed gaze on Callum. "Your pet's faith in you is commendable." His tone suggested he meant the opposite. "Sadly, also misplaced."

Oh, shit. Ezra panicked, jerking his now free hand to unbuckle the restraint around his left wrist while trying to convey to Callum that he should run the fuck away, all without drawing attention to himself.

"I'm going to enjoy listening to you tear him apart."

Ezra tore a fingernail pulling his hand free, but he hardly noticed the pain. He was too busy grabbing for the back of Darius's shirt and yanking, hoping to God he could throw off his aim. There was a whizz of air as the dart gun went off, and Darius stumbled away from Ezra, ripping away the rest of the fingernail when it caught in the fabric of his sleeve.

Ezra couldn't see Callum, but he could smell blood. His own? He didn't know. He scrambled to undo the leather strap around his neck, his fingers sliding slickly with blood and sweat. "Callum? Callum—" He heaved himself out of the chair on unsteady legs, but before he could get anywhere, that clawlike hand latched around his arm again.

There were no guards to ensure his compliance this time. Instinctively, Ezra reached out blindly with his other hand. His fingers closed around something bulky and heavy, and he swung without thinking and with all his might, praying he wouldn't lose his awkward grip.

The microscope connected with the side of Darius Maulsby's head, then slipped out of Ezra's slick fingers. It landed beside Darius as he went down, cracking and shattering, spreading shards of glass and plastic across the floor. Ezra spared one quick glance at his captor: his eyes were closed, and there was a smear of blood on his temple where Ezra had hit him, dripping down over his cheek.

Then Ezra crossed the room, heedless of the shrapnel cutting into his bare feet. "Callum!" he said again.

Callum was still standing when Ezra finally made it to his side, but his attention was clearly focused elsewhere: he didn't meet Ezra's gaze, didn't respond the first three times Ezra called his name. A cold lump of fear grew in Ezra's stomach when he saw the thin trickle of blood oozing down Callum's left arm just below the bicep.

Trembling, Ezra knelt to the floor. The dart had pierced Callum's skin, that was obvious, but it hadn't stuck—there was a possibility he'd only been grazed, that he hadn't been dosed. With unsteady hands, Ezra found the dart round and opened the casing.

"Ezra."

Ezra swallowed, his throat suddenly dry. The syringe inside was still partially loaded, but it was a huge round, and about twenty-five percent of the fluid inside was gone.

"Ezra."

Fuck. He put the vial safely to the side and leaned back, looking up at Callum looming over him. "Quarter dose," he said softly. He didn't know what a quarter dose could do, but it couldn't be good. Not when a full dose could make someone aggressive enough to kill with his bare hands.

Ezra swallowed. His own heartbeat was thunderous in his ears.

"You need to get out of here."

Obviously. "No shit," Ezra said tightly, not moving. "We all need to get out of here. These guys are—they're sadistic freaks, Callum."

"And in a few seconds I might be one of those sadistic freaks," Callum snapped. "I can already feel the hormones working. You have to get away from me before it's too late." He put a healthy pheromonal compulsion behind his words, and if Ezra hadn't been kneeling, the force of it might have made him stagger away.

"You're coming too. I won't leave you." The words were out of his mouth before Ezra could even think about them, but there was nothing to think about. Like hell he was going to leave Callum after all this shit. He slid back a few inches, ready to leverage himself to his feet.

And stopped. Looked up. The muscles in the corners of Callum's jaw were clenched; Ezra could practically hear him grinding his teeth. His hands were balled into fists. And there was also the small—or not-so-small—issue of the erection threatening to rip the seam of his pants open.

Right. So at least Callum wasn't going to beat him to death. Probably not with his fists, anyway.

Ezra licked his lips. This was so not the time and place for this. This was in fact, the part of Ezra's brain that controlled common sense pointed out, probably the worst timing ever. But Ezra's hormones weren't listening to his higher brain function; they were reacting to Callum's.

A hand landed on his shoulder, then moved in to the crook of his neck, fingers sliding into Ezra's hairline, then cradling his skull. Ezra's breath hitched. His heartbeat stuttered. His eyelids grew heavy. Everything seemed like it was happening in slow motion, through some kind of distorted glass. Reality was suddenly very far away.

Then he took a deep breath, and a flood of want hit him like a freight train, pouring in through his nose and pooling in his hindbrain, in his spine, in his throat, and between his legs. His mouth watered, and he swallowed once.

Sure hands that didn't seem to belong to Ezra appeared in his field of vision, unbuckling, unbuttoning, unzipping. But they must have been his, because Callum's were both on his head now, guiding him forward, and who really cared about *those* hands, anyway?

Not Ezra, certainly. He had just enough time to wet his lips before Callum's cock pushed past them, filling his mouth and throat without hesitation. Slow blink, look up, hollow his cheeks, and that got a growl and a press of fingernails on his scalp. Pleased, Ezra did it again, flicked his tongue along the underside, held his breath for seven seconds as Callum held him down, gasped in dazed relief when he let go again. Message received: Callum was in charge here. And if he wanted to rub the head of his dick over Ezra's lips until Ezra lost his mind and begged him to put it back in his mouth, he would.

He didn't wait that long, though, shoving back in carefully as Ezra tipped back his head with a shudder, his mind blank. Ezra registered the firm but tender hand on his neck, loose but inquisitive, like Callum wanted to feel it when he swallowed, outside and in, so he did. His own neglected cock was hard against his naked belly and leaking steadily, but he couldn't make himself peel a hand away from Callum's body.

Ezra was too tuned out to notice most of the filth streaming from Callum's mouth; for the most part it was background noise, an unnecessary part of the ambiance. Filler. But then he caught a hint: "Fuck, Ezra, your *mouth*, so good but I *need* to—" And then he was being pulled to his feet and taken in a bruising kiss, lips and tongue bitten until Callum pushed at his shoulder until he turned around and braced himself on the goddamn *chair*.

No time to think about it, though, just the sudden warmth of a body behind him and a quiet growl, then a plea, "Sorry, sorry, I can't help it, please" as that thick cock slid between his cheeks, rubbed over his hole, and *Jesus Christ* why was Callum apologizing for this?

Ezra's knees shook, but he put more weight on his arms and spread his legs and did pretty much everything except beg Callum to just fuck him already, and that only because he didn't think he could actually speak. He pushed back with his ass, wanting—something— and curled his fingers until his knuckles were white.

Callum's breath was hot on the back of his neck, loud in his ears. One hand slid up to Ezra's mouth, two fingers thick and salty pushing in, needing licking, sucking; the other down, across his oblique, diagonally over his belly, firm grip of fingers around his cock. Ezra tried to moan, but his lungs wouldn't let him, so he dropped his head, squared his shoulders, Callum's fingers painting wet smears across his lips and cheeks.

Callum made a noise something like anguish, something like joy, and the hot breath redoubled, humid air tickling Ezra's ears. He felt the moisture on the back of his neck a split second before he felt the sting of Callum's shifted teeth scraping his skin in a tease and then piercing it. Callum's thumb smeared across the head of his cock, and Ezra's eyes rolled back in his head as he came, concentrating desperately on holding himself up so Callum's teeth wouldn't maim him while he pumped his brain out through his dick.

When Ezra came to awareness the world was round again, and he had Callum's come smeared all over his ass and thighs. He was breathing like he'd just won a marathon, and his arms and legs were trembling so badly he was sure he was going to fall over.

Then he saw Darius Maulsby get up off the floor with his hand closed around the syringe full of hormones, which must have fallen when Ezra had braced himself on the chair. Ezra barely had time to open his mouth to utter a warning before Callum somehow appeared behind him and broke Darius's neck.

Callum and Ezra stared at each other for a few long seconds over Darius's cooling body. Just when Ezra's urge to heave passed, Callum threw his head back with a pained cry and crumpled to the floor, unconscious.

Fuck.

Chapter Fourteen

...That Bit You

EZRA'S first thought when he got a good look at himself in the mirror was *So that's what they were staring at*. His second was that he looked more like an extra from a graphic vampire film than a werewolf horror flick. His neck was covered in bruises—or rather, in one impressively large elliptical one.

Still, the worst of the damage could just be seen in his reflection if Ezra turned his head to the side and put the back of his neck in a better position. On either side of his neck, a curving line made up of red punctures could be seen spanning from bellow his hairline toward the tops of his shoulders.

Callum's bite, which had been hot as all hell when Ezra had been pinned between Callum and that godforsaken chair, looked nasty, raw, and painful. Unable to curb the urge, Ezra lifted a hand to press tentatively at the bite wound and hissed when he made contact. The teeth marks were large—much too large to be a human's—and set off by ringing bruises in a deeper purple. No wonder he had received concerned looks when people had seen him; it looked awful. If Ezra hadn't known how scorchingly hot it had been to get the bite mark, he, too, would have been unsettled to see it.

Sighing, Ezra turned away from the mirror and pulled on the clean scrubs that he had been given. Though it didn't much matter what he wore—nothing was going to cover up those marks.

When he emerged from the bathroom, it was to find Wyn sitting on the edge of her seat, looking small and drawn. When she caught sight of Ezra, she leapt to her feet and took several abortive steps toward him.

"Ezra, are you...?" Her gaze was frantic. She seemed to be trying to take in everything about him, maybe checking for injuries. Her expression grew pinched when her gaze fell on his neck. "Oh, Ezra." Her voice was despairing, though Ezra didn't think he warranted that level of pity.

"Wyn, I'm fine. Pretty bruised and shook up. Not sure I'll ever be able to sleep next to an open window again… but Callum got to me before they did any real damage."

Her look turned sad and disbelieving. Pitying. Damn, Ezra wished he knew what he could say to get rid of that expression.

Before either of them could say anything more, Blaise and Dannika walked into the room.

"All changed, I see." Dannika gave Ezra a sweeping look, taking in the new clothes and probably checking him over for damage. She had already done so earlier when Ezra, dragging along an unconscious Callum, had found her in Darius's lair. Fortunately she had been with Blaise then, too, and the man-mountain had taken over the task of getting Callum out.

Blaise had dragged them out, leading them away from the chaos and making sure that they were both headed off to the small pack hospital to be taken care of.

And the pack hospital had taken care of them. Callum had been carted off so that they could run tests and watch his vitals to make sure he didn't suffer from the hormonal imbalance. Ezra hadn't been thrilled when he had been held back and forced to watch Callum roll away from him into an isolation room.

Of course, the doctors hadn't left him to pine for long before they had pulled him away to his own examination. They didn't believe him the first dozen times he said he was fine and that he hadn't been injected with the same stuff as Callum. Finally, once they had been satisfied that Ezra was indeed uninjured—except for Callum-inflicted bruises—they had finally let him go to shower and change.

Ezra blinked tired eyes, suddenly aware that he had zoned out of the conversation that was still happening around him.

"He really did a number on you," Dannika was saying while eyeing the large teeth marks.

Ezra, experiencing a sudden technicolor replay of where the bite had come from, blushed. His embarrassment wasn't so deep that he didn't miss the distressed noise from Wyn.

Turning, he found that her face was as pinched as ever and that she was staring at the mark with extreme dislike.

"Wyn, it doesn't hurt."

She didn't look appeased. Instead, she stared at him with an inscrutable expression before whispering, "But he *bit* you."

Ezra wasn't sure what he could say to that, except, maybe, "He did bite me, but I came like a rocket when he did." That probably wouldn't help his cause.

Feeling lost and uncertain about how to help the situation, Ezra looked to Blaise only to find the man's face fairly expressionless. Dannika's head was tilting back and forth, her gaze ping-ponging between Ezra and Wyn. At least Ezra wasn't the only one confused.

Unfortunately, Ezra was prevented from finding answers again when Jax showed up.

"Hello," she said, her eyes looking at them all and lingering, like the others', over Ezra's neck. *She* said nothing, though. "Dannika, Siobhan thought maybe you had gotten lost."

Dannika rolled her eyes. "I'm underappreciated. Just because I can't make people just appear in front of me and actually have to go and track them down before I bring them to her…. Well, let's go. We need to go about taking statements now that everyone here has been cleared by doctors."

"Statements?" Wyn's voice rose in pitch, and she looked even more upset than before. Ezra hadn't known that that would be possible.

"For the case record? You're all witnesses. You, Ms. Wyn, are going to have to answer questions about everything before the storming of the castle. And you, Ezra… we need to know about the body."

Body. Ezra had forgotten about the body. The body of Darius Maulsby. Whom Callum had killed. In cold blood. By snapping his neck. Maybe Ezra had been infected with something after all, because suddenly he felt queasy.

CALLUM woke up that evening.

The afternoon had been interminable. Siobhan and Dannika had kept Ezra busy for hours reliving the past few days and then, worse still, the moment when Callum had snapped Darius's neck. Ezra tried to distract himself with the supreme embarrassment of recounting the sex to Siobhan and Dannika, even sparingly as he had. Fortunately, neither woman wanted to know details, though he suspected that Dannika might have pressed for information if both he and Callum had breasts, if only to distract Ezra. The only interruption to the debriefing had been the news of the lycan who'd escaped near the park. Apparently Ryan, a pack member and police officer, had found him after he'd been brought in for a mistaken drunk and disorderly. Ezra had been relieved when the women had dismissed him, and he hadn't wasted any time in running out.

In his hurry, he had almost run into Jax, who only smiled encouragingly at him before asking, "How are you?"

"Fine. Where's Callum?"

"He's still out cold." She hesitated. "Did you want to see him?"

Relieved, Ezra nodded. "Yeah. If they'll let me, I'd like to see him. He's okay, right?"

Jax nodded. "Yeah. Apparently the come-down from the hormone overload took a lot out of him, but the doctors think that he'll wake up soon."

Ezra nodded. He wanted to ask if Callum would be sane when he woke up or if he would be as crazy as Teller, but he couldn't get the words past the sudden lump in his throat. Also, he was afraid of the answer. "Will they let me stay with him?"

With a wan smile, Jax replied, "Callum's a big deal around here. Of course they will. Besides, I'm not sure anyone wants him to wake up without you near."

"What?" Ezra asked, frowning at her even as he began to follow her down the hall.

Jax looked hesitant once more. "Yesterday, when we finally found out where you were… Callum finally had a focus for his anger and fear, and he… let it all out. He scared a few people."

"Oh." Ezra couldn't find it in him to be bothered by that.

The hospital staff didn't look enthusiastic about letting Ezra into Callum's room, but Jax hadn't been wrong—Callum had pull here.

Callum looked as pale and deathly as Ezra had feared. Ezra sat in the chair by the bed and laced his fingers with Callum's. He wasn't going to move from this spot.

Without him having to say as much, Jax seemed to know. She brought him dinner and didn't suggest that Ezra eat it elsewhere.

Ezra was slumped in his chair, his fingers loosely tangled in the bed sheets, when Callum turned his head and let out a soft, mumbled "Ezra?"

"Callum!" He jumped up and leaned over the bed, positioning himself closer so that he could look Callum in his sleepy eyes and gently cup his warm face.

"You're safe." Callum's eyes fluttered shut and then opened again. He seemed to be having trouble focusing.

"Yeah, I'm safe. You came to rescue me; my hero."

"Good. Next time remind me...." Callum yawned, his eyes fluttering shut. "About jumping off of second-story balconies."

"Sure," Ezra said, smoothing Callum's hair off his forehead. He had no idea what that meant, but he'd agree to almost anything right now.

"Hmm." Callum gave a hum of apparent contentment. Then he fell silent, eyes still shut.

"Callum?" No answer.

Ezra smoothed his hand over Callum's hair once more. Callum could sleep again. Ezra was feeling much easier about the silence this time around, as he wasn't worried about whether Callum would wake up sane.

Ezra settled back down. He could wait.

"OKAY. That's it." Ezra slammed the bedroom door behind him. "I've had enough of this. We're going to talk, and *you* are going to tell me why everyone is freaking out."

Callum looked not unlike a deer in the headlights. "I don't—"

"Like hell you don't know." Ezra glared. "Blaise and Jax have been giving you the stink-eye, Wyn looks like she's going to cry, and you've been staring at me like you're a naughty puppy. So you are going to tell me: what's the big deal about the bite mark?"

Callum shifted unhappily and didn't meet Ezra's eyes. "Nothing, Ezra. It's just—"

"'Just' nothing! Tell me, Callum."

Callum sighed. "The thing is.... See—the biting isn't exactly... well, it's frowned upon."

Obviously. "Okay, I kind of got that. But why?"

Callum fiddled with a pen, keeping his eyes downcast and watching the way the pen moved side to side. "So, it used to be that alphas bit their partners all the time. It was a way of showing… ownership. Biting went out when feminism came in."

Ezra paused to think about that. He wanted to digest this before speaking. Apparently the lycan community saw the bite as a sign of alpha oppression over betas, and everyone thought Ezra's super hot and kinky bite mark was some sort of claim of domination that Callum had made. A sort of public degradation, apparently.

"So people think that you've made some caveman declaration of ownership. And this is making you feel guilty?" Ezra wanted to be sure he fully understood.

The look he got seemed to imply that Ezra was slightly unbalanced. "I should! They're right, you know. It is degrading. You're not my property, Ezra. I'm supposed to protect you, not injure you! God, when I think about how much I lost control, of how badly I could have hurt you…." Callum's expression twisted with guilt. "And now you have to walk around wearing… *it*."

Right, so this was really eating Callum up. Well, that wouldn't do.

"I'm walking around with a bite mark that I got during some *really* hot sex."

Callum blushed. "See, I know you're new to all this, but—"

"No, no buts here, Callum. You didn't hurt me, and I don't feel degraded or oppressed. If I did, I wouldn't be touching it all the time and getting hard." Callum blushed at that. "I *liked* it when you fucked my mouth, when you got us both off and especially when you bit me, and I came because of it."

"Ezra, that doesn't change—"

Ezra cut him off again, frustrated. What was it going to take to convince Callum that this lycan rule didn't fit them at all? "I *liked* it, and I don't care about your ridiculous social rules. You wouldn't hurt me or oppress me. So your bite isn't a symbol of either of those things. It's not a symbol of anything. Except maybe of really hot kinky sex. If other people have issues with being bitten… well, you'd better not be biting anyone else."

Callum still seemed uncertain, but he looked a little less anguished. Hoping that this meant progress, Ezra took several steps closer so that he could cup Callum's face in his hands. "Callum, if you see me as an equal, then you have to trust that if I ever feel like you've hurt me in *any* way, I'll let you know."

Callum still didn't look sold.

"Callum. I'm a big boy. When have I ever not told you off?"

That got a smile. "True."

"So how about you admit that the sex was hot, that I liked it when you went all butch on me."

Callum looked willing enough.

"And stop letting everyone else make you feel guilty. You're going to stop wearing that hangdog expression all the time. Okay?"

"I... all right."

"Good." Ezra sealed it with a kiss.

Still, Ezra knew that it wouldn't be over so long as others were giving Callum looks like he kicked puppies for sport. Ezra needed to have one more conversation.

Waiting until Callum was in the shower, Ezra snuck out of the house and down the street. He found Jax at Wyn's. They were sitting with Blaise at the table, eating—of course.

"We need to talk. I talked to Callum, and I get now what all the looks are about. Apparently, everyone thinks that I've been walking around with the equivalent of two black eyes." Wyn squeaked, but Ezra barreled on. "Yeah, I get it. You think that this bite mark means that Callum abused me. So I'm setting things straight."

"Straight? I don't—was it not Callum that... bit you?" asked Wyn, her eyes wide.

"No, Callum was the one who bit me." There was a brief silence, and then Jax spoke.

"Look, Ezra, I get that you're trying to defend Callum here, but, sorry, you're new and—"

"No. I may not have grown up here, but I do know that what happened between Callum and I was just that. And *this* is no worse than rug burn." Jax made a choking noise. "And you are going to stop giving Callum the cold shoulder. Because I'm the one that has to put up with the guilty boyfriend. And I'm not having my boyfriend feeling guilty about having great sex."

Blaise and Wyn both looked unhappy to hear that last comment; Jax was smirking.

"Well, it's good we had that talk. No more making Callum unhappy." Ezra stood up and pushed in the chair. "Now that that's done, I'll see you all later."

CALLUM would be lying if he ever tried to say that he was sorry to be out of the hospital. He took a deep breath, relishing the scent and taste of fresh air, and let his strides lengthen, enjoying the freedom of the outdoors. It felt good to be out. At the moment, his only regret was that Jax didn't live further away. The walk to her house didn't even take a minute.

He unlatched the door and walked in, not knocking, as usual. He opened his mouth to call out a hello when he heard a sob followed by voices coming from the living room. Pausing, he closed the door softly and then made his way quietly toward the noises.

"What the hell were you thinking!" Jax sounded distressed.

"I didn't—I didn't think anyone would get hurt." That was Lucien, Callum realized with a jolt. His voice was trembling and hoarse, but it was definitely him.

"You mean you didn't think Callum would get hurt. Of course, if anyone else was injured in the process…." Jax's voice was hard and foreboding. She did not sound pleased. Really worried now, Callum picked up his pace to get into the same room.

"N-no! I didn't know…. He just, he just said he knew Ezra, that he wanted to talk to him. He didn't say he wanted to hurt anyone. And I didn't know he was the one who…." Lucien trailed off with another sob.

"That doesn't matter! A strange Alpha wanted to know personal information about your Alpha and his boyfriend, and you were so jealous you didn't even stop to think."

"I'm sorry." Callum turned the corner in time to hear this last and to see the way Lucien's lip was trembling when he said it. His posture was hunched and his head down, though he was still looking up at Jax, probably to gauge her reactions.

"I'm not sure 'sorry' is going to cut it this time." Jax's body language was closed off.

"Hey," Callum said, letting the others know that was there.

Lucien jumped, looking spooked to see Callum. Jax's expression was still shuttered, though emotions flicked through her eyes.

"What's going on?"

"Lucien's just been confessing." Jax pursed her lips.

"Confessing?" Callum considered taking a seat at the table, but the looks on their faces made him hesitate to sit. Instead he stayed standing by the door.

"Lucien had a conversation with Darius Maulsby a few weeks ago."

Muscles stiffening, Callum demanded, "Tell me."

The pheromones that he leaked into the room would have made it nearly impossible for Lucien to not comply, but Callum refused to feel guilty for that. "He came to talk to me. He said Ezra was his ex, and he wanted to know about him and you. He kept saying that he wanted to know how serious you two were."

"Darius Maulsby told you Ezra was his ex-boyfriend," Callum said slowly, trying to fathom Darius getting past his bigotry enough to say those words or anyone believing it.

"Well... I think—he might not have said it directly, but he kept saying that he and Ezra had a past and that he wanted to know if you two were serious."

"I see. And you told a stranger everything you knew about me and Ezra because...?"

Shoulders slumped, Lucien said nothing. It was Jax who snorted and said, "Because he was jealous and hoping that Darius would take Ezra away. Of course, I'm sure that he didn't even stop to think about what it would mean if Ezra, a new lycan, had a lycan ex." That got a flinch out of Lucien.

"I didn't... didn't think it would hurt. I didn't know that he was going to hurt people."

The naïveté of that statement had Callum moving. He began to pace back and forth by the door. "Didn't know—? Doesn't matter what you thought he might do with the information. You don't start telling personal information about a pack member to an outsider!"

"I'm sorry. I really didn't—"

"Of course you didn't! You were too jealous and too busy thinking with your dick!"

Lucien whimpered, looking more distressed, and Callum's urge to hurt ramped up a level. If an alpha had put Ezra in danger like this, Callum would have been hard-pressed to ignore his impulse for physical violence. He'd probably have punched the bastard in the face by this point. But... the impulse for violence was warring with the impulse to protect a beta. It was as aggravating as it was distracting.

He didn't know what to do... so he opted to do nothing. He just turned and walked out of the room and out of the house. He didn't go far, just resumed his pacing on Jax's front lawn.

Callum wasn't a fool; he had known that Lucien's infatuation with him wasn't over. That Lucien was still entertaining thoughts about sleeping with him. But he hadn't thought that Lucien would betray him over it. It had never occurred to him that he would ever.... If Callum had thought Lucien capable of being so stupid, he would never have let things get this bad. He would have made sure that Lucien fully understood Callum's feelings on the matter without any doubt.

And now he had to deal with the aftermath of this. He had to deal with Lucien, but he had no idea how. It wasn't like he had a precedent for this.

Not to mention those warring desires to protect two betas. He wanted to avenge Ezra, but to do so, he would have to hurt a beta, and everything in him protested that almost as strongly as it protested against leaving Ezra unprotected.

Mind made up, Callum turned and headed back into the house. He marched down the hall and straight into the living room where Jax and Lucien were still talking. He didn't even bother to hear what Jax was saying or to interrupt her politely. Instead, he ran roughshod over her. With one finger pointed at Lucien, he said, "The next time you betray this pack will be the last." Then he spun around again and was out of the house. Jax could add the fine print. Callum needed to be gone, away from Lucien.

NOW that he'd been rescued—for a given value of rescued, since he'd been the one dragging Callum out of that godforsaken warehouse—Ezra was inclined to put the whole disturbing mess behind him and never speak of it again. Callum had other ideas, which—if Ezra was being honest—were probably partially due to the bruises on his legs from where Ezra had kicked him during especially horrific nightmares. Callum was insisting Ezra see Robin again for some counseling.

Ezra reluctantly agreed. The bruises made him feel guilty.

After two days straight of answering what felt like the same question over and over into a microphone, Ezra was more than ready to be done. There was just one last meeting to get through first.

Siobhan and Dannika looked just as tired as he felt. "All right, let's get this over with," Dan said, dropping a stack of folders on the table. "I have a plane to catch."

Siobhan rolled her eyes. "Is this everyone?"

"Yeah, Jax and the rest have actual work to do, so it's just the four of us." Three and a half, really, Ezra thought—the past few days, Callum had been sort of preoccupied.

"Well, let me be the first to drop a bombshell." Dannika flicked open a folder and slid it across the table. "Despite the lack of resemblance to any missing persons photos—somewhere in the Midwest there's a very well-paid plastic surgeon—we figured out who Darius Maulsby used to be before his makeover. Turns out his hips really don't lie."

Callum raised an eyebrow. "Hips?"

"Well, more like hip, singular. As in replacement." Dannika shrugged. "Coz ran the serial number, and presto! We have a match."

Siobhan rolled her eyes. "The fingerprints confirmed it first. She just wanted to use the hips don't lie line. Your Darius Maulsby used to be one Michael Feyen, US Senator for Montana."

Ezra felt his mouth drop open. Darius was really Michael Feyen, the infamous ultra-right-wing senator who'd been responsible for the untimely demise of a whole slew of pro-gay, pro-choice, pro-human-rights legislation. He couldn't exactly say he was surprised. Still—"The guy who killed his wife?" he couldn't help clarifying.

"That was never proven," Siobhan said.

Ezra looked at Callum, and then they both looked back at Siobhan. Feyen hadn't exactly been known for his PC views on women, either.

"Yes, the guy who killed his wife," she said, rolling her eyes. "Or at least the guy with the extremely 'accident-prone' spouse who died under suspicious circumstances, whereupon he disappeared along with all his money, some of which was almost certainly embezzled from the state." She shook her head. "And now we know where he went."

"He got a new identity, got someone to bite him, and continued his campaign of misogyny and homophobia as a lycanthrope." Callum let out a long breath. "Well, nobody can say he wasn't a dedicated psychopath. So what happened to that Davis Gamber guy, if Darius was really Feyen?"

"Darius injected him with lycan DNA," Dannika said.

"His idea of a promotion." Ezra wrinkled his nose. "He was probably unconscious when you came in with the cavalry—I remember how much I needed to sleep those first few hours and days."

Siobhan nodded. "Yeah, he was out cold when we found him. Well, actually he was running a fever, but anyway, he's coming back to Utah with us until we can arrange for him to be transferred to a detention facility equipped to handle lycanthropes."

There was a pause as the women shared a look. After an uncomfortable moment, Callum called them on it.

"It's about our search of the facilities," began Siobhan. "We found a refrigeration system in the basement with over 2100 cubic feet of space. It…." Siobhan turned a little green.

"They were using it to house bodies," Dannika broke in bluntly. "Preliminary autopsies suggest that they were all victims of the drug."

Callum blanched. "The drug?"

"Not of the drug directly," Siobhan assured him. "Side effects. Most of them died from injuries."

"What about the other lycans?" Ezra had figured that if Callum was recovering in the pack hospital, then so were they, but he'd never thought to check. "Isabelle and the others? I mean, did they…?" He remembered what Teller had been like. He knew it could have gone just as badly with Callum, had he taken a larger dose of alphatropin. And the other lycans *had*.

Siobhan spoke first. "The paramedics treated Isabelle on site. You wouldn't let us tear you away from Callum," she reminded him when he frowned, wondering why he didn't remember that. "She's… well, let's just say the last few months with Darius haven't been the worst of her life and leave it at that. She's fine physically…." Her words trailed off, and she shifted uncomfortably.

Callum took over. "She's staying with our pack for now so we can keep an eye on her, and she's been seeing Robin."

Well, that was something, but Ezra could see everyone was still on tenterhooks. He dreaded asking the question again. "And the others?"

"We treated them as best we could," Callum started quietly—and that explained it. He'd been helping with the other lycans. No wonder he was so tired. If the doctors had had their way, he would still be on bed rest. "Low doses of betatropin, lots of saline, casts on the broken bones. A couple of them are still under sedation until we get their hormone production back within acceptable parameters."

Ezra waited. He wasn't going to be distracted by a lot of fancy words.

"All but two of them should be okay. We think." Callum met his gaze. "It looks like Darius—Feyen—and Gamber must've adjusted the dosages down after the first few experiments failed, so nobody got quite as messed up as Teller and the ones who...." He trailed off, and Ezra filled in the blanks: *the ones who tore each other to pieces*. He cleared his throat. "The others... in one case, the alphatropin overdose exacerbated a preexisting heart condition. They're getting him set up with a pacemaker."

When he didn't immediately continue, Ezra knew what had happened to the other lycan.

"The only one who didn't make it was a female alpha. She, ah, she had broken her leg, and we think some of the marrow got into her bloodstream and caused a pulmonary embolism."

Siobhan finished, "She died in the ambulance."

Shit. Fuck! Ezra had promised he'd get help, that he'd get her out—

He was busy trying to swallow the lump in his throat when Callum put a hand on his knee and the dam broke. Jesus, hadn't he cried about this yet? Wasn't it out of his system? But no. He hadn't had time, hadn't processed any of it. And now it was there, real, everything from his father's death to his own capture and—he didn't even know that alpha's *name*—

Ezra vaguely registered Callum asking Dannika and Siobhan to give them some privacy, and he heard the door close, but he couldn't see anything through the hot mess of tears in his eyes. He didn't realize he'd crumpled into a ball until Callum touched his shoulder. Instinctively, Ezra curled into the touch, trembling, his face pressed into Callum's neck. "Sorry," he muttered thickly, fisting his hands in Callum's shirt. "I just—sorry." Jesus, how embarrassing.

Callum hushed him, running both hands soothingly up and down his back, until Ezra got it out of his system. He didn't ask if Ezra felt better, just gave him one last squeeze as Ezra pulled away to wipe at his face.

Callum caught at his hand, though, and pulled it away, then wiped Ezra's cheek with his own thumb. He held Ezra's gaze for an uncharacteristically long moment before dropping his hand away to rub at his neck instead. "Ezra... I'm sorry."

Ezra took a hitching breath. What now? Jesus, Callum wasn't going to break up with him or something, was he? "Uh," he said cautiously, voice still a little thick, "what for?"

A quick flash of warm brown as Callum met his gaze again, but it flickered away just as quickly, and he gave a minute shake of his head. "If I'd kept my hands to myself, Darius never would have taken you."

That was what this was about? Ezra had offended Darius merely by existing! "And we still wouldn't know where Darius was, and he'd still be alive and experimenting on werewolves," he pointed out gently, then added, lighter—well, he tried for lighter, but his voice was still congested—"But I'd be dead of sexual frustration."

Callum stood up and pushed his chair back so he could pace a little. "This isn't funny."

"I'm not laughing." Ezra stood, too, closing his hand around Callum's wrist to stop him and pull him closer. "You are not going to play the what-if game. That way lies madness. Besides, you're not allowed to regret me." He attempted a weak grin, feeling Callum's pulse skip-thudding under his fingertips. "I'm just too awesome to—"

"I love you." The words came tumbling out of Callum's mouth like water over a fall. Ezra blinked in surprise at the sudden declaration. Callum looked a little spooked.

Ezra inhaled deeply, the breath rattling a little. Nerves. A wave of warmth washed over him, and he squeezed Callum's hand. "All the more reason not to regret me." Ezra reached up to wind both arms around Callum's neck and determinedly ignored the way his legs were trembling. "I love you too, by the way. So I think you're stuck with me."

"Oh." Callum still looked stunned, but at least he didn't seem freaked out anymore. And that was definitely his happy smell. "Okay. In that case…."

Seriously? He was going to try to follow that? "Oh God, what is it?" Ezra teased. "Go easy on me. I'm not sure how much more emotional upheaval I can take today."

At that, Callum broke eye contact and tried to pull away a little, but Ezra tightened his grip. "That was a joke!" Mostly a joke, anyway.

He'd been played. Callum looked back up with his old easy confidence and the hint of a smile around his eyes. "Move in with me."

Okay, he hadn't been expecting that. "What?"

Callum took him by the elbows, moved him back half a step so they could see each other without hurting themselves. "Sell your apartment. Make it official. Move in with me."

It wasn't like Ezra had been in the apartment for longer than the ten minutes it had taken to gather up his more wintery things since he'd been bitten anyway. And he was pretty sure the still-healing bruise on the back of his neck was as official as it was going to get in the state of Montana. Still, he couldn't resist giving Callum a hard time. "Right. Is that the Alpha talking, or…?"

Winding Callum up like this could quickly become Ezra's new favorite hobby. He visibly reconsidered his words. "*Please* move in with me?"

Better. "Well, since you asked so nicely." He really needed to go through the apartment anyway, make his peace with his father's ghosts. "But you're helping me move my—"

Callum kissed him, and Ezra let it go.

Like many romance authors in her genre, in real life ASHLYN KANE is an overeducated, overworked, underpaid twentysomething. Writing provides a welcome distraction from her disgust with the job market, as well as a means to help buy shiny new windows for the house she just purchased with her shiny new husband.

When she's not getting up at stupid hours of the day to go to her so-called "real jobs," she can usually be found either at the gym or parked in front of her MacBook, chatting with her various co-authors and trying to create the kinds of dynamic characters she always ends up falling in love with.

MORGAN JAMES started writing fiction before she could spell it. It was in high school that she started writing her first novel about a gay character, and she thanks the Internet for helping her realize that didn't make her crazy. Coincidentally, she also thanks the Internet for the role it plays in her long-distance friendship with Ashlyn Kane. Geek, artist, archer, and fangirl, Morgan tends to while away free hours with imaginary worlds and people on pages and screens—it's an addiction. She lives in Ontario with her family and is the personal slave of three cats and a poodle (who isn't named Ringo, but who does like to poke).

Also from ASHLYN KANE & MORGAN JAMES

http://www.dreamspinnerpress.com

Also from ASHLYN KANE

http://www.dreamspinnerpress.com

From ASHLYN KANE & BETHANY BROWN

http://www.dreamspinnerpress.com

Also from DREAMSPINNER PRESS

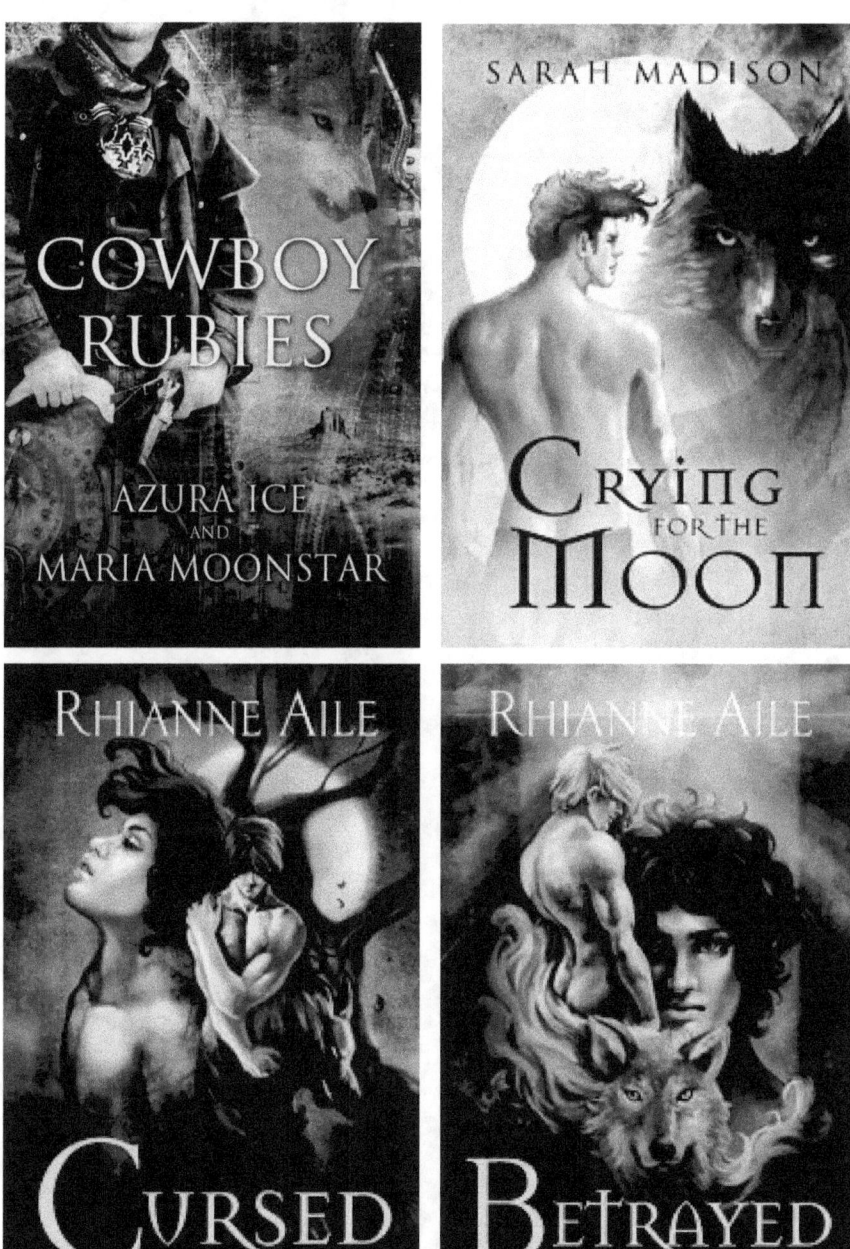

Also from DREAMSPINNER PRESS

www.ingramcontent.com/pod-product-compliance
Lightning Source LLC
Chambersburg PA
CBHW051636260626
47170CB00004B/1198